Crooked HOUSE

OTHER BOOKS AND AUDIO BOOKS
BY MARLENE BATEMAN

A Death in the Family

Motive for Murder

Light on Fire Island

Crooked HOUSE

An Erica Coleman Mystery

a novel

MARLENE BATEMAN

Covenant Communications, Inc.

Cover: *Haunted House* © Ammentorp. Courtesy of depositphotos.com.

Published by Covenant Communications, Inc.
American Fork, Utah

Printed in the United States of America
First Printing: April 2015

21 20 19 18 17 16 15 10 9 8 7 6 5 4 3 2 1

ISBN: 978-1-62108-521-8

To Jocelyn

Acknowledgments

MANY THANKS TO MONICA MILES, Jennie Stevens, Carol Berven, Janet Peacock, and Annetta Cochran, who read the manuscript and gave many helpful suggestions. I want to thank Holly Horton for her editorial expertise and insightful comments. Thanks also to Sarah at the Dover International Speedway for answering questions about the race track. A special thanks to my editor, Stacey Owen. I owe a debt of gratitude to the great cooks that tested the recipes: Dianna Frenzel, Monica Miles, Sami Miles, and an extra special thank-you a superb cook, Virginia Kendall.

Author's Note

ALTHOUGH *CROOKED HOUSE* IS A work of fiction, most of the details about Dover, including the Dover International Speedway, NASCAR races, and surrounding areas are accurate. However, a few changes were made to accommodate this story. The Dover Historical Society owns the Jeremiah Reeves House, which has been carefully restored. It houses a museum and serves as a center for historical functions.

The tour times for the lighthouses and the lightship were also adjusted. Tours for the Harbor of Refuge Lighthouse and the Delaware Breakwater Lighthouse are only available on Saturdays. Tours for the Lightship Overfalls are available every day except Tuesday and Wednesday.

Chapter One

"I'M SCARED."

Erica's heart turned over as she recalled the quaver in her young friend's voice.

"Erica, can you come?"

"Of course." Erica's reply had been automatic, though she knew it wouldn't be easy to drop everything and fly to Delaware. Although Erica Coleman often received emotionally laden phone calls in her job as a private investigator, there was a difference when the call came from the daughter of her best friend. Erica had known Megan since the girl was two, and they were almost as close as Erica was to her two daughters. She would do anything she could to help.

Erica had hurriedly made flight arrangements and now sat staring out the plane's window at the gray clouds. Megan's voice still haunted her. The very fact that Megan—who was usually so calm and composed—sounded scared had put Erica on high alert.

Upon arriving at Philadelphia International Airport, Erica took a shuttle to the Hampton Inn in Dover, Delaware. After getting a room, she hopped on the bus and rode a mile down DuPont Highway to Delaware State University, where Megan, who was a sophomore there, waited.

Still trim in her late thirties and with long chestnut hair, Erica could have passed for a student herself as she strode down the sidewalk to the Martin Luther King Jr. Student Center.

Near the entrance of the imposing red brick building, a tall young woman in black jeans paced near the front doors. On the phone, Erica had heard the anxiety in Megan's voice, but now it was fully on display as Megan marched distractedly back and forth, avoiding other students. Normally, Megan was equal to anything—poised and unruffled—but today she looked like a walking basket of nerves as she kept glancing at her watch and darting quick, hurried looks around the campus.

When she spotted Erica, Megan ran down the steps. They hugged tightly.

"Look at you!" Erica smiled as she pulled back. The last time she'd seen Megan was a little over a year ago when Erica had visited her and her family in Florida.

Megan had been an awkward and defiant teenager. She'd matured into a warm, thoughtful young woman, though she still had an undeniable independent streak. She no longer wore chains and chin-to-toe black, but she continued to dye her hair a startling black that made her fair skin look even paler.

Arms linked, they went inside to the Austin Grill and picked up chicken sandwiches and fries. After a bored clerk rang up their order, they took their food to a small table. Erica pulled out the package of moist towelettes she always carried in her pocket and wiped the table carefully before putting the towelette in a zippered plastic bag.

Megan wore a look of amused resignation. "I see you haven't changed."

"Germs are everywhere, my dear," Erica said matter-of-factly, taking a seat.

Megan popped a fry into her mouth. "I called Mom when these accidents started, and she suggested I call and see if you could come here first. Actually, I'm surprised Mom didn't call you herself. I hope it wasn't too hard to change your schedule."

Originally, the plan had been for Erica to visit Wendy in Florida for a week then fly to Dover to see Megan. "No problem. I was flying standby anyway, so I just flip-flopped destinations. I'll visit Wendy after. Thank goodness I have a brother who works for an airline so I can fly so cheaply and a great husband who'll step in and be Mr. Mom while I'm gone."

"I wish David could have come." Megan took a juicy bite, and as sauce dribbled down, she wiped her mouth with a napkin.

"Me too, but he doesn't mind me flying out once a year to visit you and Wendy. David says it gives him some one-on-one time with the kids and also 'guy time' to go fishing with my dad and brothers." As she talked, Erica expertly straightened the packets of sugar in their chrome holder.

"Your sandwich is getting cold," Megan observed.

"There, I'm done." Erica sat back with the air of a job well done. She looked at Megan with lively green eyes and nodded toward the neatly stacked packets. "Doesn't that look better?"

"It wasn't bothering *me*." Megan shrugged. "Anyway, thanks for coming. I never would have asked if you hadn't been coming in a week or two anyway. It's just that I'm scared about Liz."

That had been evident when she'd called, but Megan hadn't gone into specifics. Erica picked up her sandwich in its half-shell of paper. "Tell me again what's going on with your friend. Start at the beginning, and don't leave anything out."

Megan's chest heaved as she took a deep breath to collect herself. "Okay. Her name's Liz Johnson, and she owns this really old house she inherited from her parents, who are both dead. Liz calls it 'Crooked House' because a couple of the turrets lean."

"Turrets, eh?"

A ghost of a smile appeared on Megan's lips. "It's some house. Wait till you see it."

"And you and another girl are each renting a room from Liz, right?"

"Yeah. Beth is just as worried as I am. She was going to come with me, but we decided she should stay at the house with Liz. We don't want Liz to be alone because we think someone's trying to kill her."

It had sounded dramatic over the phone, but in person there was something so intense and earnest in Megan's startling statement that Erica swallowed wrong and began to cough. She took a drink of water and asked, "What makes you think that? Did someone threaten her?"

"No, but Liz has had a couple of accidents lately—at least she *says* they're accidents, but they were serious. She could have been killed."

It wasn't like Megan to play the drama queen, but still, the jump from accidents to murder attempts seemed a long one. Erica made an honest effort to reel in her skepticism. "Tell me about the accidents."

"Okay. First, someone tampered with her car. The brakes went out, and she ending up driving across someone's yard and hitting a tree."

"Was she hurt?"

"She hit her head. The mechanic said Liz was lucky—running over the lawn and bushes slowed her down before she ran into the tree, or it would have been a lot worse."

That did sound alarming, but again, college students were notorious for driving junk heaps. And possibly Liz had neglected regular maintenance on her car.

Megan must have detected a look of doubt on Erica's face because a note of defensiveness crept into her voice. "The second one happened when she was downtown. Liz was standing on the sidewalk waiting for the bus when someone shoved her into the road. A truck was coming, and if a guy hadn't grabbed her and pulled her back, she would have been killed."

Again, it was hard to know if this was merely an accident or something more.

Megan went on, "Liz doesn't think anything's going on, but I think someone's out to get her, and so does Beth. We're afraid something terrible is going to happen." Holding out her hand, Megan said, "Look, I'm shaking just thinking about it. I feel sick and can't sleep—it's just like that time you came to visit and found a dead man in our driveway." Megan shuddered. "That was a nightmare! I can't stand the thought of going through that again."

Reaching out, Erica took hold of one of Megan's hands. It was cold. "Don't worry. I'm here, and I'll look into it. Now, have you contacted the police?"

"Yes, and they thought I was a fruitcake."

Erica wanted to giggle. But knowing Megan would be outraged, she controlled herself. Still, the police did get all kinds of crazy calls. Certainly she had gotten her share when she had been on the police force. "Do you have any idea why someone would want to kill Liz?"

"I don't." Megan looked at Erica through tortured hazel eyes. "I've talked with Liz and Beth, and none of us can think of any reason for this."

Perhaps there wasn't one. Although Megan had seemed to recover from the trauma of the dead man at her house, Erica wondered if the girl had been so affected that it was coming out now in some sort of post-traumatic-syndrome sort of way.

"I'm really afraid for her," Megan said, tears forming in her eyes. "Liz is so awesome—I couldn't stand it if anything happened to her. She's had to make her own way and work really hard since she doesn't have any parents to help her.

"Does Liz know you called me?"

"She told me not to—said the pushing and brakes going out were just accidents and that I shouldn't bother you. But Beth and I decided we ought to call—before it's too late." There was frightening urgency in her voice.

"Let me ask you a couple of questions. Is Liz rich?"

Megan scoffed. "Just the opposite. She's dead broke. That's why she rents out rooms. Bill collectors are always calling."

"Does Liz have any enemies?"

Megan screwed up her face with a doubtful look. "Well, there's Frank—he lives next door. He doesn't like Liz, but—" She jumped when her cell phone rang.

"Hello? Yes, Erica's with me." As Megan listened, her eyes grew large. "What? Okay, okay, calm down. We'll be right there." Her chair made a sharp scraping sound as she jumped up and thrust it back. She grabbed her backpack. "That was Beth. There's been an accident at the house."

Chapter Two

As Megan screeched out of the parking lot, Erica gritted her teeth and braced herself. Erica's angst came not only from the car's sharp turns and excessive speed but because Megan had refused to give Erica time to wipe down the car seats with her wet wipes.

Megan slowed only upon reaching historic Dover, with its eclectic structures, narrow streets, and gabled houses that had been built during the last century. Nearly every house was a head-turner, with fanciful turrets, whimsical fretwork, and gingerbread woodwork done in the Victorian manner. The houses were shoehorned together on each block—usually only a few feet separated them. Most exteriors were of clapboard, brick, or stone, and each was unique. Erica stared in rapturous awe.

"There it is—Crooked House." Megan pointed at a brick home where four turrets rose from a steeply inclined roof. Two of the towers were indeed leaning, one to the south and one to the north, making it look like something out of a Dr. Seuss book. The house had a domed rotunda with cracked and peeling paint. Four marble pillars circled the bulge. Above the rotunda—on a second level—was a narrow balcony with tall French doors.

As Megan turned into the graveled driveway, Erica craned her neck to see the chimneys between ancient beech trees, whose leaves were new and shining in the golden sun of a May afternoon. The leaning turrets and rotunda made it obvious decay had set in. Further proof lay in the window shutters that hung askew and the sagging wooden veranda.

She and Megan hurried through the rusty iron fence that guarded the house. A small, slender young woman with short, dark hair came out the side door and waited for them on the porch, an anxious look on her face.

"Oh, Megan, I'm so glad you're here." The girl saw Erica and stopped, as if unsure of herself.

"Beth, this is Erica Coleman," Megan said briskly. Beth smiled timidly and opened her mouth to speak, but Megan powered on. "Is Liz okay? What happened?"

"The deck off Liz's bedroom collapsed." Beth's brown eyes were fearful.

Megan's voice stretched thin as she asked, "Was Liz—?"

"No, she wasn't on it," Beth hurried to assure her. "But she had been earlier. I was taking a shower when I heard a noise and felt a tremor. At first I thought it might be an earthquake. I ran to find Liz, and she told me the deck had collapsed. That's when I called you."

Hurrying up the wide steps, Megan flung the door open. Beth and Erica followed her into a small white kitchen. A window over the sink overlooked the driveway and flooded the kitchen with light.

"Liz?" Megan called. When there was no answer, she turned to Beth. "Where is she?"

"In her room, getting ready for work." Beth's quiet voice held a hint of exasperation.

"She must be all right then."

"Of *course* I'm all right." A bright voice came from the stairs as an attractive girl with long, light-brown hair descended. She had fair skin and delicate features and wore a trim navy-blue uniform with a name tag pinned on the left.

"I'm Liz Johnson, and you must be Erica Coleman." She flashed a bright smile and held out a hand to Erica. "I'm happy to meet you. Megan told us all about you, raving about your cooking and talents as a private eye." Then Liz frowned at Megan. "I am sorry, though, that she made you come all this way for nothing. I kept telling her not to bother you." She made a face at Megan, who scowled back. "She and Beth have vivid imaginations."

"And you have none at all," Megan shot back. "You refuse to see what's plain to everyone else."

"You see what I'm up against?" Liz said to Erica, sounding like an exasperated parent with a beloved but misbehaving child. "Megan's utterly determined to believe the worst. I think she and Beth stay up late at night, telling each other ghost stories. They're both convinced some maniac is out to kill me."

"And you're not?" Erica was curious as to what Liz thought about it all.

Liz dismissed the idea with an impatient whisk of her head. "Of course not. I think that horrible experience Megan had at her house a few years ago unhinged her, and she's talked sweet little Beth into believing there's a killer lurking about."

Looking visibly upset, Beth protested, "But . . . but the deck collapsed."

"You're forgetting that this is a *very* old house."

"I'd like to see the deck, if you don't mind," Erica asked.

"It's just a heap of wood now," Liz replied but headed compliantly toward the door.

"I'd come with you, but I've got a class," Beth said regretfully, picking up her backpack. She gave Liz an impulsive hug. "Will you please listen to Erica?" Then she turned. "Thanks for coming, Erica. I'll see you all later."

Liz, Megan, and Erica made their way to the back of the house. Wood lay in a tumbled heap. A few boards were still attached to the house and dangled dangerously, while pieces of splintered lumber hung from the two corner poles that were still upright. On a small scale, it reminded Erica of newspaper pictures of the aftermath of a tornado. They all stared at the fractured pile wordlessly.

"You could have been in that," Megan said to Liz in an accusing tone.

"But I wasn't."

Erica glanced up to the second story at French doors that would now open onto nothing but air. "Is that your bedroom?"

"Yes."

"Do you use the deck often?" Erica stepped carefully around the broken wood, where three chairs were trapped amidst the rubble.

"Every day, usually. I like to go out there to read, study, or just relax." Liz tried to pull one of the chairs out, but it was stuck, and she gave up.

"Someone knows you go out there a lot." Megan's voice was morose.

"Oh come on, how could anyone make a deck collapse?"

That was a good question, Erica thought, looking around as if that would give her answers. "You have a beautiful yard," she said, admiring the tall, shady trees, stone pathways and brightly colored flowers. Everything was trimmed, weeded, and tidy—a distinct contrast to the decaying house. It was clear Liz had taken great pains to keep it up.

"I do what I can with the yard," Liz said. "I know the house looks like it's going to fall down, but actually its sturdy underneath, even if it does need a lot of work. Unfortunately, I'm not too good at bricklaying, electricity, plumbing, or roofing."

In the far back corner was an eight-by-eight pad of concrete with four posts sticking up. A neat pile of two-by-fours were stacked nearby.

"Are you building something?"

"A friend, BJ, offered to build a shed for my lawnmower and garden tools, so I took him up on it."

"What time do you need to go to work?" Erica asked. "If you've got time, I'd like to ask you some questions."

Liz checked her watch. "I've got a few minutes."

"Let's go sit in the gazebo," Megan suggested.

They followed the stone wedges set in the lawn, which wound around neatly tended flower beds and ended in front of a small white gazebo. There were seats along four of the walls.

"You've had two accidents, and the deck collapsing makes three," Erica began. "Don't you think that's rather extraordinary?"

Megan folded her arms tightly and glared at Liz, daring her to take it lightly. For the first time, Liz's bravado weakened, and her pretty blue eyes fell.

"I don't understand it. It seems so unreal. Why would someone want to kill me?"

"That's what we need to find out." Erica said patiently, crossing her jean-covered legs. "Tell me about Frank."

"Frank Stratton? He's my next-door neighbor." Liz looked startled. "Why?"

"Are you on good terms?"

"You can't think he's behind this—"

"I wouldn't put it past him," Megan broke in heatedly. "He's a real creep—always writing letters complaining about the place to the city, trying to get Liz into trouble."

Erica's eyebrows went up. Megan sounded more vehement about Frank than she had earlier. This could be a promising lead. However, time was short, and Erica decided to go back to the topic of the deck. "Where were you when the deck collapsed?"

"In my bedroom. It nearly fell with me on it! I had just stepped out when there was a weird creaking noise, like a groan. It scared me, so I stepped back into the house, and the next thing I knew, the whole thing fell."

"How old is the deck?"

Liz stopped to think. "I'm not sure. It wasn't part of the original house. I think I was eight when my father built it. The support poles must have gotten old and decayed."

Erica had no idea how long decks were supposed to last, but offhand, she didn't think a deck that was around eighteen years old would be falling down unless it was poorly constructed. Perhaps it'd had a little help.

A purple martin hopped onto the nearby birdbath and tilted its head at them. Liz frowned as she gazed toward the house. "I'll call my insurance in the morning and file a claim. I'd like to rebuild it, if I can come up with the deductible."

"Now, tell me about the other, um, accidents."

Liz gave her friend a withering look. "I'm sure Megan's told you all about them. Did she include the time my arm was nearly cut off?" At Erica's look of alarm, Liz went on. "Oh, I'm teasing, but I'm surprised Megan didn't mention it since she tries to make everything into a drama."

"Do not," Megan muttered.

"What happened?"

"I was helping my aunt remodel her bathroom about six weeks ago. My cousin Austin had been breaking up tile in the shower with a sledgehammer, and I wanted to try. It looked like fun. It was, too, until I got careless and cut myself on a jagged piece. Took thirty stitches." Liz pushed up her sleeve and displayed a long scar on the underside of her arm.

"Wow, that's a big cut." The scar was still dark red and swollen. Erica went on. "Megan said someone pushed you into the road."

A shadow fell across Liz's face. "I was waiting for the bus, and someone shoved me. A big pickup truck was coming, but some guy yanked me back so I didn't become a human pancake. The driver honked at me like I'd done it on purpose." Liz grimaced. "But I wasn't hurt, just shaken up."

"Did you ask the guy who helped you if he saw who pushed you?"

"It all happened so quickly I didn't think to ask. The man did say that someone behind him reached out and pushed me in the back. I figured it was kids acting stupid."

"That doesn't sound like kids fooling around," Megan remarked.

"When did this happen?"

"Last Saturday, the eleventh. Around lunchtime."

"I don't suppose you got the name of the guy that pulled you back?"

"No. He just made sure I was okay then left."

Megan spoke up, "Tell Erica about your car."

In a resigned voice, Liz explained, "I have an old car. One day the brakes wouldn't work."

"Liz, would you stop it?" Megan sounded furious. "The mechanic *told* you two of the brake lines were cut!"

Looking at Megan's red face, it occurred to Erica that it might be better not to have Megan involved in the questioning. She put a hand on

Megan's knee. "Would you mind if I talk to Liz in private?" When Megan looked at her in disbelief, Erica added, "Please?"

Disgruntled, she jumped up and flounced off.

"First of all, Liz, I want to make sure it's all right with you if I investigate." Erica tilted her head toward the house. "That's part of why I asked Megan to leave—I know she wants me to look into it and didn't want her influencing you. You probably know she can be quite forceful at times." Liz smiled slightly, and Erica went on, "The odds against having two life-threatening accidents in such a short time are pretty high, but three kind of shoots it out of the ballpark."

Liz bit her lip, looking frightened and upset. "When Megan and Beth got it into their heads that someone was trying to kill me, it sounded so crazy. I didn't take them seriously. Then they became so convinced they started to scare me. But mostly, I can't believe this is real. It's just not possible that someone would want to kill me." She glanced at the pile of wood that used to be the deck and shuddered. Her eyes seemed enormous. "After this, I don't know what to think." Liz looked distraught. "But I can't afford a private eye."

"Don't worry about that," Erica reassured her. "I'm just here to visit Megan, and while I am, I'll see what I can find out. It might be nothing, but let's check it out."

Liz's face relaxed. "I feel better just talking to you."

"Megan said the brake lines were cut. When did that happen?"

"A few days ago, let's see—it was Wednesday afternoon. I'd taken the bus home from school, had lunch, and was driving to work."

"What did the mechanic say?"

"I'm not sure I can remember it all—his explanation was kind of involved. Let's see, how did he put it?" Liz thought hard. "He said the lines had been cut partway and that if the line had been cut all the way through, all the brake fluid would have leaked out and I would have noticed right off that something was wrong because the brake pedal would have gone to the floor."

It would be best to talk to the mechanic, Erica thought, so she was clear on what had happened. "Let me ask you about Crooked House." As they sat facing the house, gilded light from the setting sun shone on the century-old bricks, softening them to a muted rose color. A few bricks here and there were crumbling. Then Erica felt a prickling at the back of her neck. For a moment, she seemed to sense an atmosphere of evil—subtle and menacing. Erica shook off the feeling.

"Megan told me you inherited the house."

"That's right. Both of my parents have passed away."

"I'm sorry." An errant breeze whispered silkily through the trees. "I know the house is old, but since it's historical and in such a nice area, wouldn't it be worth a fortune?"

"I wish." Liz grinned. "Unfortunately, this crooked little house needs a lot of repairs—all of them major. The heating and plumbing need to be redone, and although I had an electrician come a year ago, more needs to be done. It would actually cost less to tear the house down and build a new one than update it, but since it's a historic house, that's not really an option. I just wish I had the money to fix it up."

"How much is it worth?"

"I'm not sure. I could ask my aunt. She sells real estate part-time and would probably know. Aunt Donna takes care of the taxes, insurance, and all that kind of stuff for me. She's always trying to get me to sell it—guess she wants the commission."

"Do you happen to have a will?"

"As a matter of fact, I do."

Erica's question had come as a matter of habit—asking common questions to determine a motive—but she was surprised. "It's unusual for someone as young as you to have a will. What made you decide to make one?"

Liz hesitated so long that Erica wondered if she was going to answer. "Aunt Donna told me I ought to have one. She said it wasn't good if you died without one. She called it something weird, can't remember now what it was."

"Intestate?"

"That's it. It made me think of interstate, you know—like the freeway. Anyway, my aunt said if I died intestate, the government would take a lot of taxes. Austin said the same thing. He's my cousin. Personally, I still didn't see why I need a will since I don't have any money, but Aunt Donna and Austin know a lot about stuff like that and thought I ought to have one."

"I see. Who did you name as your beneficiary?"

"I split it between Aunt Donna and Austin—they're the only real family I have." Liz looked at her sharply. "Now don't go suspecting them. Aunt Donna and Austin only wanted me to make a will because they're conscientious about stuff like that. They said having a will is the kind of thing responsible people do." After a quick glance at her wristwatch, Liz said regretfully, "I'm sorry, but I need to go. I can't be late." She stood and smoothed her skirt over slim hips.

"Where do you work?"

"At the Red Roof Inn. I'm at the front desk."

As they walked to the house, Erica thanked Liz for talking with her. Then Erica stood by the side door and waved as Liz backed out of the driveway.

Megan came out and stood on the porch. "So, how did it go?"

"Good. I'm going to take a closer look at the deck. Want to come?"

Staying away from any pieces of wood that were still dangling, Erica looked at the ground under the deck, which was covered with wood chips. Some of the chips were a slightly different color than the others—brighter.

"Megan, some of the chips are new."

"I can't tell any difference." Megan bent over to examine them more closely. "I think your OCD is a little off."

Erica backed away and eyed the chips from another angle. The difference in color was subtle yet clear. The newer ones were a brighter brown. And was it her imagination, or was there a slight indentation in the ground between two of the poles?

Kneeling, she brushed the chips away from one of the posts. She moved on along the indentation, moving the chips, exposing the bare ground between the two poles. Occasionally she had to move pieces of splintered wood from the deck.

"Don't do that, Erica," Megan warned her. "What if one of those pieces of wood above falls and hits you?"

After a brief upward glance, Erica kept going, although she moved quicker. When she was done, she hopped back out of danger. "Look, Megan. The dirt has been washed away from two of the poles." Erica pointed at the shallow trench she'd uncovered from one of the outside posts to the other. The trench was smoothly rounded, which could only have been caused by water. Erica looked around the yard, going to where a hose was wound around the faucet in circles. From there, Erica eyeballed the distance to the deck.

"It's a long hose," she observed. "I'm sure it's long enough to reach the deck."

Megan stood, hands on hips, a tall, perplexed figure. "Do you think someone turned on the hose to wash the dirt away?"

"Could be." Returning to the heap, Erica moved a few more pieces of wood—one of which had a rope around it. Then she bent once again to examine one of the broken poles. Could it be? With a sinking feeling in the pit of her stomach, Erica went to the second pole. "Come look at this."

Hurrying over, Megan bent down. "What am I looking for?"

Erica ran a finger over the broken end of one of the poles. "See this edge? It's smooth. But the other half is splintered. And look at that—see those thin, horizontal marks where the wood is white?"

"Yeah. So what?"

"Those are the kind of marks a saw makes when it slips. Sometimes when you first start sawing, it's hard to keep the saw in place because there isn't a groove, and if the saw slips slightly, it gouges the wood."

"You mean someone sawed through the pole?"

"Not all the way through but enough so it would break if a little extra weight was put on it." Erica went to the other outside pole. "This one is the same way." As she stood, the shadows of the evening sun slanted deeply across Crooked House. "Megan, you were right. Someone *is* trying to kill Liz."

Chapter Three

"The kids are doing great," David said the next morning; then he went on to give more specifics, even though Erica used Skype to talk to Aby, Ryan, and Kenzie every night she was away. Sitting on the bed in her motel room, Erica put another pillow behind her back as David continued. "Your mom is having us over for dinner tonight, and we're going to Chris and Amanda's house tomorrow night."

It had been a blessing for Erica and David to live so close to her parents and two married brothers in Farmington, Utah. Her parents, Howard and Barbara Taylor, had owned fifty acres before giving Erica and each of her brothers an acre building lot when they married. They were a close family, and Erica was grateful her children had uncles and aunts nearby to watch over them and lots of cousins to play with.

The conversation veered back to Liz Johnson. David said, "I'm glad you found that trench. And all because you noticed the chips were different colors."

"Whoever let the water run was a little lazy. When the water didn't make the poles collapse, they didn't bother to fill in the trench with dirt—just covered it with woodchips."

"Which means it had to be done by someone living close. Maybe a handyman or neighbor."

Erica wished it could be that easy to narrow down the suspects. "Unfortunately, Liz's yard isn't fenced, and I found several bags of wood chips leaning against the house. So really, anyone could have done it."

"What about the other roommate? What do you know about her?"

"Beth Johnson. I haven't talked to her yet, but from what Megan said, she seems really sweet. Megan's been taking her to church—it sounds like Beth is very interested."

"How did Liz take it when she found out the poles had been sawed?"

"I haven't had a chance to tell her yet. Megan's going to pick me up this afternoon when she's done with her last morning class. I offered to cook dinner tonight, so I'll tell Liz then. She's been pretty blasé about these accidents, but she's got to take them seriously now."

"You'd better contact the Dover police."

"I will. I'd like to get the deck collapsing on record as an incident, so if something else happens, the police will have a paper trail. I hope they'll take me seriously—I haven't got much to go on yet. Megan already called, and they thought she was a fruitcake."

He laughed. "I bet Megan took *that* well. Be sure and tell them you're a licensed private investigator with Pinnacle Investigations. That ought to increase your credibility."

Erica sighed. "It looks like I might be here longer than I thought. I'd better call Doug."

David knew Doug Hadfield well. "I'm sure your boss will be fine with it. Oh, one other thing, be sure to ask Liz about past boyfriends."

"I'll do that. She's very pretty—maybe some guy didn't want to give her up."

"You could also ask Super Snoop aka Megan. She ought to be able to give you names of anyone Liz has dated."

"Why do you always give Megan terrible nicknames?"

"Habit. I've been doing it since she became a teenager, and I can't seem to stop."

* * *

It was easier for Erica to appreciate the distinctive flavor of historic Dover when she wasn't worried about Megan skidding out of control and plowing into somebody's white picket fence. When Megan picked her up at Hampton Inn, she allowed Erica to quickly wipe the seats. They stopped at Safeway then went on to the historic district.

Megan drove sedately, allowing Erica time to savor the distinctive houses and Victorian architecture. In the heart of Dover's historic district was a square known as The Green, where the Delaware Supreme Court, the Old State House, and the Kent County Courthouse were located. Farther on, Erica craned her neck this way and that to take in the historic houses as Megan wound through the slender streets. Carving must have been the national pastime a century ago, Erica decided, since nearly every house was richly embellished with ornate carvings, curlicues, and jigsaw work.

Compared to other homes, Crooked House looked quite dilapidated. Last night, Erica had missed the broken fan-shaped glass at the top of the front door, and the door itself had been boarded up against the weather. A bricked pathway led to the house from the front sidewalk, but many of the bricks were cracked and uneven. Perhaps to offset this, Liz had taken pains to plant bright red petunias and yellow marigolds along the walkway.

They pulled into the graveled driveway, grabbed the groceries and Erica's briefcase from the backseat, and went through the open gate in the black, spiked fence. Megan unlocked the side door and went in. Behind her, Erica closed the door, opened it, then closed it again.

"Would it hurt you to try and act normal?" Megan shook her head.

Just inside was a sign with block letters: THIS IS AN AMERICAN HOUSE WITH JAPANESE STYLE—PLEASE REMOVE YOUR SHOES.

"I didn't see that yesterday. I have a sign just like it!" Erica cried.

"Liz pitches a fit if we forget. She's almost as nutty about keeping her house neat and clean as you are."

Ah, a compadre. Erica set her briefcase on the small kitchen table. "How do you like living here?"

"I love it. Except that I can't give in to my inner slob. Liz keeps everything picked up and cleaned to within an inch of its life."

Erica found herself liking Liz more and more.

"Beth and I help with chores," Megan explained, "but Liz won't let us touch the hardwood floors. Once, I started washing the front room floor, and Liz acted like I was hammering nails into it." Megan mimicked Liz with a high falsetto. "This home was built in 1890, and these are the *original* hardwood floors. The *only* thing I use on them is Murphy's Oil Soap."

"What *were* you using?"

"Ammonia in water."

Erica steadied herself by reaching out a hand to the counter. She informed Megan in a voice that shook a little, "You never use harsh cleaners on hardwood floors—they require special treatment."

"Whatever." Megan was unconcerned as she began putting groceries in the fridge.

"Do you have a nine-by-thirteen pan?" Erica asked. "I need to get the chicken marinating right away. " She fished around in her purse and brought out two bars of Lava soap. She set one by the sink and lathered up with the other. "I brought one for me and one for you guys."

"Did you carve your name on yours?" Megan asked with a slight smile. She got a pan out of the cupboard. "Is there anything you need before I head back to school? I've got one more class. Oh, and just so you know, Liz usually gets home an hour or so before I do."

"I'm fine."

Sounds of hammering came from the backyard.

"Sounds like BJ's working on the tool shed," Megan said. "He's always around, helping Liz."

* * *

After Megan left, Erica mixed up the marinade, covered the chicken, and put it in the fridge. She then went through the arched doorway into the adjoining front room, with its faded mossy green rug that had roses mixed in with the green. The heavy velvet draperies had faded over the years as had several chairs that were upholstered in green cut velvet. The furniture appeared antique, if a bit shabby, and matched the décor perfectly. There was a lacquered wooden desk that looked so old Erica didn't dare put her laptop on it, but she found a small folding table in the closet. Waiting for her computer to boot up, Erica glanced upward at the magnificent crystal chandelier overhead. Ornate crown molding and intricately carved rosettes adorned the upper part of the walls.

Erica spent the next few hours doing preliminary research. Finally the back door opened and Megan came in, plopping down on the patterned couch. Erica looked at her in surprise. "I thought Liz would get home before you."

"Liz texted me saying she's going to be late. Said she had a surprise."

"You don't think she's going to stop and bring something home for dinner?"

"Not unless Taco Time has started taking beads instead of money. Besides, I told her you were making dinner." There was the sound of a car crunching onto the driveway. "I bet that's her."

When Liz came in, she held her backpack in front of the upper half of her body so Megan and Erica couldn't see her head. When she got to the doorway, Liz dropped the backpack. Holding out her arms, she spun around. "Ta da! What do you think?"

"You cut your hair!" Megan exclaimed, sitting up straight. "It's *so* cute!"

"I've been wanting to for a long time. Beth looks so great with short hair; I finally got up the courage to go for it."

"It looks great," Erica said with a smile as Liz patted her hair. She was so animated. Energy seemed to flow from her in waves.

"Megan said you were making dinner," Liz said. "Is there anything I can do to help?"

Erica shut down her computer, and they went into the kitchen. "How about washing the romaine and tearing it up for the salad?"

"Sure." At the sink, Liz looked at the two bars of soap. "What's this?"

"It's Lava," Erica replied. "The original, heavy-duty hand cleaner."

Megan responded to Liz's perplexed expression. "Remember I told you about Erica and her OCD?" She twirled her index finger in circles by the side of her head. "Erica's got a thing about Lava soap. If she could marry a bar, she would."

Erica remained unruffled. "Lava is the best soap you can buy. It has moisturizers, pumice, and other cleaning agents to clean and soften even the dirtiest of hands."

"She sounds like a TV ad," Liz whispered to Megan.

"Just use the Lava, and no one will get hurt," Megan replied. "It's useless to fight her on this. Believe me, I've tried."

As they worked, Erica asked, "What time does Beth usually get home?"

Liz glanced at the clock on the wall. "Not for another hour."

"All right. Now, where's your indoor grill? Megan said you had one."

As Liz set it on the counter, she asked, "So what are you cooking?"

"Rosemary Ranch Chicken.[1] You'll love it."

As Megan started to cut up the broccoli, she told Liz, "Erica loves to cook, though I don't know why."

"It's relaxing, and it also helps me to think. Cleaning does too."

"I *told* you she had a diseased brain," Megan said to Liz. "Once Erica told me she liked cooking because it was a precise activity."

"Which is true," Erica said complacently. "And it goes right along with investigating—another precise activity. If you follow the steps exactly, everything will turn out as expected."

"Ha!" This from Megan.

"I only cook if I get tired of cereal," Liz remarked.

Erica looked at her in alarm. "Please tell me you're kidding."

"Not by much."

"Tell me, oh, precise one," Megan began, "what's your first step in finding out who's after Liz?"

"I'll go and talk to the police tomorrow."

---

1 See the appendix at the end of the book for this recipe.

"Megan already talked with them," Liz said dispiritedly. "And they didn't do anything."

"Hopefully they'll listen now that there's evidence someone sabotaged the deck." Erica told Liz about the sawed poles.

Liz stood very still, her eyes wide with shock. "So it's really true?" Her vivacity disappeared, leaving her voice flat and lifeless. "I—I can't believe it. Why would someone want to kill me?"

Erica felt for the girl. Something in Liz's voice reminded her of a child crying out for help. "That's what we need to find out." She paused then added firmly, "And we will." To distract Liz, she rinsed a cucumber and handed it to the young woman. "Dice that up, and add it to the lettuce."

Mechanically, Liz did as she was told.

Megan got plates from the cupboard then stopped. "I was going to set the table, but why bother when Erica Coleman is in the house?"

"Don't be smart," Erica said, waving a spoon at her. "I'll set it if you'll put the chicken on. I think the grill has preheated long enough."

While Erica painstakingly lined up the plates two inches from the edge of the table, Megan and Liz exchanged amused glances.

"Megan's told me about your OCD," Liz said.

Erica began setting out the utensils. "It's so much nicer when things are neat and symmetrical. It also helps the digestion."

After a blessing on the food, Liz took a bite of chicken. "Hey, this is terrific! You really *are* a gourmet cook. You must spend a lot of time in the kitchen when you're home."

"Not really. I like to cook, but I'm too busy to spend hours fixing meals. My favorite recipes are ones that are delicious, yet easy to fix."

"Speaking of dinners, that reminds me—my Aunt Donna is having a party tomorrow night, and you're invited. She gives one every year for old and hopefully new clients."

"Sounds great. Didn't you say your aunt is a Realtor?"

"Actually, she's a bookkeeper at Park Place Realty, but a few years ago, her boss, Mr. Rochford, helped Aunt Donna get her real estate license—so now she also sells. My cousin, Austin, also works there part-time. He's going to school too."

"Could you give me your aunt's phone number? I'd like to call her later." Erica dabbed at her blouse where a bit of juice from the chicken had dripped. "Rats. Oh well, I can change when I get to the motel. Megan, will you be able to take me back after dinner?"

"Sure."

Liz frowned. "We can't have you staying at a motel. Come and stay here with us."

"That's a great idea," Megan cried enthusiastically. "We can be roomies!"

"That's very nice of you, but I don't want to intrude."

"Nonsense," Liz said. "We'd love to have you."

"I'll come on one condition."

"What's that?" Liz asked.

"That you let me do the cooking while I'm here."

Throwing her head back, Liz laughed. "You'll get no argument from me." The back door opened, and Beth came in. "Hi, everyone!" She did a double take when she saw Liz. "Oh, my goodness! What did you do to your hair?" She came closer. "It's darling!"

"Thank you!" Liz preened then asked, "What are you doing home?"

"The professor let us out early. Yay!"

Megan got a plate, put a piece of chicken on it, and handed it to Beth, who inhaled deeply. "This smells wonderful!"

"And it tastes even better," Megan assured her. "*And* we'll be benefiting from Erica's culinary expertise in the future." She explained that Erica would be staying with them.

"Never turn down someone who offers to cook—that's my motto," Liz joked. Then she asked Erica, "Do you want to pick up your things and come back here tonight?"

Erica thought about it. "Thanks, but I think tomorrow would work better." Then she looked at the three girls. "You have to tell me how you all met."

Beth spoke first. "Liz and I met when we took the same English class."

"You have to tell Erica the *whole* story," Megan insisted. "It's kind of funny." In an aside to Erica, she added, "They met because they have the same name."

Erica looked puzzled. "I get that your last name is the same, but Beth and Liz are totally different."

"Beth will explain," Liz replied. "Go ahead."

Sounding a little timid, Beth began. "Liz and I were both sophomores and took the same English lit class, which had, like, two hundred students. After class, the professor told us to check the attendance roll that he'd taped to the door, to make sure there weren't any typos. When I saw the list, I thought they'd typed 'Elizabeth Johnson' twice by mistake, so I started to draw a line through the second one. Liz was standing behind me. She tapped me on the shoulder and asked what I was doing. She was really upset."

Liz giggled. "I couldn't figure out why this little mouse was crossing out my name! I hadn't noticed there were two. After a minute, we figured out we had the same name, although we go by different first names."

"Johnson *is* a common last name," Beth added with a smile. "Anyway, we got to talking and became friends. I moved in with Liz, and a year later, Liz's cousin introduced her to Megan."

"And we lived happily ever after," Megan said.

"I know Megan is majoring in liberal arts, but what are your majors?" Erica asked.

"Retail management," Liz responded.

"And I'm in elementary education," Beth said.

When they finished eating, Erica stood. "I hate to stick you guys with the dishes, but I'd like to ask Liz some questions in the front room."

"Another private interrogation?" Megan asked with a quirked eyebrow.

"Yep."

"Oh, good. Not only did I *not* have to cook, I also get out of cleaning up," Liz said, pleased, as she went in and settled on the end of the couch.

Erica took the green chair by the desk. "I know I asked before, but I need you to really think. Is there any reason why someone would want to harm you?"

"I've thought and thought, and I can't think of a thing." Liz rubbed her forehead.

"Do you have any enemies?"

"No, not unless you count Frank Stratton—but I don't really think of him as an enemy. He's just a crazy old man. And I can't imagine him trying to try kill me, even if he is a major jerk."

Erica was tempted to smile. "All right. I need to ask you some personal questions."

"Go ahead."

"Do you take drugs?"

"No."

"I'm sorry I had to ask, but a lot of murders happen over drug deals. Next, do you owe anybody money?"

"Just the utility companies—and the government for student loans."

"Have you been or are you now involved in anything shady or illegal?" That question didn't always get honest answers, but Erica had to ask.

Affronted, Liz replied, "Of course not."

"Have you got a boyfriend?"

"Why do you ask that?" Liz shot out, her voice unexpectedly strong.

"Sometimes boyfriends can be jealous."

Bowing her head, Liz stared at her lap. "No boyfriend." Her voice was strangely dull and mechanical.

"What about past boyfriends? Have you had any relationships with a man who had been convicted of a crime, or have you broken up with anyone who was jealous or upset when the relationship ended?"

Liz paused then replied, "No."

"Tell me about yourself and your family."

"I don't have a lot of family. I was nine when my father was killed in a car crash. My mother died seven years ago from cancer and left me this house. I've lived here all my life. My father had two brothers. Uncle Lee was in the army and retired a few years ago. He lives in Vermont. We're not close, but we do talk once every six or eight months. I've lost track of my other uncle, Ron. I never really knew him. There was some sort of trouble when my grandfather died and left the house to my father. From what I've been told, Uncle Ron was upset about it and took off. I haven't seen or heard from him since my mother's funeral."

"What about your mother's side of the family?"

"My mom had two sisters. My aunt Betty lives in Kansas. We talk occasionally, and she comes to visit once in a while. Then there's Aunt Donna, who lives here in Dover."

"Is Donna married?"

"She's a widow. Her husband died four years ago. They had three children. The oldest son, Jerry, lives in Nevada, and Shelly lives in Georgia. I don't know them very well. Austin is the youngest and has an apartment on the other side of Dover. We're pretty close, probably since he's only a couple years older than me."

Erica ran through the list of standard questions, but they shed little light on Liz's predicament.

When the interview was over, Megan drove Erica to the motel. She called David and talked to him and the children. When she said goodnight, Erica had to blink the tears away—she missed her family so much.

As she got ready for bed, Erica went over Liz's answers in her mind. There didn't seem much to go on, but she would just keep digging until something turned up. It always did.

* * *

The next morning, after breakfast, Erica called Liz's aunt, Donna Phillips, hoping she might be able to provide some information that would help identify Liz's would-be killer.

"Hello, Donna? This is Erica Coleman. I'm a private investigator, and I'd like—"

"Hold on," Donna interrupted brusquely. In a moment she was back. "What do you want?" Her tone was unexpectedly harsh.

Taken aback, Erica replied, "I had some questions I wanted to ask."

"I know why you're calling, but I'd prefer you didn't call me at work."

"This is the number Liz gave me. Do you have a cell phone number? I wondered if we could meet today and—"

Again, Donna cut her off, sounding upset. "Liz gave you this number?"

"Yes. She thought I could meet you at your office. She's worried about what's going on, and I hoped you might be able to give me some information."

"Liz is worried?" Donna sounded flabbergasted.

Erica couldn't understand it. Why *wouldn't* Liz be worried? "Very—and scared. Her roommates are too. I'm a friend of Megan Kemp. She's the one who called me."

Sounding bewildered, Donna asked, "Why on earth would Megan call you?"

Erica was just as confused and hardly knew what to say. "Because she's scared about what's been going on."

"Megan's scared? I don't understand."

That made two of them. Perhaps she'd better start at the beginning. "Megan called me because she thinks someone is trying to kill Liz."

A long silence. Then Donna asked, "Is this about the accidents Liz has been having?"

The woman finally got it. "Yes, it is."

"And that's what Megan talked to you about investigating?"

What is it that makes this so hard to understand? "Megan's worried, and so is Liz. I hoped you'd be able to help."

The frostiness melted out of Donna's voice. "I'm sorry. I didn't mean to be rude. It's just that I didn't know Liz had hired a private investigator."

"She didn't. I'm a good friend of Megan's, and she asked me to come. Could I meet with you today or tomorrow?"

"Today's not good—I'm having a party at my house tonight. But you can call me tomorrow or just stop by the office. Did Liz give you the address for Park Place Realty?"

"She did. Thanks." When Erica hung up, she wondered if she might be able to talk with Donna tonight. Probably not. A party wasn't a good time to ask penetrating questions—especially from someone who had seemed so antagonistic. Erica frowned. Why was that? Altogether it had been a strange phone call. Why had Donna been so unfriendly—almost hostile? And why had Donna claimed she knew why Erica was calling?

Chapter Four

THE LADY AT THE FRONT desk of the Hampton Inn seemed a little surprised when Erica asked which bus to take to the police station, but she recovered quickly and gave efficient directions. From the bus stop, it was a short walk to the corner of Bank Lane and South Queen to a large, red-brick building with two imposing white columns. Erica went up the wide, red-brick stairway to the door. Above it was a metal sign that read, *Dover City Police Department.*

After explaining what she wanted, Erica was shown into a cubicle, where an officer listened to her story. He then directed her to another policeman. After relating her tale again, that officer sent her on to yet another officer, this time a detective.

Detective Ranquist was an intelligent-looking man in his late forties, with gray hair at the temples. He was fit—athletic, even—and had shrewd eyes. When she entered his office, Erica closed the door, opened it slightly, then closed it again. Detective Ranquist looked at her questioningly but greeted her pleasantly and made no comment on her actions. The office was small. The blinds of the two south-facing windows were open, allowing the spring sunshine to stream inside. Erica went over Liz's story once again.

Detective Ranquist's manner was relaxed, agreeable, and absolutely noncommittal. "I understand your concern, and certainly three accidents in such a short amount of time would worry anyone."

Erica willed herself not to frown at the "but" she knew was coming.

"But the incidents you're describing could very well be accidents."

"It's not an accident when someone saws almost all the way through the support poles of an often-used deck."

Wearing a skeptical look, Detective Ranquist said condescendingly, "It's more likely the poles simply rotted away with age, or the braces connecting the deck to the house failed. And those marks on the poles could have been there since it was built."

"What about Liz being pushed in front of a pickup truck?"

"Kids horse around."

"And the car losing its brakes?"

Detective Ranquist didn't have a glib answer this time. "Cars do break down," he said finally, rubbing his chin thoughtfully.

Erica pressed her point. "Three 'accidents' in less than a week is a coincidence of gigantic proportions."

"Stranger things have happened." The detective's lack of enthusiasm was exceeded only by that of the previous police officers who had talked with Erica. Then he went on the offense. "Why hasn't Liz Johnson called the police herself if she's so worried?"

"Because she didn't want to believe someone was trying to kill her."

"And you do."

"Yes, sir. I wasn't sure at first, but the sawed poles convinced me."

Detective Ranquist leaned back in his chair and studied his visitor. "Are you related to Liz Johnson?"

"No, I'm a close friend of her roommate, Megan Kemp. Megan asked me to come because I'm a private investigator with Pinnacle Investigations, an agency in Utah."

There was a glimmer of interest in his dark brown eyes, and he leaned forward, elbows on his desk. "How long have you been a private eye?"

"Twelve years. Before that, I served as a police officer for two years. My husband is a police officer in Farmington, Utah."

Erica sensed a thawing in Detective Ranquist's manner, and he began asking pertinent questions. "Has anyone made any threats to Liz? Is she a drug dealer? Has she recently obtained a restraining order against anyone?"

Rats. Just when Erica had been making headway. "No, no, and no." It was evident the small window of opportunity had slammed shut.

The detective leaned back again. "There's not much we can do without more to go on."

Erica stood and shook hands with Detective Ranquist, whose face was once again back to the "polite but impersonal" setting. Cordially, he said, "I appreciate your coming in to see us. I'll write up an incident report so it's on record, and I'll have an officer contact Liz. That's the most I can do."

Knowing police budgets were tight everywhere and that no threats had been made, Erica was grateful Detective Ranquist would at least have someone talk to Liz. For now, the rest was up to Erica.

* * *

When Megan texted that she was on the way to the hotel, Erica brought her bags down the elevator and waited out front. The weather was mild and pleasant, the sun warm, as Megan pulled up.

"Is this Liz's car?" Erica asked as Megan opened the trunk.

"Yeah, but don't worry—the brakes are fixed. I asked if I could borrow it. Now watch this." Megan held out the car remote and pushed a button. The engine started up, and Megan smiled broadly. "Is that cool or what? In the winter, you can turn it on and warm up the car without even leaving the house. Liz just points the remote out the kitchen window when the car's in the driveway."

At Crooked House, Megan lifted out the larger suitcase with a groan. "What have you got in here? A case of Lava?" Megan never failed to tease Erica about her fanatical devotion to the soap.

"Don't you wish!"

They carted the suitcases up the stairs, and Megan sat on the edge of the bed as Erica unpacked. "How did it go with the police? They sure didn't listen to me when I called."

"I think it helped to talk to them in person. I had to tell my story three times, but the last officer, Detective Ranquist, finally said he'd send an officer out to talk to Liz."

Megan was impressed. "You got a lot further with them than I did."

"That's because you're a fruitcake."

Megan stuck out her tongue.

"And so mature for your age."

When Erica pulled out a nightlight from her case and plugged it in, she saw a flash of sympathy cross Megan's face. Megan was one of the few who knew about Erica's fear of the dark. Years ago, when trying to help a teenage Megan find the strength to fight her own fears, Erica had divulged her secret—that when she was six, a prank-playing cousin had locked her in a pitch-black basement closet and left her screaming there for five mind-numbing hours. It was an incident Erica kept tightly guarded because—despite counseling—it had left her with a profound fear of the dark.

Megan went to the dresser and held up her long, black hair, tilting her head one way then another. "Maybe I ought to cut my hair too."

"I like it the way it is."

"But Liz looks so cute. I'm surprised she cut it, though—she told me once she didn't like short hair." Megan let her hair fall. "Of course, when you're as pretty as she is, you could wear a skunk on your head and get compliments."

"You're just as cute."

"Oh yeah, right," she said skeptically. "I'd love to be tiny and petite like Liz."

A big girl, Megan had always been self-conscious about her size, inherited from her father, who had been a tall, husky man. Self-consciousness had made Megan awkward during her adolescent years, and Erica was glad when she'd outgrown most of her self-consciousness and become comfortable with herself. She decided to add a little reassurance.

"You're perfect the way you are. Everybody stares when you come into a room because you're so tall and graceful and pretty." Looking into the mirror, Erica held up her own hair so it fell just to her shoulders. "Do you think I should cut *my* hair?"

"Absolutely not." Megan gently slapped at her hand so Erica's hair fell in bouncy waves. "It's perfect the way it is, and I love the color—brown with a lot of red."

"The word is *auburn,*" Erica informed her. She laid her scriptures on the nightstand then went over to gaze into the wire cage on the dresser, where a furry little hamster peered about inquisitively.

"I can't believe you have a hamster." Erica still remembered the sweet moment during her visit to Florida two years ago when Megan's little brother, Brandon, had brought his hamster into his sister's room. Megan had just been released from the hospital, and Brandon told her he didn't want her to be alone at night.

"I got used to the stupid wheel going 'round and 'round at night, so when Brandon took his hamster back to his room, I couldn't sleep and got one of my own."

What's his name?"

"Hamlet."

"Are you serious?" Erica giggled and put her finger to where the honey-brown hamster had wrapped his delicate little paws around the wire of the cage. She straightened and turned around. "I wanted to ask you about Beth and Liz. Do they get along all right?"

"Yeah, fine."

"No jealousy, rivalry, arguments? Could Beth have any reason to want Liz dead?"

Megan shook her head. "None. Beth is the sweetest person I know. Plus, she'd never have the nerve—she's way too timid. Besides, she's the one who told me she thought Liz was in danger. No, you can cross Beth off your list. She's nice—sometimes too nice."

"Is that possible?"

"It sure is. I can never measure up to her, so I gave up trying."

"You mentioned once that Beth had started going to church with you. Has Liz shown any interest?"

"No, I keep asking, but she keeps saying no. But her aunt and cousin are members and keep encouraging her—so maybe she'll join the Church someday."

"So, how's it going with Beth?"

Megan's face glowed as she sat on the bed. "Really good. She loves it and has even started taking the missionary discussions."

"Awesome."

"Beth was scared to tell her parents that she was thinking about becoming a member, but it turned out all right. They were worried at first—thought Mormonism was some kind of a cult."

"Oh dear." Overcoming preconceived notions could be difficult, Erica knew.

"They're okay with it now that they know more. Sometimes I go and stay with Beth at her house on weekends, and a couple of times, I've asked her parents to come to church with us."

"Did they?"

"Yep, but not for the reasons I'd hoped." Megan grinned. "They wanted to check it out for Beth, double-check what I'd told them—that Mormons didn't practice polygamy, have blood sacrifices—that sort of thing. They thought sacrament meeting was a little noisy, but other than that, they were surprised—and relieved—to find out it was just a regular church. And the members were friendly. They were impressed by that."

"Oh good—that can make a big difference."

* * *

Late that afternoon, Erica went downstairs to find Beth at the kitchen table, studying a thick textbook, *Activities for Developing Mathematical Thinking*. "Ah, doing a little light reading, I see."

Beth closed her book and smiled. "I wish. Are Megan and Liz about ready to go to Donna's?"

"Almost." Then Erica sat next to her. "Do you know Liz's aunt very well?"

"Not really, but she's always seemed nice whenever I have talked with her."

"When I called Donna this morning, she sounded—um, strange. Like she was upset or confused."

"The upset part could be that she's stressed about the party." Beth thought hard. "Or else she's worried about Liz."

"Maybe." Erica wondered if either of those would be enough to put that hard edge in Donna's voice.

Putting her book aside, Beth said, "You ought to do some sightseeing while you're here."

What Erica wanted to do most was solve the case and go home, but still . . . "Do you have any suggestions?"

Beth's face lit up. "First, go to the Air Force Museum. It's great. My father was in the air force, so maybe that's why I love it. There are also a lot of great beaches around and a bunch of lighthouses."

The last one caught Erica's attention. "Oh, I love lighthouses!"

"Me too. Another one of the big draws around here is the Dover International Speedway. The NASCAR Sprint Cup is coming up soon, if you like to watch racing. You could also go see the governor's mansion in Woodburn. And there's Dover Downs if you like horse racing and gambling."

"I'm not too big on gambling." Erica smiled.

"Oh that's right. Megan told me you were LDS. I've gone to church with her a few times."

"How's that going?"

"I like it," Beth said sincerely. "I've really enjoyed the meetings, and the people have been so nice."

"I wanted to ask you about Liz. Do you know why someone would want to hurt her?"

"You're asking me?" Meek little Beth seemed surprised that someone would ask her opinion. "Liz is so wonderful; I can't see why anyone would want to hurt her."

There was a clatter on the stairs, and Liz burst into the kitchen, wearing a brown blouse under a lime-green sweater.

"All set?" Liz asked, full of energy. "You guys are great to go over early with me and help Aunt Donna get things ready for the barbecue. She's a little stressed right now, what with Grandpa and all."

"What's going on with her father?" Erica asked.

"His health has been going downhill the past couple of years, and he finally got to where he couldn't live alone, so Aunt Donna took him in about four months ago. It's been really hard."

Perhaps that was why Donna had been short with her, Erica thought, glad she had offered to go help.

As Megan came down the stairs, Liz went on. "Austin will be there too, so you'll be able to meet my handsome cousin. You'll like him—everyone does. Okay, people, let's go!" She picked up a plate of brownies and headed outside, clicking the remote starter. Beth followed Megan, who carried a grocery sack with three bags of potato chips.

As they approached the car, Erica pulled out her ever-present packet of wet wipes. "Hold on, this'll just take a minute."

Liz stared. "You carry wet wipes around with you?"

"Of course."

As Erica industriously wiped the seats, Liz sidled over to Megan and whispered, "What's up with this?"

"One of Erica's little quirks."

"Like lining up the plates and that Lava soap?"

Megan nodded. "Erica's OCD makes her catch a lot of stuff that other people miss, which makes her a great detective, but it comes at a price—she can drive you crazy."

"I heard that." Erica's muffled voice came from deep inside the car.

"I wasn't whispering," Megan replied.

They climbed in, and as Liz backed out onto the road, she called over her shoulder, "Hey, Megan, is Todd coming?" There was archness to the question that made Erica pay attention.

"Yes," Megan mumbled.

Liz winked at Erica. "What was that? Couldn't quite hear you."

"He's coming," Megan snapped. "All right?"

Erica turned around to look at Megan. "Who's Todd? You've never mentioned him before."

"He's just a friend," Megan murmured, turning to look out the window. Her nose practically touched the glass.

"Nice of you to invite your 'friend.'" Liz sounded amused.

"That's because I'm the sweetest thing that ever lived," Megan retorted. "Todd said he didn't have anything to do and that a barbecue sounded wonderful—blah, blah, blah. I *had* to ask him. It was either that or throw up."

Beth giggled, and soon Liz pulled up in front of a cream brick house that had two rectangular flower beds on either side of the sidewalk leading to the door.

"What a great yard," Erica remarked. "It's perfectly symmetrical."

"Glad it's got your seal of approval."

They left the food in the kitchen and went out a sliding door to the patio. Donna, a middle-aged woman with short, highlighted hair, stood at a table, pulling tablecloths out of a box. Liz waved at a young man in back, who was setting up round, wooden tables. He waved back. The long rectangle of lawn was bordered on the east side by a neighbor's trim yard and flowerbeds. On the west, the neighbor's yard consisted of a thick tangle of trees, overgrown mountain laurel, bayberry, and rhododendrons.

Donna, wearing a bright-orange top and flowered capris, hugged Liz then pulled back to look at her more closely. "When did you cut your hair?"

"Yesterday. I stopped by the office to show you and Austin, but you were gone."

"Well, it looks great. Thanks for coming over early to help set up." Erica noticed dark circles under Donna's eyes as she added, "I see you've brought reinforcements, but there's not all that much left to do."

"You've met Megan and Beth," Liz said. "And this is Erica, a friend of Megan's."

There was an air of reserve about Donna, and her eyes had a wary, searching look when she looked at Erica. Why would that be? Erica wondered. Then again, that was a fairly common reaction to meeting a private investigator. Then, as quickly as flipping a switch, Donna's manner changed.

"So you're Erica." Donna gave her a warm, sunny smile as she took Erica's proffered hand.

"I hope you don't mind Liz inviting me."

"Glad to have you. I want to apologize for the misunderstanding when you called. I thought you were someone else."

Apparently that someone else had to be high on Donna's list of people she disliked—or perhaps was afraid of.

The young man with crisply curling brown hair came up to meet them. Liz introduced her cousin to Erica. Austin had a boyish, appealing smile, and the hand that clasped hers was firm and warm.

"Nice to meet you, Erica. Good to see you, Beth and Megan." The timbre of Austin's voice was attractive—deep and resonant—and Erica noticed that his eyes lingered on Megan.

Donna turned brisk. “Austin could use some help with the lights, and one of you could put the tablecloths on and set a citronella candle in the middle. And I could use a hand with the vegetable trays after I check on my father.”

“How is Grandpa today?” Liz asked.

“As well as can be expected. His nurse is really so good with him.” Donna’s voice sounded mired in sadness, as if she was making a determined effort to be cheerful.

Liz volunteered to help her aunt, and they went into the house

“Megan, could you help me with the lights?” Austin asked. Megan nodded, her cheeks unusually pink as she began pulling strings of lights from the box.

“Looks like we’ll have to untangle them first,” Erica said.

There were two boxes, one with strands of miniature bulbs and one with strands of larger light bulbs. Beth separated the sets while Austin, Erica, and Megan began untangling individual strands. To prevent them from tangling again, the trio draped the strands over a lilac bush on the corner of the patio, which was heavy with purple blossoms and gave off a heavenly scent.

“So, Austin,” Erica began, “tell me about yourself.”

“I’m not sure how much I should tell a private detective.” Austin winked at Megan as he deftly unknotted tangles. “Let’s see, I’m in the master’s program at Delaware State University and *really* looking forward to graduating in a few weeks. I work at Park Place Realty—”

Megan jumped in. “He’s one of their top salesmen, although he only works part-time.”

When Austin beamed at her, Megan flushed and bent low over a knotted strand.

“Park Place—that’s the same place your mother works, isn’t it?” Erica asked.

He nodded and chatted on, seeming to have limitless patience with the knots, while Megan kept muttering darkly under her breath.

Finally they were done. Austin went to get a ladder, while Erica grabbed an armload of tablecloths. Megan followed, carrying a box of candles.

“I’m glad Austin was here to help with those stupid lights,” she said. “He’s so patient. If it had been left to me, I’d have thrown them all in the garbage.”

Erica smoothed a cloth and walked around the table to make sure it was even on all sides. “You can tell a lot about a person by the way he handles three things: a rainy day, lost luggage, and tangled Christmas tree lights." Erica spread out another tablecloth. "How long have you known Austin?"

"About a year. I went with a girlfriend to a singles' fireside and met him there."

Erica went around the table, pulling the cloth this way and that while Megan waited. "Erica! It's fine. Nobody cares if one side is a centimeter longer than the other."

"Au contraire! If the tablecloths are uneven, everyone would feel uncomfortable."

"I don't suppose you want me to put the candles on, since I don't have a measuring tape to make sure they're precisely in the middle of the table."

"I'll do it. I don't need a tape measure," Erica said smugly.

"That's right. Dead-eye Erica. How could I have forgotten?" With a roll of her eyes, Megan went to hold the ladder for Austin, who was teetering as Beth handed him lights.

Liz opened the patio door. "Hold on, Beth. Use the small lights."

Perplexed, Beth glanced at the lights in her hand. "I thought the larger ones would give more light."

"The smaller ones will be cuter though."

With a small shrug, Beth acquiesced and carried the larger lights back to the patio.

* * *

They went home to change then returned to set out the food. Megan had wrapped a red scarf around her head, tying it at the back of her neck. Her long hair flowed over her shoulders in rippling black waves as she helped Liz set up the chocolate fountain. Beth, wearing a tan blouse and a sweater, carried out plastic-wrapped platters of strawberries, pineapple, marshmallows, and brownie bites for guests to dip in chocolate. As Austin tended to ribs on the grill, the aroma of barbecue sashayed through the yard, drifting on the air and causing a rippling sensation deep in the stomach.

Megan and Erica were chatting on the patio when a tall, handsome man came through the open gate. His eyes grazed the yard as if searching for someone.

"Oh! There's Todd!" Megan waved at the man, who wore a pale-yellow, button-down shirt that brought out his deep tan. He was solid, muscular, handsome—and the center of attention as he moved through the guests with the easy grace of an athlete. He came over and slipped an arm around Megan's waist as she introduced him.

"This is Erica Coleman. Erica, this is Todd McCauley. He's a race car driver." Megan sounded proud. Todd was the male equivalent of Danica Patrick, the attractive female race car driver. Erica was sure female fans swooned over him.

"You certainly have an exciting job," Erica remarked. "Do you love it?"

"It's awesome," Todd admitted with a flash of white teeth. "I wouldn't do anything else."

"He'll be racing in the NASCAR races," Megan said.

"I came to town a little early so I could see the sights," Todd said, looking at Megan with such arresting blue eyes that she seemed discombobulated. She broke the ensuing silence by blurting out, "Erica's from Utah."

Todd turned his attention to her. "What brings you to Dover, Erica?"

For a moment Erica debated between stating the truth or sugarcoating it. She settled on the former. "I'm here to find a killer."

Todd's tanned face went blank. "Excuse me?"

Megan made a scoffing sound. "And she calls *me* blunt." Then she explained to Todd, "Erica's here because of those accidents Liz has been having. She's a private investigator."

Understanding dawned. "Oh, I see. But if you're worried, why don't you just call the cops?"

"I have," Megan said irritably, "but they won't listen to me."

"That's because you're a fruitcake," Erica said teasingly then laughed.

Megan scowled and grabbed Todd's hand. "Come on; let's get something to eat."

Erica followed them through the buffet line, which was shaded by an immense oak, creating a zone of cool, sweet air. They went over and sat at a table with Beth and Austin. A few minutes later, Donna and Liz carried their plates over. As Liz came around the table to sit by Megan, her toe caught on the leg of Todd's chair, and she pitched forward, sending her plate flying toward Beth.

Todd jumped up to help Liz, who had fallen to her knees. Grabbing a napkin, Megan dabbed at the baked beans that ran down Beth's sweater.

"I am so sorry," Liz said as Beth took off her dripping sweater. Still apologizing profusely, Liz went to get a new plate.

Darkness settled in, and the group chatted over a leisurely dinner as stars came out—pinpoints of light against the sky. Then Liz and Donna collected plates while Austin left to check the grill. The air turned cool as Megan, Todd, Beth, and Erica continued to talk.

When Beth shivered in her thin blouse, Todd noticed and inclined his head toward a green sweater draped over a chair at their table. "Why don't you put that on?"

"It's Liz's."

He shrugged lightly. "She's not wearing it."

"Put it on," Megan said. "You've got goose bumps."

Beth slipped it on. When Liz came back with a saucer of chocolate-dipped fruit, Beth asked, "Do you want your sweater back? I got cold."

"Keep it; I'm fine."

It was a beautiful evening, Erica thought, with the soft fragrance of flowers, tables with flickering candles, and women wearing bright colors. Everybody seemed happy and full of life.

Todd glanced at Liz's plate then at Megan. "Those chocolate-dipped strawberries look good, but I thought I also saw brownies. You can't beat chocolate on chocolate. Come on, Megan, let's go get a chocolate fix."

When Erica returned to the buffet line, the fruit salad was nearly gone, so she carried the bowl into the house. Beth stood at the counter, cutting up apples for the chocolate fountain.

"This has really been a nice evening," Erica said, getting more salad from the fridge.

"It has," Beth agreed, with a sweet smile. "It's been a good distraction for Liz. She tries to hide it, but she's really been on edge lately."

That reminded Erica of a question she'd wanted to ask. "You've been living at Crooked House awhile. Is Liz dating anyone?"

"Not now. She stopped dating after she and Todd broke up."

"She and *Todd* were dating?"

"Yeah. I was surprised when they broke up. But lately, Todd seems interested in Megan. They've started dating."

They went outside, and Erica set the fruit salad in place then went over to Megan. She was talking and laughing with Austin, whose hands were black from scraping the grill. He made a move as if to smear his blackened hands on Megan, who squealed and stepped back.

Then he grinned at Erica. "Guess I'd better go wash up."

Standing in the deep shadows of a dogwood tree with its fragrant white blossoms, Erica inclined her head toward Todd, who was talking to a couple on the patio. "He's very good-looking, isn't he?"

"You can say that again."

"Do you like him?"

"He's all right. We've gone out a few times."

"Austin seems nice too."

Something softened in Megan's face, and there was a sudden blush on her cheeks that told Erica all she needed to know. Austin started lighting the tiki lights that lined the yard.

"I'll go see if Austin needs any help," Megan said and was gone.

People were content to mingle, standing in groups or clustered around tables. The citronella candles made it so people could hear the hum of the mosquitoes but not be bothered by them. Todd came over to talk to Erica, and in the flickering light, she could see the planes of his face, and the flash of his teeth. He was attentive and interesting—a man who would make every woman he talked to feel special.

Unexpectedly, a shot rang out.

There were screams, and a man in a panicked voice shouted, "She's been shot! Someone call 911."

Chapter Five

A WOMAN SCREAMED—A HIGH, thin sound—and Erica raced to the woman lying crumpled on the ground.

It was Beth.

Shocked, Erica fell to her knees and put her fingers to the young woman's neck. Nothing. A cacophony of anguished cries, shocked murmurs, and sobbing filled the air. Beth had fallen backward, and a spreading red stain seeped through the front of her blouse as Erica began CPR. Megan dropped beside Erica, sobbing as Austin tried to pull her back.

An eternity passed before the wail of sirens signaled the arrival of the police. Shortly after, the paramedics arrived. One of them took over CPR, giving up only when it became obvious Beth was beyond help. An officer handed Erica a towel to wipe her hands, and the police ordered people back. Erica complied, though she continued to stare at the still, white figure on the ground. Her chest felt tight, and her eyes were blurry with tears as she tried to take it in. Megan stood nearby, tears streaming down her cheeks, as Austin held her in his arms.

Other officers arrived—among them, Detective Ranquist. He recognized Erica, gave a surprised lift of his eyebrows, and made his way to her.

"They tell me the girl's name is Beth Johnson." He stared at Erica in sympathy then asked, "I'm sorry; did you know her?"

Through lips numb and tasting of salt, Erica whispered, "I met her a few days ago."

An officer called to Detective Ranquist, and he responded, "Be right there." Then he told Erica, "I'd like to talk with you after the crime scene investigators are done." He strode away.

Erica encouraged Austin to take Megan in the house. The girl was so weak and disoriented that Austin had to keep his arm tightly around her for support as they moved haltingly across the lawn. Donna opened the sliding door for them.

It was hard to move—to think—but Erica forced herself to go inside and ask Donna for a notebook and pen. Unobtrusively, as police questioned the guests, Erica did the same. She got names and phone numbers for everyone, including those who were too overwhelmed right then to talk about the shooting. Several times, Erica had to turn for a moment to wipe away tears and collect herself.

How could this have happened? And why, *why* had a beautiful, sweet young girl like Beth been murdered? Yet even as she asked herself the question, Erica felt like she already knew the answer.

After Beth's body was taken away, Detective Ranquist found Erica. As they talked, she told him the shot seemed to come from the west but that she hadn't seen anyone with a gun.

"No one else did either." The detective gloomily studied the neighbor's tangled yard. "It's a jungle over there—a hundred people could have hidden there." He looked back at Erica. "I was told the victim was Liz Johnson's roommate."

"That's right. Megan Kemp is the other roommate—I told you about her. I'm staying with them at Crooked House." Then she said, "When Beth was shot, she was wearing Liz's sweater."

A sudden immobility came over Detective Ranquist, a listening stillness.

"The sweater was lime-green. Very distinctive. And Beth and Liz both have short hair and are about the same size." She looked at him intently.

"You think someone meant to shoot Liz but got Beth instead?"

"It's possible. Liz had been wearing that sweater most of the evening. Beth put it on just an hour ago. It was dark. And they were both wearing dark pants."

"I'll keep that in mind," the detective stated grimly.

When Erica trailed into the house, Liz, Megan, and Donna were sitting around the dining room table. Liz sat as if in a trance, staring at nothing, silver tear tracks on her face. Austin was filling glasses of water, and when he came to sit beside his mother, he put an arm around her shoulders.

Donna's eyes were rimmed with tears as she asked Erica, "Do the police know who did it?"

"Not as far as I know."

"Do they think it was one of the people who were here tonight?"

"I don't think so. No one saw anybody with a gun; although I guess someone could have slipped away for a few minutes. The shot seemed to come from your neighbor's yard."

Shakily, Megan took a sip of water. "But who would want to kill Beth?"

There was no easy way to say it, so Erica just said softly, "Beth was wearing Liz's sweater. The shooter might have mistaken her for Liz."

All eyes turned to Liz, who looked pale and shaken.

"It's my fault," she whispered.

"Of course it wasn't your fault," Megan said, a touch of anger making her voice rough.

"Whose fault is it, then?" Liz's voice was high and held a note of hysteria as she locked eyes with Megan. "You told me over and over that someone was trying to kill me. And I came to a party with a lot of innocent people, exposing them all to danger." Her face was blanched white, and there were hectic spots of red high on each cheekbone. "But I never really thought anyone would get hurt because of me." Liz glanced at the others beseechingly, as if asking forgiveness.

"Of course you didn't," Donna said sharply. "No one knew something like this would happen."

Silence fell. Then Erica said, "I know it's a difficult time, but I'd like to know where all of you were when you heard the shot? Austin?"

"I was in the back of the yard, relighting one of the tiki lights that had gone out."

"Megan, weren't you helping Austin?"

"I was, but he sent me into the house to find a new lighter. His wasn't working very well." Megan's voice was ragged and raw. "I heard a pop, and when people screamed, I ran outside."

"Donna? Where were you?"

"With my father. The nurse had just left." Donna's hand trembled as she set down her glass of water. "The door was shut. I thought I heard a noise but didn't think much of it at the time."

"What about you Liz?"

Liz spoke up. "I was in the bathroom. When I came out, people were running all over and shouting."

* * *

That night, after long hours spent with Liz and Megan, Erica changed into pajamas and padded down the steps to the front room. Feeling a need to connect with someone and put the horror of the night behind her, she curled up on the end of the couch, where the lamp cast a soft yellow glow, and called David.

His first concern was for Erica. After being assured she was fine, he listened intently as she rambled on, releasing the pent-up emotions she'd tried to hide from Liz and Megan.

At one point, Erica stopped and gulped. To the end of her days, she would never forget Beth's startlingly pale face as she lay on the grass. There was a vast, tight place inside Erica's rib cage, and she wondered how an empty space could feel so heavy. Erica started to speak again, but her voice broke, and she fell silent

"What can I do?" David asked, his voice full of concern.

"Pray for Liz, Megan, and Beth's family."

"I will—and I'll also pray for you."

"Thank you," she whispered. Then David switched into policeman mode, asking her a number of pertinent questions. When he was done, Erica explained that the police thought it could have been a random shooting.

"I doubt that," David said. "It appears that someone's after Liz. It's possible that person followed her to the party."

When Erica told him her theory that Beth had been mistaken for Liz, David agreed. "I'm with you. It seems likely the killer simply shot the wrong person. That bright-green sweater made Beth an easy target."

"The shooter had to be someone at the party, don't you think? To know what Liz was wearing?"

"He could have been watching from the neighbor's yard."

Erica finally went to bed. She must have slept, but her slumber was so fitful and shallow she seemed to remain partly conscious throughout.

The morning sun was pressing against the windows when Erica woke. Disoriented at first, she lay still—listening to the chirping of birds in the trees. Inside, everything was still and empty—Megan and Liz had both left. With no need to be brave for others, Erica cried for Beth—that sweet, gentle girl who was no more on earth.

In the bathroom, Erica splashed cold water on her face. As she hung up the towel, a deep-seated determination rose. She would *not* allow Beth's murderer to go free. Erica would find out who killed her and do everything possible to protect Liz.

She made toast and took it out into the gazebo. As she nibbled, Erica looked toward the house. The windows seemed to be eyes watching her. For no reason at all, a chill touched Erica, as though there was something there to frighten her. To dispel such fanciful notions, Erica pulled out her cell phone and called David, needing the anchor her husband always provided. Hearing his voice would help her cope.

David answered on the second ring. "Hi, sweetheart. How are you doing today? I've been worried—you sounded so upset last night."

"I still can't believe it," Erica said mournfully. "Beth was so sweet, so young. And I'm worried about Liz. The killer isn't going to stop just because he got the wrong person. And what about Megan? She might be in danger too."

"You might be too. I'm really worried about you." David sounded agitated. "I'm glad you have your gun."

"After the hassle I went through in Florida to have you send it, I don't ever travel without my Glock anymore."

"You've got to be very careful."

"I will, but I have to find out who did this before anything else happens."

"You will. You're a brilliant detective."

It was nice to hear, but David was always a complimentary and supportive husband. "Thanks, honey."

"I mean it," David insisted. "You notice things most people don't. I know I tease you about your OCD, but that's what makes you such a great detective. It helps you see little details and make connections other people don't notice or ignore because they think those things are too random to be part of the solution."

As Erica listened, she saw a movement next door. She hadn't met him yet, but it had to be Frank. He was on his knees—presumably weeding. He must pluck the weeds as mere sprouts, since Erica had yet to see a single one in his entire yard. A weed would have to have uncommon temerity to germinate in Frank Stratton's yard.

Erica pulled her feet up and drew her knees to her chest. "I never expected someone would try to kill Liz at the party."

"That was pretty daring," David stated flatly. "You're dealing with someone very cool, very professional. Each attempt has been well thought out and well planned—and this one most of all. I'm glad you were able to talk to Detective Ranquist last night. It sounds like he'll be willing to work with you now."

"I think the shooting convinced him someone really is out to get Liz."

"What are you going to do now?"

"First, I'll do a neighborhood investigation around Donna's house. One of the neighbors might have seen something. And, even though I don't think it was a random shooting, I ought to check if there are any gang members living nearby or a drug house in the area."

"What about the people at the party?"

"I'll check with Donna today to make sure I have the names of everyone who was there. I'll talk with them and see if I can come up with anything."

"Did the police interview them last night?" David asked.

"Most of them. Some were too upset to talk, but people react differently to cops. Most of the people saw me at the party, and I'm hoping that will create a feeling of camaraderie so they'll talk openly with me."

"You know, it's possible the shooter *meant* to kill Beth."

"I'll check that out too," Erica said. "And it could be that the killer is a terrible shot and was aiming for someone else."

"Sounds like you have your hands full."

"Amen. But first, I'm going to call Detective Ranquist and see when I can meet with him."

* * *

Erica spent a long and tiring morning knocking on doors in Donna's neighborhood. She was walking to the bus stop to go home for lunch when Wendy, Megan's mother, called. Wendy's voice was tight with concern. "I talked to Megan this morning. She's devastated. She and Beth were such good friends."

"I know. It's horrible."

"I'm scared for her."

A little shiver went down Erica's back. How eerie was *that*—to have Wendy say nearly the same thing Megan had when she'd first called?

Wendy went on. "Megan told me Beth was wearing Liz's sweater and that's probably why she got shot. *What if Megan had put on Liz's sweater*?" Wendy's voice broke.

"Megan looks a lot different from Liz—with her long, black hair and her height. I don't think anyone would mistake her for Liz, but I'll watch out for her."

"I'm glad you're there, Erica, but I'm so *scared*. What if something like this happens again and Megan gets in the way?" Wendy sounded helpless and frightened. "I've asked Megan to come home, but she won't. Erica, will you talk to her?"

"I will." Still, Erica didn't hold out a lot of hope that she could talk Megan into leaving. Megan had always had a mind of her own.

"Please protect her, Erica. And Liz too, of course. I'm praying for both of them."

"I'll do my best."

"But will that be good enough?"

* * *

That afternoon, the side door slammed, and Liz came into the kitchen. Lifting her chin, she sniffed. "What *is* that? It smells good. And bad."

"You can't have it both ways," Erica informed her.

Liz sniffed again. "I smell bread and . . . and lemon cleaner."

"Those are *both* good smells."

"If you say so." Liz's voice sounded doubtful as she slipped her backpack off and let it slide to the floor.

"I needed to unwind, so I polished the furniture, which explains the lemon smell. And I made some Cranberry Walnut Bread[2] because cooking also helps me relax. I'm going to take a loaf over to Frank when I talk to him tonight."

They went into the front room, and Liz sat heavily on the green couch. Her face was pale and upset.

"Aren't you home early?" Erica remarked.

"Yeah, my boss told me to go home. It's been a horrible day. All anyone could talk about at work is Beth getting shot. And they all had tons of questions for me, especially after Detective Ranquist came by to talk to me." Liz looked around. "Where's Megan?"

"She went to visit Beth's parents. She's going to spend the night."

Disconsolate, Liz covered her face with her hands.

"Liz, you might as well know I'm going to ask Megan to stay somewhere else for a while, and I think it would be best if you left Dover. I don't like how bold the killer was last night—shooting when there were so many people around. Whoever is doing this is getting more daring, taking more chances."

When Liz dropped her hands, her big, blue eyes were bright with tears. "I've thought about leaving, but I can't drop out of school. Tuition is

---

2 See the appendix at the end of the book for this recipe.

too expensive. It would mean wasting an entire semester, and I only have a few weeks left."

Erica had thought Liz would balk at leaving. With a sigh, she eyed the stone fireplace. There were tin plates and a teapot on the mantle, black fireplace tools on the hearth, and a sprinkling of soot on the floor of the firebox. Then she had another idea.

"What if you stayed somewhere else in Dover?"

Liz thought about it. "I could, but I can't see that it would make much of a difference. If someone is stalking me, it wouldn't be hard to find out my school and work schedule."

She had a point. "One thing you *can* do is be extra careful." Erica gave Liz a list of precautions to take, including always walking in a group, parking in a different place every day, and taking different routes to work and school. When Liz nodded solemnly, Erica asked, "Now could you tell me more about Frank Stratton?"

"Oh, Frank." Liz rolled her eyes. "According to him, I rank right up with Osama bin Laden. My crime is desecration of a historic landmark—Crooked House. He's always on me to fix the turrets, restore the front door, hire a bricklayer, and a hundred other things. Frank doesn't seem to understand it costs money for all of that." Liz's mouth was set in a hard, white line. "When I tell him I can't afford it, Frank calls city council members and complains about me. His latest act is to try to have the city condemn my house."

Erica's eyes went wide. "That's awful. Why does he care so much about Crooked House?"

"You mean besides the fact that he's a nut?" When Erica smiled, Liz went on. "There's a fine line between hobby and obsession, and Frank crossed it long ago. He's on the board of the Dover Historical Society, which works to preserve historical houses. And boy, does he take his job seriously. Aunt Donna is a member, too, and has lots of stories to tell about how Frank goes off at the meetings."

"Your aunt is a very busy lady."

"I'll say. The past few months, she's been working all hours of the day and night. When she got her real estate license, her boss said she could show houses during the day as long as she made up her hours as a bookkeeper by staying late, coming in early, or working Saturdays."

Liz sat back and crossed her legs. "But, getting back to Frank—he says if I can't fix Crooked House, I should sell it to him. I keep telling him no, but it's like he doesn't even hear me." Liz's eyes perused the room, and there was tenderness as she viewed the windows, furniture, and fireplace. "Maybe I should sell, but I doubt anyone would buy the house because of all the expensive repairs it needs."

"Can Frank afford those repairs?"

Liz scoffed. "I doubt it. The only reason he wants the house is because I told him he can't have it."

"Surely there's more to it than that."

"He and his wife were both history buffs and loved old houses. Frank's always been strange, but ever since his wife died three years ago, he's become a real nutcase." Liz frowned. "Being a bigwig in the Dover Historical Society, Frank thinks living next to a historic home that's in such bad shape reflects poorly on him. In its present condition, Crooked House is a personal affront to him. If he lived a few streets away, I doubt he'd feel so strongly about it. But now Frank's gotten to the point where he feels I'm insulting him personally because I can't afford to maintain the house the way he thinks it ought to be maintained. But I keep it up as well as I can with BJ's help."

"It'll be interesting to talk with Frank."

"Be careful, or he'll chew you up and spit you out."

Erica leaned forward and turned on a lamp. "One other thing. Are any of the antiques or paintings in the house valuable?"

Liz looked doubtful. "I don't think so. They're not in very good shape."

"Has Frank or anyone else ever asked about any of the furnishings in the house?"

She thought. "Aunt Donna has, but just because she wants me to take better care of them. Once she told me that the desk and cabinet in the corner ought to be in storage or donated to a museum. But I grew up with this furniture and want to keep it."

"Have you ever had anything appraised?"

"I can barely afford groceries, and appraisers are expensive. Aunt Donna called around once to get an appraiser, but she couldn't afford it either."

"What if I could talk someone into coming out and giving us a complementary appraisal?"

"How would you do that?"

"By dropping a hint or two that you might be willing to sell some things in the future if they'd do us a favor and come take a look."

"Sure. I guess that'd be all right." Liz gave a small shrug. "But actually, I don't really care if the furniture or paintings are valuable. I like them, and that's what matters." A look of amusement crossed her face. "Some of the people I've rented rooms to thought I ought to take everything to the junkyard."

"That's another thing I wanted to ask you about. Were you on good terms with all of your renters?"

"For the most part. There were a few who stopped paying rent but always had money to go to the movies and out to dinner. I finally told them to leave."

"Did any of them get angry about it or threaten you?"

"They weren't happy, but no one ever threatened me."

"Even so, I'd like to get a list of everyone who's rented from you in the past three years. And put a checkmark next to anyone you kicked out."

* * *

While Liz went to study, Erica put one of the golden brown loaves she'd baked on a paper plate and covered it with plastic wrap. She peeked out the window at Frank's house. Was it possible a killer resided within those walls? From what Liz had said, Frank Stratton seemed a likely suspect.

Frank's house sat far back on a velvet lawn under a canopy of gnarled, mossy oaks. Its rose-hued bricks were similar to those used for Crooked House, but there, all similarities ended. Where Liz's house was derelict and crumbling, Frank's house was well maintained, with fresh paint on the front door, neat window shutters, and a three-foot black iron fence that circled the yard. The front lawn was mowed short and had been crisply edged. Each tree stood in a circle of fresh redwood chips. Lovely.

The yard was also perfectly symmetrical, with an identical number of trees planted the same distance from the house. Such a man couldn't be all bad, Erica decided, strolling down the sidewalk that was flanked by perfectly pruned bayberry hedges.

She knocked and waited.

Then knocked again.

Erica had seen Frank pull in hours ago. Maybe he didn't like visitors. Suddenly the door cracked open two inches. A chain ran across the opening from the doorframe to the door. A wary eye with a gray caterpillar eyebrow stared at her.

"Mr. Stratton? My name is Erica Coleman." That single, faded-blue eye was a bit unnerving. "I'm a friend of Liz Johnson, next door."

"Then you're no friend of mine." The eye disappeared, and the door began to shut.

"Mr. Stratton, I've brought you some cranberry walnut bread. I wondered if I could talk to you."

The door remained open a bare inch. "Are you crazy like her?"

"I passed my last evaluation with flying colors."

The door opened as far as the chain would allow, and the eye examined the plate.

"I wanted to talk to you about The Dover Historical Society. I've only been here a few days, but I'm fascinated by all the amazing houses I've seen. I'd like to know more about Dover's history."

A shaggy gray eyebrow raised. "Good try, but if you're a friend of Liz Johnson, I have nothing to say to you."

The door began to shut and would have—if Erica hadn't put her foot in it at the last second.

Chapter Six

"GET YOUR FOOT OUT OF my door!" Frank Stratton's voice blasted through the gap.

"I really *am* interested in Dover's history and all the beautiful homes here." The pressure on her foot eased. "And I'd really love to see *your* house." Erica put all the sincerity she could muster into her voice. "I love old houses, and it's so beautiful from the outside that I know the inside must be amazing too."

There was a long pause.

"Move your foot, then, so I can undo the chain," Frank ordered. The door shut, and there was the sound of the chain sliding in the bolt. He opened the door. "Come on in, and don't take all day about it."

Frank stood on the tiled foyer, a solidly built man with an impressive nose that looked remarkably like a pickle. His hair was short, white, and bristly.

"Go on in there." Frank thrust a thick arm toward the small drawing room that held a red couch and a stone fireplace. She took a seat on one of the red-cushioned wooden chairs. Frank sat across from her, giving her an appraising look that was far from friendly. There were pouches of dark skin beneath his eyes.

"This is a lovely room," Erica said, admiring the highboy with brass pulls that stood in the corner. "Liz told me you're a member of The Dover Historical Society."

"I'm on the board, not just a member, like Liz's addlepated aunt. Irresponsible woman."

Erica was curious to know what lay behind his statement. "Why do you say that?"

"She's done absolutely nothing to make Liz take care of her house."

"As I understand it, Liz doesn't have the money for repairs."

"She could take out a loan—*if* she wanted to take proper care of a very important house." He made it sound as if Liz was not only negligent but foolish. Frank thrust out his chin. "Donna shouldn't let her get away with it. She needs to put some pressure on that niece of hers. That's a historical house over there, and Liz Johnson is letting it go to wrack and ruin." Frank's face turned a mottled red and white with upset.

Thinking it best to give him a moment to cool down, Erica glanced upward at the gold leaves painted on the carved crown molding. "You must love being in the historical society and seeing so many wonderful old homes."

There was a softening of those blunt features. "Each and every one is a slice of history. We've got to do what we can to preserve them." Frank rubbed the silvery bristles that glistened on his jaw. "Would you like to see the rest of the house?"

"I'd love to."

In the kitchen, Erica laid the bread on the wooden table as Frank listed the unique features of the room, which included a small fireplace where a round kettle hung from a hook.

"That's the original fireplace," Frank said. "Can you imagine cooking on that?"

She couldn't. They went upstairs on narrow steps that curved in a spiral, and Frank proudly pointed out various authentic features and offered historical tidbits. Flattered by Erica's genuine admiration, Frank became positively loquacious.

When they went back downstairs, Erica asked, "Do you mind if I see the backyard?"

Frank's gruff manner reappeared. "You can see it from the yard of that Philistine you're staying with."

"I'd hoped to see it up close. The wishing well is so unique, and your stone shed looks so interesting. Was it built at the same time as the house?"

Unable to help himself, Frank led the way down the cobbled pathway, which had moss in between the stones. When Frank finished his discourse on how he'd restored the well, Erica felt qualified to write a paper on the subject.

Approaching the shed, Frank said, "You wouldn't believe the condition this place was in when my wife and I bought it. It was even worse than Crooked House. The shed roof was caved in, but I completely restored it. The walls were decayed, too, and had to be replaced."

Inside were neat shelves on three sides, while a fourth was taken up with a wheelbarrow, lawn mower, and fertilizer. "Everything's so neat and organized," Erica praised, admiring how the hand tools were neatly arranged on pegboard. Two wrenches were out of order, and Erica deftly rearranged them so they went from large to small. An assortment of saws hung on the wall. Noticing sawdust below on the work bench, Erica took a pinch and closed it in her fist.

"Houses and sheds don't keep themselves in shape—it's up to responsible homeowners to do that," Frank pontificated, heavily emphasizing the word responsible.

"Liz wishes she had the money to do more."

Frank turned to face her, his legs braced far apart, reminding her of a wrestler's stance. "It's a crime the way she's letting it go. She's got a historical house, and it's falling apart."

"Have you ever thought about buying it?"

"I've asked her many times, but that flibbertigibbet won't sell. Shortsighted. Doesn't care that she's destroying something priceless and that it's crumbling into ruins." It was alarming how quickly Frank's face could turn red and white.

"I hear you've written letters to the city, trying to get it condemned."

"So Liz tattled to you about that, did she? Well, I did, and I'll keep writing until they do something. I've got three council members on my side so far."

They stepped out into a stiff breeze, and Frank put a crossbar in place to secure the shed door. His eyes went to Crooked House's leaning turrets. "Look at that. It's a disgrace to the neighborhood. The historical society ought to buy it. As it is now, it's an eyesore to Dover." He flung out his arms towards the street. "Look at all the houses around here! Historic! Beautiful! Well-maintained. Then you come to that thing and wonder what happened."

As they walked toward the house, Erica casually asked, "Did you know there have been several attempts on Liz's life?" Frank stopped abruptly and stared at her. "The last one happened last night, at Donna's house. Someone took a shot at Liz, missed, and killed another girl."

Frank's eyes took on a baleful expression. "I heard about that on the radio. And you think I did it, right? That's the whole purpose behind your little 'visit,' isn't it? To snoop and see if you can pin it on me. Well, this visit is over." With that, Frank stomped away.

* * *

The next morning, Megan returned earlier than Erica had expected. It was good to have her back. The house had seemed cold and empty without her bright presence. She and Erica sat on the couch and talked—and cried—at length.

Finally, Erica patted Megan's knee and asked, "Can I get you something to eat?"

"Thanks, but I had breakfast with Beth's parents." Megan's eyes were red and swollen as she blew into a tissue. "What are you going to do today?"

"Let's see, I've got a bazillion phone calls to make and a few people from Donna's barbecue that I'd like to talk with in person. I'm also going to see Detective Ranquist. Then this afternoon, I'd like to go to Park Place Realty and talk to Donna. If I have time, I'll take the bus to the Red Roof Inn and talk with Liz's coworkers."

"When are you going to Park Place? If you can wait until three, I'll be home and can drive you over. I know where it is." Megan seemed unusually helpful.

"Yeah, I can wait. That'd be great."

Yesterday's wind had ushered in clouds, and a light rain was falling as Erica walked to the bus station later that morning, but she didn't mind. She loved the smell of rain-washed air. Exiting the bus, Erica opened her umbrella for the short walk to the police station. She went through security then down the hall.

Detective Ranquist looked at her oddly when she shut his office door, opened it, and shut it again. "What's up with the door?" he asked, reaching out to shake her hand.

"Just making sure it's shut."

"You did the same thing last time. Do you always do that?"

"Unless it's a revolving door."

He chuckled. "I can see how that might be a problem."

The window caught her attention, and she looked at it uneasily until he asked, "Is something wrong?"

"Do you mind if I adjust the blinds?"

"Be my guest."

Erica strode to the windows and twisted the wands so each set of blinds were open at the same angle. "They look so much better now, don't you think?" Erica settled into a chair with a sigh of satisfaction.

"How are you all doing?" His deep voice was compassionate. "It's got to be difficult."

"It's really been hard on Megan and Liz, but they're doing their best to cope. Beth and Megan were especially close. Beth's parents have even asked Megan to speak at the funeral."

"And how are *you* doing?"

She thought a moment. "Although I believe in God and know Beth's in a better place, it still hurts. It was horrible that night, but I have my police training to help me through that. And now I'm staying busy investigating. It's been harder on Liz and Megan, since they knew Beth so well. I'm trying to get them to talk about their feelings so they can process their grief, but they're really struggling."

They were quiet a few moments, then Erica asked, "Did you find out if anyone left Donna's party early?"

"Two or three, but all of them had people who vouched for their presence elsewhere."

"Someone at the party could have left long enough to shoot Beth then come back without anyone noticing they had been gone."

Detective Ranquist nodded. "I agree. All the shooter had to do is go out the front way and slip around into the neighbor's backyard. The people who live east of Donna were at the party, but the couple on the west—the ones with the overgrown yard—are on a cruise."

Erica nodded. Liz had mentioned that. "I did a neighborhood investigation, and there aren't any signs of a drug house nearby, nor of any gangs. I've also been talking to people at the party, asking if anyone had threatened them recently."

"You do realize we've already questioned the guests." The detective's voice had a pinched, steely quality.

Oops. Apparently she had overstepped her bounds. Time to soothe ruffled feathers. "Yes, sir. I just thought it was worth a shot. Since most of the guests saw me at the party, I thought they might be more open with me." Erica went on in a businesslike manner. "I also wanted to ask if any of the guests had enemies or had been threatened by someone. That would help us determine if someone else was the intended target."

"I see." Detective Ranquist appeared mollified. "If I was a gambling man, and I am, I'd say Liz was the target because of the prior incidents. I assigned detectives to talk to Beth's parents, friends, and coworkers, but so far, there's nothing. Everyone seemed to like her."

His use of past tense made Erica's throat tighten. Her voice turned husky as she tried to move past the pain. "The big question is motive. Without that, it's hard to come up with suspects. Have your detectives uncovered anything?" It was a shot in the dark, but Erica was hoping he'd be willing to share information.

"They're still investigating," Detective Ranquist said carefully. "For now, we'll work on the premise that the murder was premeditated."

"Although Liz said she didn't have any enemies, she mentioned that she and her neighbor, Frank Stratton, have an ongoing feud. I talked with him last night." Erica went over her visit in detail.

"Sounds like a possible lead." There was hope in the detective's voice as he jotted down the name. "But does Frank want Liz out of the house bad enough to kill her? Sounds a bit far-fetched." His shrewd eyes met Erica's.

"I thought so too until I talked to him. Frank is very upset that Crooked House—a historical house—is falling down because of Liz's neglect. Frank thinks he might be able to get the house condemned if he puts enough pressure on the city council. Then he'd either buy it or have the Dover Historical Society buy it."

"Ah, a fanatic with a plan and a purpose."

"I talked with my boss at Pinnacle Investigations, and he'll let me use the agency's databases to look into Frank's background, but I know you have access to more databases." Erica's keen, green eyes studied the detective, hoping Detective Ranquist would offer to check Frank's background.

"I'll put someone on it."

"Great." Erica pulled a baggie from her purse and set it on the desk. "When I was in Frank's shed, I got this—sawdust. I wondered if you could have it analyzed to see if it matches the poles on Liz's deck."

"We'll need a sample from one of the poles."

"Of course." Erica rummaged in her purse and brought out another neatly labeled baggie. "I sawed a piece off. Thought it would save time." Erica set her purse on the floor. "In addition to Frank, other people might have their own reasons for wanting Crooked House. Liz has a lot of antique furniture and old paintings. I asked her if anything was valuable, but she wasn't sure."

Detective Ranquist leaned forward, a serious look on his intelligent face. "You might have something there. It could be that she owns something valuable."

"I'll call around to see if I can get an appraiser to come out, pro bono."

He nodded.

"Liz said she couldn't think of why anyone would want to kill her, but I keep coming back to the house. Surely Crooked House is worth a fortune, being located in historic Dover."

"I had the same thought," Detective Ranquist admitted. "But when I interviewed Liz, she said it needs a lot of major repairs, and the cost of renovating would be astronomical. Who would get the house if Liz died?"

"It would go to her aunt, Donna Phillips, and her cousin, Austin Phillips."

"And yet, they don't stand to gain much. The cost of restorations would apparently cancel out anything they would gain by getting the house."

"There's an answer somewhere—we just have to find it." Erica said determinedly. "Liz is also going to get me a list of her old renters, and I'll check them out."

"I'd like to talk to them first. Get me a copy of that list." Detective Ranquist's voice brooked no dissent.

Police privilege, but it still rankled Erica. After all, it *had* been her idea.

He went on. "When I interviewed Liz, she said she didn't have a boyfriend. Is that true?"

"As far as I know."

"Liz is a pretty girl. I'd have thought she'd have to beat the boys off with a stick."

"She stays pretty busy with school and work," Erica said. "Megan told me Liz's last boyfriend was Todd McCauley. After they broke up, Todd started dating Megan."

The detective's eyebrows shot up. "And is Liz okay with her ex-boyfriend dating her current roommate?"

"I don't really know."

"Hmm. Tell me about Megan."

Erica went over Megan's background, adding that she had known the girl since Megan was two years old and that in her mid teens she used to be moody, insecure, and rebellious.

"But now, she's more confident, independent, and spunky? Interesting. Any jealousy or animosity between her and Liz?"

"Not that I've seen. Megan's been very worried about Liz." After a moment's thought, Erica said, "I wonder if Liz could have been targeted because she saw or heard something that somebody doesn't want known. It could be something she isn't even aware of knowing."

"That's a long shot." Detective Ranquist checked his notes. "Let's see, Liz works at the front desk at the Red Roof Inn. Not exactly a place for high rollers, but I suppose she could have overhead something. But it seems unlikely."

"If you don't mind, I thought I'd go there and ask around."

He considered then gave her the go-ahead. "Let me know if you find out anything." He paused then asked, "Is there anything else? You look like you're thinking of something."

"All day today, whenever I've thought about Beth's murder, something's been niggling at me, but for the life of me I can't remember what." Erica frowned. "I don't know how to explain it, but I saw or heard something that struck me as wrong or unlikely. I didn't have time to think about it right then."

"And now you can't remember what it was."

"Exactly. All I can remember is thinking it was odd."

"And this happened at the barbecue?"

"I'm not sure. It could have been before or after."

"It'll come back to you." Detective Ranquist sounded sure.

"Maybe." Erica hoped so because whatever it was left her feeling extremely uneasy.

* * *

Before leaving for Park Place Realty that afternoon, Megan spent an inordinate amount of time in the bathroom getting ready. "You're going to an awful lot of trouble," Erica said. "It can't be to impress Donna, so it must be Austin."

"Don't be stupid."

They got in the car. The windshield wipers beat a steady rhythm against the rain as Megan drove past The Green, the city's central grassy square. Megan pulled into a spot and hurried with Erica through the parking lot, avoiding puddles, and into a small office building on North Dupont.

Dolores Martinez, the friendly young receptionist with curly hair, sympathized with their dampness then dialed Donna. She pointed with one of her long orange nails. "That way. It's the third door on your right."

Donna was at her desk. To her right were a pair of rain-streaked windows. File cabinets and cupboards lined another wall. She paused her typing to glance up with a faintly annoyed expression. "Just let me finish this e-mail."

A few more keystrokes, then Donna swung round with a flourish to face them. Her navy suit looked good on her stout figure, but there was an unbecoming tightness to her face. "I thought you'd call before you came. I have to go show a house in a few minutes."

Evidently Donna didn't remember telling Erica to stop by anytime. "I'm sorry. I thought it would be all right to stop in."

Megan stood awkwardly near the door. "Is Austin around?"

"No, he's showing a property."

"Oh." Megan's face fell. "Well, I'll just wait for you out front, Erica."

Erica took a seat under Donna's impatient eye. "I know you're in a hurry, but I have a couple of questions." When Donna nodded, Erica asked, "Are you and Liz close?"

Giving a good imitation of a guppy, Donna's mouth opened and closed several times. Then she asked sharply, "What kind of a question is that? Liz is my niece, for goodness sake."

My, someone was touchy today. Then again, maybe she had been too abrupt. While Donna's reply had been no answer at all, it served as a warning to tread carefully.

"I suppose Liz has told you about her 'accidents'?" Erica said.

"Yes, and she laughed them off."

"She's not laughing now."

Donna thought about that a moment. "I know you think someone mistook Beth for Liz, but one of the policemen said he thought it was a random shooting."

"Everyone is entitled to their own opinion, but I think the shooter was after Liz. She's had too many near-fatal accidents."

Donna bit her lip. "I hesitate to say anything, but there's something you ought to know. I love Liz, but all her life, she's majored in drama. She often exaggerates, and when she told me about her so-called accidents, I figured she was doing it again—as a way of drawing attention to herself. Liz does like the spotlight. That's why I have a hard time believing someone's trying to kill her. I'm sure those accidents are just coincidences."

That's what Erica had thought when she first arrived in Dover. "I wondered myself, until the deck collapsed. But the odds of having three potentially fatal accidents in the span of just a few weeks are astronomical."

"It was a very old deck," Donna protested. "I've heard about decks collapsing before."

"This one had a little help." When Donna appeared puzzled, Erica asked, "Didn't Liz tell you that two of the support poles had been sawed almost all the way through?" Donna shook her head.

Erica felt that Liz not mentioning the sawed poles effectively refuted Donna's theory about her niece being a drama queen. If Liz craved the spotlight as much as her aunt said, she surely would have told anyone and everyone that the poles had been sawed.

However, Donna was still skeptical. "So Liz told you the poles had been sawed?" She gave Erica the same indulgent look one would give a gullible child. "This is just what I've been telling you. Ever since Liz was small, she's had a tendency to overstate things. I've learned to take anything she says with a grain of salt. You should too. It's possible Liz is putting on a little act. She saw the broken poles and jumped to conclusions."

"Actually, I'm the one who noticed they had been sawed."

Taken aback, Donna recovered quickly. "You could have been mistaken."

"I'm not." It would be fruitless to try and convince her, so Erica moved on. "I'm afraid whoever is doing this might try again. There were three attempts on Liz's life before Beth was shot, and I don't think the killer is going to stop trying."

Erica leaned forward. "Would you mind telling me where you were when Liz lost the brakes on her car? That would have been last Wednesday afternoon."

A flush crept up Donna's face and neck. "You think I tried to kill my own niece?" Her tone was glacial.

"I'm asking everyone their whereabouts at the time of the incidents."

After a short staring contest, Donna relented. Turning to her smartphone, she swiped the screen then tapped her calendar. "I was here at work."

"What about when Liz was pushed into traffic? It happened last Saturday around noon."

An angry look. She studied her calendar as though it was written in Egyptian.

"I was showing a home to Mr. and Mrs. Brinton in Middleton that day. And on Monday night, when the deck collapsed, I was at home."

"Thank you. Can you think of anyone who might want to kill Liz?"

"If I knew that, don't you think I'd tell the police?"

"Not if you believe all these incidents are accidents or a product of Liz's imagination. Has Liz had any jealous ex-boyfriends?"

Donna considered. "She hasn't mentioned it, but maybe. Liz attracts men like flies. They're always swarming around her."

"She's very attractive."

"And she knows it. Plus, Liz can 'turn on the charming' when she wants."

Erica felt suddenly annoyed. What was it with Donna? Why was she so nasty about her own niece? Liz seemed like a genuinely caring person—not someone who turned the charm on and off to suit herself. Liz had always spoken highly of her aunt—it was too bad Donna didn't return the favor.

There was a flush in Donna's cheeks when she stood. "I need to go. I can't be late, or else my clients might think I'm unreliable, and if they think that, then I've lost the sale, which I cannot afford." She picked up her purse and came around the desk.

It must be a very important sale, Erica thought, as Donna's foot tapped out an impatient staccato beat. Standing, Erica said, "I'd like to talk with you again."

Donna's hand snaked toward the doorknob as she flashed Erica a strange look. "I'm here every day except Sunday. Saturdays are my lightest days."

"I'll give you a call first."

In the waiting area, they found Austin perched on the arm of the loveseat, with Megan smiling brightly up at him, her cheeks pink.

"Why hello, Austin. I didn't know you were back." Donna sounded aggrieved.

Austin looked up with that friendly expression Erica was getting to know. "I got back a few minutes ago."

Donna eyed Megan from under hooded eyes. "I'm going to show a house. Austin, did you call Mr. Shaffer back about that earnest money agreement? I know he was anxious about it."

"I'll go call him now." Austin rose. "It was good to see you, Megan." He nodded at Erica before disappearing down the hall.

The rain had eased a bit as the three of them went through the parking lot. Donna gave a small wave and went to her car, which was farther down the lot.

"What's up with Donna?" Megan asked as she merged into traffic. "She was acting kind of weird."

"I thought the same thing."

"Maybe she's worried about Liz."

"Possibly." Erica recalled that strange look she'd seen on Donna's face. It had almost looked like fear. If so, exactly what was Donna afraid of?

Chapter Seven

Hearing the sound of a hammer early Saturday morning, Erica decided BJ must be hard at work in the backyard. Time to meet him. Outside, the sky was overcast, the day gray and brown. Seeing Frank as she went down the porch steps, Erica called hello then waved when he looked up from picking yellowed leaves off shrubs that were still moist from yesterday's rain. Amazing. There was never a thing out of place in his immaculate yard. It was perfection squared.

The handyman, his long hair caught back in a ponytail, was atop the shed, pounding shingles into the black, felt-papered roof. A dog with long, brownish-red hair and a black muzzle barked when it saw her then lollopped over. Must have some German Shepherd and Irish Setter in his blood, Erica figured.

"Don't worry about the dog," BJ called from his perch. "He's friendly."

Erica pulled out a pair of the disposable gloves she kept in her pocket, slipped them on, and let the dog sniff the back of her hand.

When BJ looked at the gloves curiously, Erica explained, "Just a precaution. I'm sure you understand."

Although it was evident from his baffled look that he didn't, BJ didn't pursue the matter. "His name's Duke," he said, climbing down the ladder. His jeans were torn at the knees, and his checkered shirt was frayed at the collar. The sleeves were rolled up above his elbows.

"Ah. And how are we today, Duke?" Bending over, Erica scratched the dog around the ears then looked up. "I'm Erica Coleman. I'm staying with Liz and Megan." When this was met with a slight nod and nothing else, Erica added, "And you must be BJ."

He nodded again. Obviously BJ was a man of few words, so Erica tried again. "Liz told me you were building a shed and that you help her with the yard work."

"Sometimes."

No one would ever accuse BJ of being a chatterbox, Erica thought wryly. She guessed the tall, lean man was in his early thirties, but he still had an awkward air about him, and his Adam's apple jutted above his collar like a half-grown boy's. A bristle of dark hairs sprouted from his jaw and chin. She gestured toward the pile of splintered wood that used to be the deck. "I guess you saw that."

"I asked Liz about it. The insurance adjuster came out and told her to get three bids before any work is done on it. I already gave her mine."

She eyed the mess. "Did you take down those dangling pieces of wood?"

"Yeah. It was too dangerous to leave them hanging that way."

"Could I ask you a question over here?" Erica walked over to the deck. She pointed out the trench in the dirt between the broken poles. "It looks like the hose was left running and washed away some of the dirt. Could that have made the deck collapse?"

After an examination, BJ concluded, "Nah. Liz must have forgot to turn off the water, but it didn't hurt them poles—they're set in concrete. Go down a long ways."

She squatted by one of the broken poles. Duke came closer to see what was so interesting, and she patted him absently. "Any ideas on what would make the deck collapse like that?"

"Wood rotted away, I guess. Them poles are redwood, which is good, but they didn't have metal wrapped around them." He shook his head as if annoyed by the poor construction techniques the builder had employed.

Curious to see his reaction, Erica showed him how one of the broken poles had jagged splinters while the other side was smooth. "It looks like someone sawed this pole."

BJ's brows came together in puzzlement as he hunkered down, pushing Duke aside. "Why would someone do that?"

"Hasn't Liz told you about the 'accidents' she's been having?"

"What accidents?" He stared at her fixedly.

When she told him, BJ's jaw dropped. "Who'd want to hurt Liz?"

* * *

Liz was kind enough to let Erica borrow her car for errands, so she didn't have to figure out bus routes. Everyone at the Red Roof Inn was concerned about Liz and more than willing to talk to Erica. They spoke of Liz's intelligence, resourcefulness, and take-charge attitude. But after several hours of interviewing everyone from the concierge to the valets, Erica had no more real information than before.

Next stop was Park Place Realty, where Erica hoped Donna would be in and have time to talk. She'd called from the Red Roof Inn, but the line had been busy, and since Erica was close by, she decided to take a chance and stop in. Dolores wasn't there, but that came as no surprise since it was Saturday. Erica went down the hall to Donna's office. Since the door was open, she stepped inside, surprised to see Liz in the corner, bent over an open drawer in the file cabinet.

"Hi, Liz," Erica said. "Now I feel guilty for borrowing your car. I didn't know you needed to come here."

Startled, Liz swung around. "Oh, hi! It was just a spur-of-the-moment thing, and I don't mind riding the bus." She shut the drawer and stood. "I was just returning my insurance policy on the house. Aunt Donna keeps all my important papers here. Are you meeting her?"

"I dropped in hoping she'd be here. If she isn't, I have another errand to run, and then I'll check back."

"Austin's here. He might know when she'll be back."

Liz went with Erica to her cousin's office. Austin was on the computer and paused to give them a friendly smile. His office was rather austere—two blue-cushioned chairs in front of a white-washed desk with a computer and two monitors. Against one wall was a single pine bookshelf filled sparsely with binders and books.

"Good to see you, Erica. Come on in."

"I'm headed home," Liz told Austin. "Don't forget you promised to stop by later and help me move that dresser."

"I'll be there."

After Liz left, Erica asked, "Do you know when your mom will be back?"

"I'm not sure. Grandpa had some kind of medical emergency."

"Oh, I'm sorry! I hope he'll be all right."

"It wasn't anything serious, but when the nurse called, Mom wanted to check on him."

"I'm sorry about your grandfather. Liz said his health was failing."

"He also has Alzheimer's. Mom had to hire a full-time nurse a few months ago."

"That's hard," Erica sympathized. "My grandmother had Alzheimer's, and eventually my dad had to put her in an assisted living center. They couldn't afford a full-time nurse."

"Grandpa made Mom promise over and over that she'd never put him in a home. He even got insurance to pay for his care, just in case, which is good because he certainly needs it now."

Erica stepped over to a framed poster hanging on the wall. It was of the Dover International Raceway. "What's with the monster?" she asked, pointing to the corner where a hulking gray monster held a race car in one outstretched hand.

"Oh, that's Miles," Austin said. "He's very popular here in Dover. Miles is the official mascot for the 'Monster Mile,' which is a nickname for the Dover International Raceway."

"Do you go to the races much?"

"Not too often, but I do try to catch the Sprint Cup Series. They race in Dover twice a year—June and September."

"That would be fun to watch," Erica said. "At home in Utah, we have the Miller Motorsports Park, but I've never gone—even though I do like racing. Sometimes I'll watch part of the Indianapolis 500 or the Daytona 500 on TV."

"Dover isn't a super speedway like the Indy 500, but it's a pretty awesome track. If you're still around the first weekend in June, ask Liz or Megan to take you. Or better yet, we could all go. It's great. NASCAR only holds races on really good race tracks, and the Dover has one of the best in the country."

"You sound like an expert."

"I wouldn't say that, but it is exciting to watch. NASCAR holds three other series in Dover besides the Sprint Cup."

"Wow. Then you can take your pick." Erica glanced toward the door.

"Let me call Mom and see when she plans on being back." Austin dialed, but there was no answer. "She must be busy. Sorry."

"That's okay," Erica said. "I'll leave her a message and come back another day."

At the receptionist's desk, Erica pulled over the pink notepad. When she was done, Erica ripped the page off and put it with the other messages, straightening them into one neat pile. As she did, Erica saw that one of the notes had the name Brinton on it. It took only a moment for her to recall where she had heard that name before. Erica read the message several times then left her note on top.

* * *

When Erica got home, Liz wasn't there, but she breezed in an hour later. "Do you know if BJ's around?" Liz asked. "I hoped he could help Austin move a dresser into your room."

"It seems like I heard him sawing a while ago, but I haven't really been paying attention—I've been listening to music while I worked on the computer."

"I'll go out back and see if he's here."

Erica went out with her, and when Duke galloped over, Erica slipped on her gloves and offered Liz a pair.

"No, thanks." Then Liz asked slyly, "Do you also carry extra water and a first-aid kit?"

"I would if I could." Erica smiled, stroking Duke's head. She crooned, "You're a good old dog, aren't you?" He followed them to the shed. BJ's eyes lit up when he saw Liz.

Straightening from where he had been picking up pieces of tar paper, BJ smoothed back loose strands of hair. "Sorry I haven't been around lately—it's been too rainy, but I finished the roof today." He eyed his handiwork proudly.

There was a look of admiration on Liz's face as she walked around the shed. "It looks wonderful, BJ! You did a great job; thank you so much." She turned to Erica. "I don't know what I'd do without BJ. He's my right-hand man and helps me with all the heavy work."

BJ's look of pride changed to one of worry. "Erica told me about the accidents you've been having."

Liz shot Erica a sharp look. "She shouldn't have done that." Then her eyes went to the heap of lumber that used to be the deck. "I'm just glad I wasn't on that when it fell."

"Me too," BJ said forcefully. Then, incredibly, he blushed beneath his tan.

The tender smile Liz offered BJ made the handyman blush even more. He seemed to have a hard time catching his breath.

"Thanks for getting me your bid, BJ. I'm sure yours will be the lowest, although I'm still waiting for the third one. But yours is way lower than the other guy. I'm afraid you've underbid it."

"I wanted to make sure I got the job."

Liz laid a hand on his arm. "You will. You're very kind, BJ, but you have bills to pay just like everyone else, and I'm not going to have you working for nothing."

"Doesn't matter." His face reddened. "I'd help you without getting paid."

Liz put a hand on a slim hip and shook her head. "What am I going to do with you? You are just *so* sweet. You know what? Let me make you dinner one night. Would you like that?"

BJ gazed at Liz as if it was his birthday and she was bringing him an armload of gifts.

"What night are you free?" Liz asked.

"Anytime."

"All right, let's say next Thursday. Will that be all right?"

BJ nodded happily, like a small child. "I'll be here."

A car pulled into the driveway. "That'll be Austin," Liz said. "BJ, would you mind helping move a dresser and a chest of drawers in the house?"

They walked to the driveway. When Liz gave Austin a big hug, BJ's face turned dark. Liz pulled back and told him, "BJ, I don't believe you've ever met my cousin, Austin. And Austin, this is BJ—he's the one I'm always telling you about." The storm cloud left BJ's face.

Inside, Austin looked around, then asked Erica, "Is Megan home?"

"She went on a date with Todd."

"Todd? Is he the guy that was at the barbecue? The one with the spray-on tan?"

Erica giggled. "I think it was the real thing, but that's the one."

Liz directed the men to take the chest of drawers from Megan and Erica's room and trade it with the large dresser in Beth's old room. Liz had offered to let Erica stay in Beth's room, but Erica just couldn't.

"What's this?" Erica asked, curious about towels that had been taped to the doorframes of both rooms with painter's tape.

"It's to protect the woodwork," Liz explained. "It's all original, and I don't want it damaged."

The men took opposite ends of the dresser and began shuffling to Erica's room.

"Watch out!" Liz cried. "You're too close to the doorframe, Austin! Be careful!"

Austin shook his head and asked Erica, "Got any earplugs? If not, a gag will do."

Erica insisted on sweeping before the men put the dresser down. There were impatient looks, but she explained, "Megan and I will be able to sleep better knowing the floor is clean."

When they went downstairs, Austin looked around, as if viewing the house for the first time. "You know what you ought to do, Liz? Knock out some walls. That would open things up—make the house more modern."

Liz's jaw dropped. Then she quipped, "And while we're at it, let's remodel the kitchen in the Betsy Ross home, carpet the Edgar Allen Poe house, and put up siding on Mount Vernon."

Austin grinned. "Just a suggestion, cousin."

"One of your poorer ones."

* * *

That night, Erica settled happily in bed, propping pillows behind her back to watch *North by Northwest*, with Cary Grant as the debonair hero.

When David called, Erica pushed the mute button on the remote. "So, what are the kids up to?"

"What kids? Didn't they go with you?" He chuckled at his own wit then went on to say that Aby had gone to watch a movie with friends and Kenzie was at a sleepover. "Just me and Ryan tonight. On Monday, for family home evening, we're going to a baseball game in Salt Lake. Your parents are going, and Chris and his family. The Bees are playing the Sacramento River Cats."

"Sounds fun. Wish I was going."

Her husband knew Erica was being sarcastic. More than once, Erica had told him that for sheer excitement, watching baseball ranked right up there with watching bread dough rise. David went on, "Other than that, it's the same old thing. Your mom takes the kids to piano lessons and soccer games and has us over for dinner as often as we want."

Erica was grateful her parents were almost always available as a backup, despite their busy schedule. In addition, Erica's two brothers and sisters-in-law lived a few houses away, and their children loved to play together.

David continued, "Today, the kids helped me plant the garden. Tomatoes, corn, beets, carrots, and green peppers." David was ever cautious and refused to plant anything before mid-May.

"Yeah, they told me about it when we talked on Skype earlier." Erica missed her children and looked forward to talking with them each day. Again, Erica wished she was home. She loved planting—it was the only time of the year when the garden was weed-free.

"We didn't talk much about the case last night," David said. "How's it coming?"

"I'm glad I kept a log of everyone I've talked to or else I'd never be able to keep all the people from the barbecue straight. Unfortunately, there's nothing much there, but I've just about eliminated the idea that someone else might have been the target. When I can, I'm going to talk to the mechanic who worked on Liz's car after her brakes failed. Speaking of which, Megan's car died, which scared us a little, after Liz's car was tampered with, but it turns out it just had a dead battery."

"How's Megan doing?"

"It's been really hard on her. Today she boxed up Beth's things so Beth's parents didn't have to do it; then she went out with Todd, which is good. It'll take her mind off things. Liz is also struggling and seems down." What Erica didn't mention was that sometimes at night, even she would wake from a nightmare and be unable to go back to sleep. Often, she used those times to work on her laptop. She had pored over her notes so much it was as though she hoped the screen would tell her the answer if she stared at it long enough.

"Oh, I also talked to BJ." Erica went over her conversations and mentioned his low bid.

"Sounds like he really likes Liz."

"I'll say. You should have seen him when Austin gave Liz a hug—BJ looked like he wanted to punch the guy. But then he found out Austin was her cousin. One other thing, I stopped to talk to Donna this afternoon. She wasn't there, but I found out something interesting."

"What was that?"

"She lied to me. On my way out, I stopped to leave a note for her at the front desk, and I saw a message for Donna from the Brintons. They wanted to reschedule their appointment since Donna was sick last Saturday when she was supposed to show them a house."

"And this is significant, why?"

"Because when I asked Donna where she was when Liz was pushed into traffic, she said she was showing a house to the Brintons."

"Ahha! Busted." David sounded triumphant.

"Exactly. Why would Donna lie about her whereabouts?

"Can't think of a single good reason."

* * *

Sunday was a sad, sober day. During church, Erica's thoughts were often on Beth, and she knew, from Megan's near-constant sniffling, that it was the same for her. Liz spent the day in her bedroom, only coming out that night to attend the viewing with Megan and Erica.

Early Monday morning, Erica woke to gray clouds and a drizzling sky that seemed somehow fitting for Beth's funeral. Water dripped off the eaves and formed glassy pools in the driveway. Donna came with Austin, who stopped to pick up Liz, Megan, and Erica in his Grand Cherokee Jeep. As he drove to Beth's hometown, Selbyville, which was at the southernmost tip of Delaware, gloom permeated the atmosphere. Erica spent most of her time staring out the window at housing estates, which were interspersed with staid old farmhouses and fields where herds of cows lazily chomped and stared at nothing.

Beth's parents, Gary and Brenda Johnson, had decided to follow what they felt their daughter would have wanted and held the funeral at an LDS church. Inside the Relief Society room, they stood close by the casket, their sides touching as if for strength.

Megan had told them Erica was working with the police. Gary clutched Erica's hand with both of his, thanked her for coming, then asked briefly, "Do they know anything?"

Brenda's eyes were puffy and red, and she held her breath, waiting for Erica's answer. Her face had the gray, worn look of a person overwhelmed with sorrow. Erica hated to cause further sorrow but had to shake her head.

During the funeral, Erica worried about Megan being able to control her emotions when she spoke. But although she paused a few times to collect herself, Megan spoke movingly about her friendship with Beth and related experiences they'd had together. When Megan's voice trembled as she talked about how grateful she was to know their friendship would endure to the next life, tears flooded Erica's eyes.

After the service, Austin took Megan's hand. "You did a wonderful job." The tears Megan had held back suddenly gushed, and she clung to Austin, burying her face in his chest. He held her tightly and patted Megan's back comfortingly.

They drove to the green stretches of the cemetery and parked on the edge of the road. The clouds were dark, and a stiff breeze blew Erica's hair in tangles. In the far distance, lightning forked silently to earth while a great, purple thunderhead swelled and spread.

When Beth's father laid his boutonniere on the casket, he seemed to break. Leaning forward, he placed both hands on the casket and began to sob. The sounds were dry and rough, like he did not know how to do it properly. A quiver of pain shot across Brenda's face as she laid a lone white rose on the casket. She didn't cry though—it was as if she'd struck the bottom of a well and used up all the tears, though a few clung to her bottom lashes.

Friends and neighbors had prepared a luncheon at Beth's home. A crew of women efficiently replenished the buffet table and washed dishes in the kitchen.

In the front room, Erica and Megan went to look at the family photographs that hung on the wall. Some were old, while a few were newer, such as a wedding picture of a young woman who looked remarkably like Beth. There was a family portrait of Beth's older brother with his wife and two young children, whom Erica and Megan had talked with at the viewing and the house.

"One of these must be Beth's father," Megan said, pointing at a picture of six men in uniform, standing in front of a plane. "Beth told me he was in the air force."

When it was time to go, she and Megan threaded their way past the mourners to say good-bye to Beth's parents. Brenda, her face white and haggard, clasped Megan's hands and pulled her down to sit on the couch. "Thank you so much, dear, for everything. You've been a real friend to Beth, and you gave a wonderful talk."

Megan gulped and nodded, unable to speak.

Brenda went on, her eyes brimming with tears. "I found it very comforting to hear that we can be with our Beth again." She paused. "Still, it's hard to realize we'll never see her married or hold her first baby—" Her face crumpled like a used paper bag.

Leaning over, Gary patted his wife's hand and told the girls, "She's thinking of Sophia, Beth's sister. Sophia got married last year."

"And now Beth will never have that chance." Brenda's voice quavered.

"Oh, but she will!" Erica burst out. "She'll have that opportunity in heaven."

Both parents turned startled eyes on her. Brenda was the first to speak. "She was in love, you know," she said sadly. "Beth told us she'd found someone special. But we never got to meet him."

Erica held out a gift sack to Brenda. "I wanted to give you this."

Pulling out the tissue paper, Brenda withdrew a framed picture of a wooden covered bridge, which showed light at both ends. She read the quote at the bottom out loud: "'The grave is but a covered bridge, leading from light to light, through a brief darkness.' Henry Wadsworth Longfellow. The thought was very comforting to me," Erica said.

Brenda squeezed her hand. "That's lovely. And you all believe that, I know."

Erica knew she was referring to Mormons. "We do," she replied softly.

"Beth was very interested in your church," Brenda said. "Gary and I worried about it at first." Her husband gave her a look, and she added hastily, "No offense. We just didn't know much about your religion. But after we went to church with Beth and Megan, we felt better. Being there for three hours was kind of, um, *long*, but it wasn't so bad."

"You get used to it," Erica said with a smile. "Megan said Beth was meeting with the missionaries." She tilted her head toward the far side of the room, where two young men in suits with nametags were talking to Liz and Donna. "Are those the ones who were teaching her?"

"Yep," Gary answered. "They came to the house every once in a while—on the weekends Beth came home from school."

"They're nice young men," Brenda said. "A bit earnest—but very polite. And laws, can they eat! They came to see us after—after Beth was killed. They said we'll see her again. Of course, our church believes that too." She paused. "We don't go very often, but we're going to do better." This was said in a significant tone, seemingly aimed at her husband. Gary nodded in agreement.

"Would you like to come with me to LDS services if I came out to visit on a weekend?" Megan asked softly.

The parents exchanged glances, and when Gary nodded at his wife, Brenda smiled tremulously at Megan. "We'd like that. I liked those things you said in your talk, you know, about families being together forever." She glanced at her husband and gave a gentle smile.

Then she turned to Erica. "I'm very appreciative of what you're doing to investigate." When Erica nodded, Brenda clasped both of Erica's hands tightly. "Please find out who did this to our little girl. I can't understand . . ." Her voice trailed off, and though her mouth was parted slightly as if she wanted to say more, nothing came out.

Gary put an arm around his wife and said simply, "It would mean a lot to us to know why. That's what eats at us day and night. Not knowing why. It makes no sense."

When they left, clouds were still moving restlessly across the sky, their underbellies dark. But on the horizon, a few bright rays from the sun percolated through the clouds. On the drive home, Megan and Austin talked quietly, and after a while, Liz and Donna fell asleep. Erica looked over at Liz, whose head rested on her aunt's shoulder. Her peaceful expression contrasted with the anxiety Erica felt in the pit of her stomach. They could so easily have been attending Liz's funeral. Erica felt a new resolve. She couldn't bear another funeral. She had to find out who wanted Liz dead before another tragedy occurred.

Chapter Eight

When Liz came downstairs the next morning and saw the waffles, a small smile appeared. "This is the life I've always dreamed of—having a live-in chef. Usually I just have yogurt or cereal for breakfast." Despite her determinedly cheerful tone, Erica felt a weariness coming from her.

Erica poured some juice. "And these are no ordinary waffles. They're Lemon Poppy Seed Waffles."[3] Erica set a glass bowl and ladle on the table. "And this nectar to drizzle over them is Blackberry Maple Syrup."[4]

Once they were seated, Erica asked if she could say a blessing on the food.

Liz agreed then afterward asked, "Do you always do that?"

"Yeah. I do. It's a habit now—and a nice way to thank Heavenly Father for having food to eat."

"Should we wait for Megan?"

"She already ate. Had an early study group." Erica noticed dark circles under Liz's eyes. "You look tired."

"It shows, does it?"

"A little."

"You're kind, but I've seen myself in the mirror." Liz sipped her juice. "It's hard to get to sleep at night, and just when I do, I wake up with my heart racing, thinking about Beth, and—" She stopped abruptly.

"I know you're scared. You just have to be extra careful."

Liz stared at her plate. "It doesn't matter. Nothing really matters now."

It was unusual to see Liz so downcast. The young woman was usually so positive, so upbeat. Yet lately, she'd been silent and preoccupied. The pressure was definitely getting to her.

3 See the appendix at the end of the book for this recipe.

4 See the appendix at the end of the book for this recipe.

"I wish you'd go away," Erica said. "I think you'd be safer somewhere else. You wouldn't have to stay away long, but it would give me and the police time to figure things out."

With her elbow on the table, Liz used a hand to support her head. It was as if her neck was too tired to support it. Speaking slowly, she said, "I can't go." Her eyes grazed the kitchen and looked into the front room. "This is my home. I won't give it up." Despite her brave words, Liz looked vulnerable. As if making a determined effort to be upbeat, she added, "Besides, how could I be any safer than living with a private eye who has her own gun?"

It was good to see a bit of sparkle in her eyes.

Liz went on. "I was talking with a girl at work, and she thinks I'm overreacting big time. I told her everything that's happened, and she's convinced it's just a series of coincidences. But whenever I leave the house, I feel like someone is watching me—and waiting." She shivered.

"We've got to do something to take your mind off this, even if it's just for a day," Erica said. "Let's go to Philadelphia or the beach. We could even go look at lighthouses." She giggled. "But that's my thing—I love lighthouses."

"Really? So do I!" Liz brightened. "And there are tons of them around here."

"That's what Beth said." Erica spoke without thinking, and the comment brought their conversation to a grinding halt as they thought of Beth.

Then Liz began counting off lighthouses on her fingers. "There's Fenwick Island Light, the Fourteen-Foot Light, and there are a bunch of them by Lewes Beach."

"What are we waiting for? Check with your boss, and see if you can take a day off, and we'll have Megan do the same. Lewes sounds good; we can see lighthouses *and* soak up the sun."

Liz's eyes came alive with new interest and anticipation. "That does sound like fun. Could we invite Austin? I'd feel safer having a man around. His Jeep will fit all of us. Megan's car is big enough, but it's still out of commission."

"She hasn't got a new battery yet? Why doesn't she have it fixed?"

"Because it's cheaper to borrow my car."

Erica giggled. "Okay, you call Austin, and I'll pack a picnic lunch and dinner."

"I can help with that," Liz said, rinsing off her plate. "By the way, how did your talk with Frank go? I'm surprised you came back with your head intact."

"We got along pretty well—at least until Frank thought I was accusing him of murder."

Liz's eyes went wide. "Did you?"

"Not in so many words, but that's what I was getting at. For some reason, he took offense."

It was great to hear Liz's light, bubbly laughter.

* * *

After Liz left for school, Erica caught the bus and, with the help of the kindly driver, found the auto repair shop that had fixed Liz's car. A skinny young man wearing dirty blue coveralls listened as Erica explained that she was a private investigator and had some questions. She gave him the date of service and Liz's name, and he looked up the record.

"Dennis worked on this," he said, eyes on the computer screen. "He's really good—knows manifolds and intake valves, shocks, struts and pistons, and radiators inside and out." The young man caught himself. "I'll, uh, go get him."

In a few minutes, Dennis, a short, thickset man, strolled in from the garage, wiping his hands on a rag before stuffing it in a back pocket. His dark eyes widened appreciatively when he saw Erica then became wary when she handed him the invoice the young man had printed out. He reviewed it, holding it with fingers that appeared to have been permanently stained black.

"Okay, I remember this now," Dennis said. "We had to tow the car in. The lady"—he glanced at the paper—"ah, Liz Johnson, said she didn't want me to do any body work because she had a high deductible. So, what do you want to know?" He looked at her with pleasant curiosity.

"Anything you can tell me. I'm a private investigator and think someone is trying to kill Liz and make it look like an accident." Dennis raised thick eyebrows, and Erica went on. "Liz told me the brake lines had been cut. How can you tell they were cut and not just worn and faulty?"

"'Cause I'm a mechanic." This wasn't said with conceit, but with an air of calm confidence. "First, though, Liz is a little confused. I never said her lines had been cut."

That was a surprise. "Then what did happen?"

"You know anything about brakes?" When Erica shook her head, Dennis said, "I'll have to explain a little, then, so you can understand. You see, brakes run through rubber flex lines on the front brakes, and metal ones on the rear—usually, that is. They all go to the ABS system and from there to the master cylinder. When a car is old, the rubber flex lines, after years of moving back and forth, can develop weak spots that crack and leak fluid. That gives you a spongy pedal."

"And it's different if the line is cut?"

"The only part you can cut that would lead to brake failure would be the metal brake lines or possibly the rubber flex lines. But the cut would have to be very precise. A person would have to just barely cut the line to where it still holds some pressure, and that's next to impossible."

"Why is that?"

"Because if someone cut the metal line, you're going to get air in there, and the driver would notice a spongy pedal before he even put the car in drive. What I told Liz is that it looked like someone had put a few *holes* in her brake line. I figured someone punctured it, hoping the brakes wouldn't feel spongy right off but that the brakes would fail when Liz was out on the road."

"Would it take special knowledge to put those holes in the brake line? I mean, would someone have to be an expert with cars?"

"Yes and no. I'd say a person would need a fair amount of experience with cars to know how to do it. But then again, a person could ask around and find out how to do it."

"Does it make a difference that Liz's car was old?"

"Not really," Dennis said. "Most newer cars have a two-piston master cylinder so if you lose one brake line, you can still stop on the other wheels. You see, 80 percent of braking is done on your front brakes. So if someone really was trying to kill Liz, they would have to make sure the brakes lost hydraulic pressure all at once by draining the entire system." His eyes narrowed. "But whoever made those holes didn't do that. Either they didn't know what they were doing, or they were hoping Liz wouldn't notice the bad brakes until she was in a serious situation. I remember thinking she was real lucky to be able to slow down before running into a tree. It could have been a really serious accident."

* * *

At Park Place Realty, Austin welcomed Erica with a smile even as he looked past her, out the glass doors, as if hoping to see someone else.

Austin looked nice in a blue blazer, gray slacks, and a dark blue tie with thin red stripes. Megan would have been drooling.

He went so far as to ask, "So, uh, Megan didn't come with you?"

"Not today; she had class. I just came from the mechanic who fixed Liz's car. I wanted to talk with you—if you've got time."

"I'm good—come on back." Austin was always friendly. They went past Donna's office. Her door was shut today. Erica sat in one of the blue cushioned chairs, and Austin rolled his chair out from behind his desk to sit closer. "So you talked to the mechanic. Find out anything?"

"I'm now a fountain of knowledge about brakes, lines, and master cylinders. Brakes work on hydraulics—you push the pedal, and that pumps fluid through the lines to the brakes, which squeeze the brake pads against a disc to stop the car."

"Any high school auto-shop student knows that." Austin appeared amused.

"I never took shop, so it was news to me," Erica said with a grin. "Anyway, the mechanic said someone put holes in the brake's lines. Apparently the idea was to have the brakes fail while Liz was driving."

Alarm showed in Austin's brown eyes. "Liz told me the lines had been cut, but I have to admit, I thought she was exaggerating."

"This is serious business. I need to know more about Liz, and since you two seem pretty close, I thought you might be able to give me a little more information."

"What do you want to know?"

"Does Liz take drugs, or has she ever experimented with them?"

When Austin blinked, Erica hurried to add, "I'm sorry; I should have warned you the questions would be personal."

"Well, that's all right." Austin composed himself. "As far as I know, Liz hasn't ever used drugs. She's smoked a joint or two, but that was years ago."

"Okay. Has Liz ever been involved in any illegal activities?"

"No." He sounded irritated. "Why are you asking me this? Surely the police have checked out her background."

"They did, but sometimes things occur under the radar."

"So the police still don't have a clue who's trying to kill her?"

"Not yet. Now, does Liz ever talk to you about her job? I talked with her coworkers but didn't find out anything that would suggest she has an enemy there."

"She hasn't mentioned any problems."

"Do you know any of Liz's friends? Any sleaziness there?"

"Not really, though I have to admit I didn't care much for Todd. But they broke it off almost before their relationship started."

"Why doesn't Liz go out on dates?"

"I don't know." Austin looked baffled. "She used to, but the past six months or so, she just hasn't been interested. She's kind of weird about it. I keep trying to set her up, but each time I ask, it's like I'm hitting a nerve. She keeps saying no."

"Let me ask you something else. Do you know if any of the old furniture or paintings in Crooked House are valuable?"

Austin scoffed. "Most of it is junk that Liz refuses to part with."

"Has she ever had any of it appraised?"

Was there a shade of hesitation on his part? Erica thought so.

"Why are you asking me?" Austin narrowed his eyes. "You already talked with Liz and told her you were going to get an appraiser to come to the house."

Busted. Liz and Austin talked together more than Erica thought.

He went on. "So you're either double-checking, or else you think I might be the one trying to kill Liz."

"Double-checking. You see, people lie all the time, sometimes for reasons that aren't important, but I have to check everything out."

"I notice you didn't deny suspecting me. Liz must have told you I'm one of the beneficiaries of her will."

"She did. But I'm checking everyone."

"Even my mother. Mom told me she'd talked with you." Austin's manner turned cool. "Check me out all you want, but my mom has enough stress in her life without the accusations you're making. She has a lot on her mind with my grandpa. I think there might be more wrong than she's telling me there, but regardless, I'd appreciate it if you'd leave her out of this."

That was not something Erica could do, but rather than saying so, she returned to the subject of appraisers. "I've been trying to talk an appraiser into coming out to Crooked House, but so far, no luck."

"Really, Erica, there isn't anything in Liz's house worth killing for. While some of the furniture is very old and might be worth something, I doubt anything is *that* valuable."

"But if you haven't had it appraised, there's no way to be sure, is there?"

Austin sat quietly, fingers laced together. "I guess not. I'm no expert. But I wouldn't hurt Liz to get my hands on her furniture, and neither would my mother. Actually, no one else would either, because if Liz were killed, the house and everything in it would go to me and my mom."

That was the dead end Erica kept coming to. Or was it a dead end? Sometimes the simplest answers were the correct ones. In that case, it could be that either Donna or Austin was a cold-blooded killer.

Picking up her purse, Erica thanked Austin. On her way out the door, she glanced back. Austin was staring at the wall, and the expression on his face was revealing. He looked apprehensive. It appeared Austin knew something he hadn't told her. But what?

* * *

That afternoon, Erica was on her hands and knees scrubbing deep inside a cabinet when she heard a noise. Backing out carefully so she didn't hit her head, Erica looked up to see Liz standing over her.

"What are you doing?" Liz looked both exasperated and amused.

"Cleaning." Erica put her rag in the bucket and sat cross-legged. "I figured I deserved a break after spending hours on the computer checking the background of your old renters. Pinnacle has a lot of databases, but they're all different, and I have to check each one."

"And cleaning cupboards is your break? You're kidding, right?"

"I thought it would be fun to clean and organize them."

"You must like root canals too." Liz opened an upper cabinet to get a glass. "Hey! Where are the glasses?"

Apparently Liz hadn't been listening. "I rearranged things a bit."

After opening a few cupboards, Liz found the glasses. "Am I going to have to search for everything?"

"I could label the cabinets if you want. What do you say?" Erica smiled at the very idea.

When Megan came in carrying a box, Liz announced, "Erica's been cleaning again—*and* rearranging the cupboards."

"Oh, Erica!" Megan put the box on the table. "Don't you know how rude it is to rearrange someone else's kitchen without asking?"

"Oh, I don't mind, really," Liz said.

"You think that now, but once Erica gets started she doesn't know how to stop," Megan cautioned her. "She'll go through the entire house, cleaning, organizing, labeling. It's like a disease with her."

"All I can say is, be my guest." Liz headed for the stairs. "I'm going to take a nap."

"Don't say I didn't warn you," Megan called after her darkly. Then she turned back. "Erica, this box is for you. It was on the porch. It's from David."

After stripping off her yellow gloves, Erica used a paring knife to slice through the strapping tape. She folded back the cardboard to reveal a folded sheet of paper lying on top. She smoothed it out and read, "'So noble a confection, more than nectar & ambrosia, the true food of the gods.' Dr. Bachot."

When Megan appeared perplexed, Erica explained, "David and I have a little hobby of coming up with unique quotes."

"That's right; I remember that now. What does that quote mean, anyway?"

"It means he sent me *chocolate*!" Digging into the box, Erica pulled out a small box of individual chocolates, a bag of truffles, and an assortment of chocolate bars. She ran her fingers through them like they were gold coins. "That sweetheart!" She beamed at Megan. "It's always been kind of a joke between us that chocolate helps me think, so David buys me some if I'm on a tough case."

She shook a fistful of chocolate bars at Megan. "If you're ever feeling down, eat chocolate. It's a lot cheaper than therapy, and you don't need an appointment."

Megan took a bar. "Thanks. I'll try it. Bring the box upstairs, and visit with me. You can look through it while I get ready. Todd and I are going to see a play this afternoon. He should be here any minute."

Erica got some tiny pieces of carrot out of a plastic baggie in the fridge then followed Megan upstairs. She lifted the lid on the hamster cage and dropped the bits inside.

"You're not giving him chocolate, are you?" Megan asked as she changed.

"No. Carrot. Hamlet was a good hamster last night—only woke me up twice by running around on his wheel."

"I hate to break it to you, but Hamlet didn't do it because he likes you. You're just getting used to the noise."

"You're underestimating your hamster." While Hamlet stuffed his cheeks, Erica sat on the end of the bed and dug deeper into the box. "Look! David sent some Dilbert comic books."

"Those *are* funny. Dogbert is so evil."

"And hilarious." Erica chuckled just thinking about the tail-wagging little dog.

As Megan brushed her black hair into a ponytail, Erica asked, "So, do you like Todd?"

"He's awesome. And almost as handsome as David." Then Megan paused, her brush drooping. "But sometimes I wonder if he really likes me. He talks about Liz so much I wonder sometimes. I'd tell him to knock it off, but I don't want to be rude."

"Of course. You're *never* rude."

Megan made a face. "Why do I even like you? You're so sarcastic."

There was a knock from downstairs. Megan set down her brush. "That'll be Todd. See you later."

Going to the window, Erica watched Megan and Todd pass through the gate to his low-slung silver sports car. It matched him very well, Erica thought. Both were well-made, powerful, and caught and held the eye. But Erica was disturbed by Megan's words. Could Todd still be interested in Liz? Todd opened the passenger door, and Megan folded her long legs out of sight. He moved lithely to the driver's side, and with a tightly knit snarling sound, the car backed out and raced off.

* * *

The last cabinet to clean was the one under the sink. Erica pulled out cutting boards and the dish drainer, then recoiled in disgust when she found a mousetrap in the back corner, complete with a dried-out mouse carcass. Using a plastic knife, she slid the trap onto a piece of cardboard and carried it out to the backyard.

BJ was next door cutting out sod in Frank's backyard. When Erica called out a friendly hello, he straightened his lanky form and waved. He watched as she retrieved a shovel from the shed. Curiosity got the best of him, and he came over to where Erica was digging.

"Whatcha doing?"

"I found a dead mouse in the house. I wanted to give it a suitable burial."

He stared, unsure if she was joking or not. "Liz usually asks me to get rid of them for her."

Obviously Liz didn't check the traps often. "Does Liz get a lot of mice in the house?" Erica tilted the cardboard and slid the mouse into its grave.

He nodded. "I put out a bunch of traps." When Erica started filling in the hole, he yelled, "Hey, you're burying the trap!"

"Yes, I am. Mouse traps are barbaric," Erica declared firmly. She tamped the dirt down and put a little stick at the head of the grave. Then she asked, "Where are the other mouse traps?"

He stared at her, a bit slack-jawed. "In the house."

"Um, yes, but where, exactly? It would save me time if you could point them out."

A movement from next door caused him to glance over at Frank, who had come out of his house and stood watching them, a ferocious look on his face. "I can't right now—I've got to get back. I'm makin' a pond."

"When you're done, can you can come over and show me the traps?"

"Sure. But Liz isn't going to like it if you get rid of them."

"Then let's not tell her." She winked. When BJ blinked in surprise, Erica added, "Don't worry. I've got an idea." Once BJ showed her where he'd placed the traps, she would take measures to prevent any future burials. But her plan would have to remain a secret—for now.

* * *

That night, Megan rushed around like a maniac. She'd gotten home later from the play than expected and was going to meet Austin on campus.

"That's what you get for packing two dates into one day," Erica remarked as Megan double-checked her makeup in the mirror in the front room. She used a finger to smudge her eyeliner.

"Can I help it if the play *and* the concert are on the same day?" She grabbed her purse and called upstairs, "Hey Liz, can I still borrow your car? I promise to get the battery on my car fixed soon."

"I've heard that before," Liz said. "The keys are in my backpack."

"Thanks. I'll put some gas in it. See you later, Erica," Megan said as she opened the door.

"Have a good time." Erica bent back over the kitchen sink, where she was washing dishes.

Seconds later, an explosion from outside caused Erica to duck instinctively. She straightened and, from the window, saw a fireball rising from Liz's car. For a split second, Erica was stricken to stone by the flames licking upwards. Then, screaming, she ran outside.

Chapter Nine

MEGAN WAS LYING ON THE ground at the bottom of the porch stairs. Erica grabbed Megan under her arms and dragged her backward, away from the scorching flames. Liz nearly tore the door off as she ran out and pounded down the cobbled sidewalk to the front lawn, where Megan lay. Liz looked panicked as Erica patted Megan's face and called her name over and over. A passerby ran over, and Erica begged her to dial 911.

Megan's eyes fluttered open, but her face was blank and dazed. She tried to rise, but Erica gently told her to lie still.

Megan blinked in bewilderment. "What happened?" Her voice was weak and confused. "I pressed the remote starter, and then . . . I'm not sure."

People were gathering. One lady with a spaniel on a leash took off her sweater and put its soft folds under Megan's head. When the ambulance arrived, Liz and Erica stepped back as the EMTs examined Megan.

Then a gruff voice called out, "What happened here?"

It was Frank.

Liz launched herself at him, her face wild as she struck at him with balled up fists. "Why can't you leave me alone? You almost killed her!"

"What are you doing?" Frank exclaimed as he fended her off. "Are you crazy?"

Erica started to pull Liz back as a police car slid to a screeching stop. The officer ran over and helped separate them. Frank backed off a few steps.

Liz was shaking all over, tears of fury streaming down her face. "You did this! You did something to my car. You wanted to kill me, and instead you almost killed Megan!"

"What are you talking about?" Frank's eyes were popping out of his head.

She made another lunge at him, but the policeman restrained her. Liz continued to scream at Frank, her slender body trembling with rage. At one point, Liz kicked out at Frank, but the policeman forcibly lifted her off her feet and moved her away.

Another officer escorted Frank out of Liz's sight. As the fire engine arrived, someone threw a blanket around Liz's shoulders.

Making Liz sit on the lawn, Erica told her, "I'll be right back. I'm going to get my cell phone." She ran into the house.

When she returned, an officer called out loudly, "Anyone know who lives here?"

Raising her arm, Erica answered a bit shakily. "I do." She tilted her head toward Liz. "And she does too. She owns the house."

The policeman came over and was still writing down information when Detective Ranquist arrived. He headed straight for Erica. "I heard the call. What's going on?"

"Megan was going to borrow Liz's car. She went outside and pressed the remote car starter, and there was an explosion. It must have been a bomb."

"Is Megan the girl on the stretcher?"

"Yes. She's coherent and doesn't seem to be badly hurt. She must have pushed the button when she was going down the porch steps. Thank goodness the car was parked all the way down the driveway instead of alongside the porch."

"That may have saved her life," Detective Ranquist said, eyeing the car as firemen put out the last of the flames.

The police officer who had separated Liz and Frank asked to talk to Detective Ranquist. After a minute, Detective Ranquist called Erica over. Eyeing Liz, he said, "I take it she thinks Frank planted the bomb."

"I think Liz said that out of shock."

"Then again, it's a possibility."

Austin came running down the sidewalk and kneeled beside Megan, heedless of his dress pants. "Megan! Are you all right?" His face was anxious as he stroked her black hair.

"I would be if they'd just leave me alone. What are you doing here?"

"Erica texted me. I was waiting for you at the university."

"We're going to miss the concert."

He stared at her; then the corners of his mouth turned up. "You know, if you don't want to go out with me, all you have to do is say so."

Megan grinned.

"Sir, would you please move back?" It was the second time one of the EMTs had asked Austin.

"I want him here." Megan reached out and clutched his hand.

Gently he let go of her hand. "I'll be right over here."

Detective Ranquist took a closer look at Erica. "You're shaking." He had Erica sit by Liz and waved one of the policemen over. "Get a blanket for her too."

Someone gave Liz and Erica bottles of water, and gradually Erica stopped shaking, but her mind raced. Who could have done this? She kept one eye on Megan, grateful she hadn't been hurt seriously. The EMTs decided to take Megan to the hospital as a precaution. She protested, but after Austin talked to her, she gave in.

Just as the ambulance was leaving, Donna arrived, flushed and out of breath. "I had to park a mile away," she explained. She gave Erica a grateful look. "Thanks for texting me." Donna turned and helped Liz into the house.

After the fire truck left, Erica found Detective Ranquist. "Do you mind if I look around? If I find anything, I'll let your detectives bag it."

He hesitated then gave in. "All right, if you're feeling up to it."

Erica's nerves were stretched to the limit, but she knew it would do her good to stay busy. She thought again of that night when a sheet had covered Beth and said a silent prayer of gratitude that Megan was all right.

A large area had been cordoned off with yellow plastic tape that read, *CRIME SCENE—DO NOT CROSS*, in black letters. As Erica stepped inside, a policeman stopped her. Detective Ranquist came over.

"It's all right," he told the officer. "She's a private eye working on the case and has my permission to be here."

Erica went over the area carefully, starting at the center then spreading out, avoiding other crime scene investigators and detectives. Then she went beyond the cordoned-off area into Frank's yard. He was watching from the window.

Erica saw something white at the base of one of the rhododendrons that formed a hedge between Frank's yard and Liz's driveway. She pulled out her Leatherman pocket tool and used the tweezers to pick up the small rectangle. It was a ticket stub. Interesting. Erica beckoned to a detective, and he put it in a bag.

* * *

"Yes, Megan's fine," Erica assured David as she folded the chocolate chips and walnuts into the cookie dough. Erica always made cookies when one of her own children needed a boost, and she figured Megan was definitely in need of a pick-me-up. One of her all-time favorite cookie recipes was Applesauce Cookies.[5] As far as it was possible for a cookie to be healthful, this one was, using whole-wheat flour and applesauce. She'd talked with David last night but called him again this morning, wanting the reassurance of hearing his voice.

"Donna, Liz, and I went to the ER last night after I talked with you," she explained. "They checked Megan over and released her."

"I'm glad she's okay. Do the police know what kind of a bomb it was?"

"A pipe bomb. Thank goodness Megan always uses the remote starter." Erica couldn't bear to think what would have happened if Megan had started the car while sitting inside it. She didn't dare tell David that she had borrowed Liz's car from time to time.

"These murder attempts are getting more deadly." David said. "I'm scared for you. It doesn't look like the murderer is going to stop until either you find out who it is or until Liz is dead."

But, hey, no pressure, Erica thought dismally. "I hope I can do this. I have some ideas, but nothing's really come together yet."

"You'll find out." David sounded confident. "You've done it before. Besides, you're the best investigator I've ever seen."

The compliment was nice to hear, even though it came from someone who was heavily biased in her favor. There was a beep on her phone, and Erica glanced to see who was calling.

Rats.

"Hey, David, can I call you back later?" Erica asked. "Wendy's calling, and I'd better take it. She was beside herself last night."

"Sure. Give me a call at lunch."

She clicked over and put all the brightness she could muster into her voice. "Hi, Wendy." Erica worked as she talked, comforting her friend while smoothing the dough onto the cookie sheet and washing bowls.

What Wendy needed most was to vent and be reassured. Erica did her best—it was a role she was used to filling with her friend.

Yes, Megan looked fine today. She was able to stay awake, and no, there was no grogginess, slurred speech, or glazed eyes. Yes, she would watch Megan more carefully. Yes, Erica was working hard on the case and doing all she could to solve it quickly.

---

5 See the appendix at the end of the book for this recipe.

As Wendy poured out her fears, Erica put the dishes away and cut the still-warm cookies into squares. At the end of their conversation, Wendy's fear had dimmed, and her voice sounded calmer.

"I'm so glad you're there with Megan," Wendy said fervently. "I couldn't bear it if anything happened to her."

"Nothing is going to happen," Erica promised. "I'll take care of her."

Later, when Megan came down to breakfast, Erica put some cookies in a baggie for her to take to school.

"I see each one is two inches square. So two is still the magic number?"

"Always and forever."

With a glint in her eye, Megan asked, "Do you ever make round cookies?"

"Never. Square ones taste better."

Megan laughed, a sound that lifted Erica's heart. "I hate to break it to you," Megan said, "but round ones taste exactly the same."

"I know they're supposed to, but they just don't for some reason."

"Oh, Erica." Megan gave her an unexpected hug. "You're one in a million."

* * *

Pulling on a pair of gloves in advance, Erica put two doggie treats in her pocket and carried two plates of plastic-wrapped cookies next door. BJ and Frank were in his backyard, laying heavy black liner in the huge hole BJ had dug for a pond. Or at least BJ was working the liner into place. Sweat glistened on his brow while Frank told him, "It needs to be more that way," while doing nothing to help shift it.

"Hello, Frank, BJ!" Erica glanced around. "Where's Duke?"

"I left him home," BJ replied—a bit gloomily, Erica thought.

"I'm not going to have a dog digging up my flowers and pooping on my lawn." Frank looked at her suspiciously. "What do you want?"

"I brought you some cookies." She handed over the plates and gave BJ two doggie treats. "You can give these to Duke when you get home.

"Why are you giving me cookies when you think I tried to kill Liz?" Frank asked gruffly.

"Liz is the one who said that. And it was just because she was so upset about Megan."

"I'm surprised they didn't cart her off in a rubber truck last night."

"You were the first person on the scene—someone Liz could blame. She's calmed down now, but she's scared. You've told Liz you want her house, so it's natural for her to wonder how far you'd go to get it." Erica spoke as if it was the easiest thing in the world to understand.

Frank rubbed his chin, considering her words. "I'd never do something like that. How's that other girl?"

"Megan's fine, although, she has a headache and some bruises from when she fell."

"And Liz is okay?" BJ asked, wanting to make sure.

"Yeah. Just scared."

When BJ started to open one side of the plastic wrap to reach for a cookie, Erica pulled out her wipes and handed him one. He leaned the shovel handle against his shoulder and wiped his hands.

"Hope Liz didn't break any of her nails." Frank's hand went to his face, where a few red scratches showed.

"Did you see or hear anything last night before the explosion?"

Frank glared at Erica. "I suppose you think I planted that bomb."

"Did you?"

"Course not." The square line of his jaw seemed a little grimmer. "The police already asked, and I told 'em I didn't do it."

Munching on a cookie, BJ watched the interplay between Frank and Erica with apparent interest.

"I'm not saying you did. All I wanted to know is if you saw anyone around Liz's car yesterday afternoon."

"Why should I tell *you*?" Frank said evasively, faint color appearing in his cheeks. "I'd call the police if I saw someone strapping a bomb to the engine, not you. You're just a private eye." Then he seemed to think better of his words. "Besides, I was gone most of the day."

"Do you have anyone who can verify that?"

Veins corded on Frank's neck. "That's none of your business."

"Do you have any idea why or how Liz's deck collapsed?"

"Of course not."

High emotion turned Frank's face red and white. Erica felt sure that even if he knew something, Frank would never tell her. Yet she had to try.

"There were saw marks on the poles. And when I was in your shed the other day, I noticed you had a number of saws."

"There's hardly a person in Dover who *doesn't* have a saw. You're determined to make me the scapegoat, aren't you?" Frank's eyes were ringed with white, and his fists clenched. This was a man who had a serious issue with anger. She was tempted to take a step back, but she held her ground.

Erica turned to the younger man. "How about you, BJ? Did you see anyone around yesterday? You were working over here, weren't you?"

A wary look came into BJ's eyes. "I was here, but I didn't see anybody."

She looked toward the back of Crooked House. "I see you've already started working on the deck."

"Yep. In a day or two, I'll have the wood hauled off. I might be able to salvage some of it. Liz said I could have it."

"You've been working for Liz for quite a while, haven't you? Do you know any of Liz's old roommates?"

"I talked to some of them."

"Did any of them ever get upset with Liz for any reason?"

He blinked, thought hard, then shook his head.

Frank jumped in. "You like stirring up trouble, don't you?"

It was an accusation Erica heard frequently and that came with the job. A lot of her work involved asking hard questions and trying to pick out anything that could relate to the case.

"Confucius had a saying that makes a good axiom for private investigators," Erica responded calmly. "He said, 'Study the past, if you would divine the future.' That's what I'm trying to do—find out if there's something in Liz's past that would make someone want to kill her."

* * *

When the receptionist at Park Place Realty recognized Erica, she smiled cheerfully. "Donna's in her office if you want to go back."

"Thanks, Dolores."

The door was open, and Donna was on the phone in the midst of a heated discussion. She looked up at Erica's discreet knock and waved her in. To give the older woman a little privacy, Erica went over to look out the window. Still, it was impossible not to overhear the conversation, which seemed to be with her banker about a loan.

As the minutes ticked by, Donna's voice became increasingly strained, then angry. Finally she burst out, "Oh, go foreclose on something," and hung up.

After a few seconds, Erica turned and took a seat. Resilient as tempered steel, Donna took a deep breath and swiveled round, trying to recover her normal, unassailable dignity.

When she had rearranged her features into a semblance of calmness, Donna asked, "All right, what can I do for you?"

Erica got right to the point. "Last night's car bomb made it clear that whoever is out to kill Liz is not going to stop until he or she succeeds. We're in a race against time, here. I need to find out who is doing this, and to do that, I need the truth. You were not honest with me."

Looking irritated, Donna drew her brows together. "What are you talking about?"

"You told me you were showing a house to the Brintons when Liz was pushed into traffic. But you called the Brintons and cancelled your appointment, telling them you were ill and that you'd show them the house another day."

Erica could almost see the wheels churning in Donna's head as she struggled to come up with a response.

"Actually, I had an emergency that day."

"What kind of emergency?"

"The none-of-your-business kind." There was cold fury in Donna's voice.

Erica said nothing.

Finally, Donna stirred uneasily in her chair. "I suppose this makes me a suspect."

"Oh, you were always a suspect. Do you want to tell me where you were?"

An instant coldness passed like a mask over Donna's face. "It had nothing to do with Liz."

"That's not good enough."

"Bite me."

"After I talk to Detective Ranquist, I'm sure the police will want to talk with you."

Alarm flared in those brown eyes, and it was surprising how quickly Donna capitulated. "It was nothing, really. I—I just had to go home and check on my father."

Was this another lie? If that was the truth, there was no reason to lie about it in the first place. Donna had to be hiding something.

"Would the nurse be able to vouch for you?" Erica asked.

A pause. "I'm sure she would."

Right. Especially if Donna got to her before Erica could. She wouldn't get very far with this kind of tension between them. Trying to find safer ground, Erica said, "I'm sorry about your father. You're in a very difficult situation."

Donna sighed. "Yes, it is hard."

This conversation was exactly why it was always good to talk to a number of people. Erica hadn't gotten this depth of information from Liz. "I understand Frank is on the board of the Dover Historical Society."

"He's passionate—some say obsessed—about saving historical homes in Dover. Frank's approached me a number of times, trying to get me to 'talk sense' into Liz. He doesn't seem to realize that Liz would fix up Crooked House if she could."

"What about the paintings and furniture? Some of the pieces look like they could be valuable."

"I don't think the furniture is worth much. I was going to get an appraiser once but decided it wasn't worth the cost."

Erica thought hard. Hadn't Liz told her that Donna was concerned about the valuable antiques? "Didn't you tell Liz that she ought to donate some things to a museum or put them in storage?"

Donna looked surprised. "No. If Liz told you that, she misunderstood. Oh, there might be a few good pieces, but most of it isn't worth anything."

When Erica left and headed for the bus stop, she had a lot to think about. What Donna had said about the furniture differed substantially from what Liz had said. Who was telling the truth?

Chapter Ten

When Erica returned from Donna's office, she found Megan in the front room, a book in her lap. "What are you reading?" Erica asked, sitting by her on the couch.

"One of Beth's books. *An American Tragedy*. She liked older books and was reading this one when she died."

"Did you know they made a movie based on it, called *A Place in the Sun*?"

Megan shook her head. "When I saw Beth's parents Saturday, I asked them if I could keep the book until I was done, and they said I could have it."

"How are they doing?"

"Not so good. They're leaving in a few days to visit their son and his family in Illinois."

"That'll be good for them."

"I think so. While I was there, Gary and Brenda asked me some questions about baptism. They were curious because Beth had told them she wanted to be baptized." Megan frowned slightly. "I'm not sure I explained it very well."

"I'm sure you did just fine. Are the missionaries still teaching them?"

The girl's face brightened. "Yeah, and it sounds like they're really enjoying it. They also started reading the Book of Mormon."

"Great." The sun had begun to set, and Erica reached over to turn on the light. She was grateful Megan didn't seem to have any lingering emotional trauma from the explosion. "Didn't you say you're going out with Austin tonight? You certainly stay busy. One night, Todd; another night, Austin," she said teasingly. "Where are you going?"

"There's a documentary on campus in the Education & Humanities Theater: *Just Like Us*. It's directed by a comedian, Ahmed Ahmed, and it's supposed to be really good."

"Sounds interesting."

"I think it will be. I like learning about different cultures, and Austin heard it was very funny. Afterwards we're going out to dinner at Lonestar."

Erica gave her a sidelong glance. "So, is Austin at the head of your pack of admirers?"

There was a great snort from Megan. "Two isn't a pack." Then she frowned. "The only thing is that his mother doesn't like me."

"Donna?"

"I keep getting weird vibes from her. Oh, she says all the right things; it's just that she says one thing, but it sounds like she means something else. She's a hard person to get to know."

Erica could believe that. She'd had the same feeling. "Maybe that's just how Donna is. And to be fair, it could be that Donna is just stressed about her father and Liz."

"Who wants to be fair?" Megan grinned.

At first, Erica thought Donna was unfriendly because she had a thing about private eyes, but now, she thought there could be more to it than that. But maybe she was too suspicious. "Say, did you know BJ is going to build a new deck for Liz? The insurance adjustor accepted his bid."

Megan scoffed. "I knew BJ would give her a super-low bid. That man would do anything for Liz. But at least he'll get paid *something* this time." Megan marked her spot and put the book on the table. "I feel sorry for him. I know he has lots of other customers, but I sometimes wonder how he can afford to spend so much time here and get paid next to nothing."

Erica hesitated to say what she was thinking but went ahead anyway. "Sometimes I get the feeling BJ is not the sharpest quill on the porcupine—at least when it comes to social interactions."

"You can say that again. He's so in love with Liz it's affected his brain. The poor guy keeps thinking up projects so he can be around her. I think he'd cut the grass with scissors if it would buy him some time with Liz."

"I could tell he liked her, but . . ."

"I'm not sure Liz is even aware of it—she's so used to having men fall at her feet. I wonder sometimes if BJ will ever get up the courage to do something crazy—like ask her out." Megan grinned; then she rose and stretched. "I'd better go get ready."

Erica stayed on the couch. If BJ was head over heels about Liz, Erica could probably mark him off her list of suspects. BJ couldn't be the one trying to kill her, not unless there was some weird, hidden reason.

Idly, Erica picked up the book Megan had set down. Megan had marked her place with a small piece of white paper. With a quick intake of air, Erica opened the book and examined the paper. It was a ticket stub. And it matched the one she'd found in Frank's yard.

* * *

The next morning, Erica rode the bus to the police station. She looked forward to soon having a car to borrow again, since Austin was putting a new battery in Megan's car today.

Detective Ranquist's black chair creaked as he swung around to greet Erica. Pearly light streamed into the office as she pulled a chair closer to the desk.

The detective's face showed concern. "How's Megan today?"

"She's good—considering what could have happened." Whenever Erica thought about the horrible possibilities, she felt like there was a knot in her solar plexus. "She's a little sore from where she fell and still has a headache, but basically she's fine."

"And what about Liz?"

"She's seriously freaked out. This whole thing has been hard on her, but now it's even worse. Liz won't step outside the house until she's looked out all the windows. She refuses to take the bus, so her cousin, Austin, drives her to classes and picks her up." Erica crossed her arms and sighed. "Liz, Megan, and I are going to Lewes Beach next week to get away for a day and relax. Austin is coming along to provide a male presence." Detective Ranquist leaned forward, about to speak, but Erica added quickly, "Yes, I'll watch Liz *and* Austin, and yes, I'll make sure we're not followed."

Satisfied, he leaned back in his chair. "Good."

"So, have you found out anything about the bomb yet?"

"It was a galvanized pipe bomb. Black powder, with an electric blasting cap wired to the ignition. Very simple. Very crude."

"You forgot effective."

The grim lines around Detective Ranquist's brown eyes deepened. "That too."

"So we're looking for someone with technical know-how on bomb-making."

"Not really. It was a simple bomb—anyone who can navigate the Internet could have made it." The detective looked at Erica. "Did you ever borrow Liz's car?"

"A few times."

"I don't want to worry you, but the bomb might have been meant for you. You've been doing a lot of digging. You might be making somebody uneasy."

That idea had already occurred to her. "That's possible, but I still think Liz was the target—she's the one who drove the car the most."

"All the same, you need to take more precautions yourself. Beth Johnson got shot. Megan almost got blown to pieces. You'd be safer if you weren't living at Crooked House."

"Perhaps, but there's no way I'm going to leave Liz and Megan alone. If I'm there, I can protect them. Me and Little Suzie." Then she explained, "I carry a Glock 19."

Detective Ranquist's eyebrows raised.

"I think I told you my husband's a policeman. He checked to make sure Delaware honors Utah's license to carry a concealed weapon. I also have a black belt in karate."

"Karate won't do a whole lot to protect you from a bullet or bomb." He scratched his chin. "I've been thinking about BJ. What's your opinion of him?"

"Well, he seems devoted to Liz."

"I got that feeling when I talked to him," Detective Ranquist said. "He's a different sort of guy—looks like a chewed-out bit of string and acts like he's not quite firing on all cylinders."

"He's very quiet—I think he's more comfortable building things than interacting with people. I've talked to him a little, and so far, he seems harmless." Erica went on, "I keep trying to think who would benefit from Liz's death, but so far, the only people who stand out are Donna and Austin, and maybe Frank. By the way, I talked with Frank the morning after the bombing."

"What did he have to say?"

"He claims he didn't plant the bomb. His opinion is that Liz is crazy."

"Liz is lucky she didn't get arrested for assault. Frank could have pressed charges if he'd wanted." The detective tapped on his computer. "I did a background check on Frank—let me pull up the results. Okay, he had one parking ticket six months ago—argued it before a judge and got it dropped. He was also charged with trespassing two years ago and, a month later, had a restraining order put on him by Roxanne Cortman."

That sounded serious. "What was that about?"

Detective Ranquist squinted at the screen. "Doesn't say, other than Ms. Cortman said Frank was bothering her and wouldn't leave her alone. The order was lifted after a year."

"When I asked if he'd seen anybody in the driveway, Frank said he didn't see anyone strapping a bomb *to the engine*. How did he know where the bomb was planted?"

"Either it was a lucky guess, or he's our boy."

"Did you get the lab results back on the sawdust and wood?"

"Yep. The sawdust was a mixture of redwood, pine, and fir, so nothing conclusive, unless Frank doesn't have any redwood around his place."

"What about getting a search warrant? You could look for black powder, pipe—things related to the car bomb—as well as the gun he might have used to kill Beth. The car bombing next door to him would give you probable cause."

He mulled that over and nodded. "I'll prepare an affidavit and send it to a judge."

"I also found something you might find interesting." Erica opened her purse, took out a baggie, and set it on the desk. "When I searched the ground after Liz's car was bombed, I found a piece of paper stuck in the bushes—a ticket stub."

Ranquist leaned forward. "The detective told me. I thought you turned that in."

"I did. I got this one from Megan. She was using it as a bookmark. When I saw it, I realized the stub I found in the bush had to be Todd's. That afternoon, Megan and Todd went to a play."

He looked at the ticket and read, "*Les Belles Soeurs*," then looked up. "He probably dropped it when he brought Megan home."

"I don't think so. Frank keeps his yard immaculate. I look over there every time I come home or leave. I would have noticed if the stub had been there before." She was very sure.

"If anyone else told me that, I'll call them crazy, but with you—" Detective Ranquist moved the bagged ticket closer. "Mind if I keep it?" She shook her head; then he said, "I believe I'll call Mr. Todd McCauley and ask him a few questions. Like how his ticket got from his car to the neighbor's yard, and if he happens to know anything about pipe bombs."

* * *

"What time is BJ coming for dinner?" Erica asked when Liz came in the front room that afternoon.

Liz's eyes widened. "Oh no! Is that tonight? I'd forgotten all about it." She looked around as if hoping a magical dinner would appear. "What am I going to do?"

Liz was so flustered, Erica had to smile. "Don't worry about it; I'll make dinner."

"You can't do that! I'm the one that invited him. Besides, you've been running around today and doing investigating stuff on your computer. You must be tired."

Erica followed Liz into the kitchen and watched as Liz buried her head in the fridge. "Half a carton of sour cream, yogurt, a bowl of chicken noodle soup, wilted lettuce." She backed out. "I'd better run to the store."

Erica picked a paper off the counter and handed it to Liz. "I made a list—just in case."

"You *knew* I'd forgotten," Liz said ruefully. "You're so organized it's disgusting."

Just then, Megan came down the stairs. Liz looked at her and Erica entreatingly. "You'll both be here for dinner with BJ, won't you?"

"I won't be," Megan declared. "BJ creeps me out. I called Todd and told him he was taking me out to dinner tonight."

Liz gave Erica a beseeching look.

"I think BJ would like it much better if it was just the two of you," Erica responded.

"That's just what I'm afraid of! Lately, I've been getting the feeling that BJ has a crush on me, and if it's just the two of us, he'll get the wrong idea. It would be so much better if you were here, Erica. He's a great friend, but that's it. And I don't want to hurt him, you know?"

Erica understood. And even though she didn't like being a third wheel, she gave in.

"Megan, can I take your car to get some groceries?" Liz grinned. "Hey, I like the sound of that—*me* asking to borrow *your* car for a change."

* * *

A few hours later, when the doorbell rang, Erica opened the door. Todd smiled—white teeth flashing. "Hi Erica, how are you doing?"

"Good. Come on in. I'll go get Megan."

She hurried up the stairs. When Erica stepped into the bedroom and shut the door, Megan was pulling a blouse over her head. "Was that Todd?"

"Yep."

Standing in front of the mirror, Megan brushed her thick hair. "Sometimes I wonder what I'm doing going out with Todd. What does he see in me? He's totally out of my league—successful, older, and *so* good-looking."

"I think it's obvious." Erica gazed at the tall girl. It seemed only yesterday Megan had been an awkward girl, and now she was a graceful young beauty. "You're smart, fun, *and* pretty. Plus, he loves your scintillating personality."

"Good thing you added personality to that, or I'd think you were talking dirty." Then one corner of Megan's mouth turned down. "Todd could have any woman he wants, and sometimes I get the feeling he wants Liz." She set down the brush. "Well, I'd better get down there."

Todd and Liz were on the couch, deep in conversation. Jumping up, Todd crossed the room as gracefully as a cat and gave Megan a long hug.

"I've been so worried about you," he said. "I don't know why you wouldn't let me come and see you yesterday."

"I was busy with school and had to work. Besides, I'm fine."

"But you could have been killed."

"Oh yeah, I forgot," Megan said dryly.

Todd turned to Liz. "Is she really doing okay?"

"So she says. Megan's always upbeat."

He then asked Erica, "Have the police found out anything about the bomb?"

Erica hesitated. Was his question as casual as he made it seem? She wasn't sure, but she filled him in on the basics.

Then Todd asked Liz, "And how are you holding up?"

"Not well," Liz admitted. Then she brightened a bit. "But Erica is taking me and Megan away for a day. We're going to the beach next Tuesday."

Taking Megan's hand and smiling that devastating smile, Todd asked, "Got room for one more? I'd love to come." He glanced at Liz. "That would be all right, wouldn't it?" The inquiry was warm and courteous, but Erica noticed the way their eyes locked and the faint look of alarm that crossed Liz's face. When Todd turned back to Megan, Liz shook her head slightly at Erica.

Message received. “It’s going to be just us girls,” Erica replied easily. “Although Austin is going to be the designated driver.”

“What about a *professional* driver?” Todd asked with another charming smile.

“We’d never fit in your car, but thanks,” Erica said. “Maybe another time.”

* * *

BJ arrived fifteen minutes early in clean jeans, a fresh T-shirt, and jaws that had been scraped of their usual stubble. His long hair was slicked back in a neat ponytail, and he looked different without his ball cap. Stiff-armed, BJ held out a bouquet of roses to Liz, along with the box of heart-shaped chocolates he’d held tightly under his arm.

“Oh my goodness,” she exclaimed, giving Erica a glance of apprehension as she gathered them in her arms. “You didn’t have to do all this. The flowers are lovely, though.”

“I can take the chocolates,” Erica offered.

“That’s all right,” Liz said with a smile. Tonight she looked especially pretty, in jeans and a white blouse, and she’d curled her hair. She turned. “BJ, would you help me light the grill? I hope you like steak.”

He gave Liz an adoring look. “Steak’s my favorite.”

When they came back in, BJ noticed the table Erica had set. “There’s three places.” He looked at Liz, puzzled. “I thought we were going to have dinner alone.”

“Ah, well—Megan had a date, and I didn’t want Erica to eat alone.”

BJ’s face fell a little, but he accepted it with good grace. When the steaks were done, BJ gallantly pulled out Liz’s chair, and when she thanked him, his face split with a smile.

“So, BJ, where are you from?” Erica asked, passing the glazed carrots.

“Sweetwater, Tennessee.” The pride in his voice was evident.

“Do you have a lot of family there?”

“My parents and two of my brothers are there.”

Liz spoke up. “Are you able to go back and see them very often?”

“I go a couple of times a year. And in the fall, everyone gets together for a week-long hunting trip. I always get a deer,” he informed Liz proudly.

“You must be a good shot,” Erica said. “I went hunting with my dad a few times. But he stopped taking me when I saw a deer and hollered, ‘Run, Bambi, run!’”

Liz giggled then asked BJ, "What do you do with the meat?"

"I leave most of it with my folks, unless my dad gets a deer too. They need the meat more than me. My dad raises chickens and a hog each year, and my mom has a big garden—does a lot of canning."

Erica asked about his mom's canning, then Liz asked, "Want more potatoes? I added some sour cream and a little garlic."

"That must be why they taste so good." BJ had such a besotted look on his face that Erica wanted to giggle. As he dished up more, Liz mentioned their upcoming trip.

"Who's going?"

"Just Megan, Erica, and me. Oh, and Austin."

"So that Todd fella isn't going?" When told no, BJ seemed to relax. "I've always wanted to see those lighthouses. Never have been."

"Oh, look, you're out of water," Liz said quickly, jumping up. "I'll get you some more." When she returned, she handed him the basket of rolls. "How's the deck coming along?"

"Good. I've got a friend lined up to help me when I get ready to put the floor in."

"That's wonderful." Liz turned to Erica. "It's so nice to have BJ here in the afternoon. Whenever I hear the sound of his saw or hammer and know he's here, I feel safe."

BJ's face gave off light like the sun.

Liz asked, "The other night, I thought I saw someone in the backyard. You aren't missing any tools, are you?"

"Nah. I take everything with me or else lock it in the shed."

"I wondered if it was a burglar."

"You should have called me. I would have come out."

"That's very nice, but I didn't want to bother you." Liz brought over apple pie and vanilla bean ice cream. "Hope you don't mind store-bought."

He didn't, especially when Liz was the one dishing it up. His fingers brushed her hand as she handed him the plate.

It was sad to feel a sense of relief when BJ left, but it had been almost heartrending to see his adoration for Liz.

When Liz closed the door, she put a hand over her heart. "Oh dear. I think BJ read a lot more into this dinner than I meant. What am I going to do?"

Chapter Eleven

Birdsong poured from the trees, and the sun was directly overhead, brushing the tops of the dogwoods and oaks with light as Erica wandered about the backyard with her cell phone.

"So how did you sleep?" Erica asked David, even as she admired how the masses of deep red petunias contrasted with the emerald lawn.

"Not good. I keep reaching for you in the night and waking up when I realize you're gone. I miss you. A lot."

"Me too. Hopefully I can figure things out soon." Erica stepped into the shady gazebo and took a seat on the white bench.

"Can't be soon enough for me." Then David asked, "What did you do this morning?"

"I called Roxanne Cortland—she's the one who had a restraining order issued against Frank."

"What's her story? Was Frank stalking her?"

"Yes and no. It didn't sound like a real stalking case, but he was bugging Roxanne about her house. I guess it's on the national register and is practically falling down. He kept calling her and stopping by to try and get her to do something about it."

"Sounds familiar."

"Roxanne doesn't hold any grudge—but she was tired of dealing with a fanatic." Erica brushed away an annoying fly. "Oh, and I finally talked an appraiser into coming out. He'll be here tomorrow."

"On Saturday?"

"Yeah, apparently he's the low man on the totem pole, and his boss wouldn't give him time off to come out during the week. But he wanted to see what we had."

"Let me know how that goes."

"I will. Then I went to the pet store. They had the cutest puppies and kittens."

"The answer is no. And what were you doing at a pet store anyway?"

"I needed a cage and some food."

"Erica—"

"It's nothing you need to worry about. Just a secret little project."

"Those five little words are enough to strike fear into anyone's heart—anyone who *knows* you, that is."

Time to change the subject. "How are the kids?"

"You tell me—I think you talk with them more than I do."

She laughed. "It's been interesting helping Ryan and Kenzie with their homework over Skype. Unfortunately I can't do much for Aby. Calculus is beyond me."

"Me too," David admitted. "She's working hard to get a good GPA for college next year. On the other hand, Ryan and Kenzie are coasting, just waiting for school to get out."

"I miss them."

"They miss you too, although they're enjoying the novelty of having round pancakes instead of square ones. And they enjoy throwing their socks in their drawers instead of having you line them up."

Erica sighed deeply. "What other bad habits are they getting into?"

"It's best you don't know. So how did the dinner go with BJ last night?"

"BJ brought Liz roses *and* chocolates. He's in *love* with a capital L." She told about the rest of the evening.

David remarked, "I'm not sure I like this guy. He sounds a little off. What does Detective Ranquist think?"

"About the same as you—he thinks BJ is someone to keep an eye on. I'd consider BJ a strong suspect except that he obviously adores Liz."

"Maybe he loves her so much he wants to keep her all to himself," David said. "It could be that BJ would rather see Liz dead rather than with someone else."

"But Liz isn't seeing anyone."

"And my brilliant theory goes down in flames."

"Tonight we're having another suitor over for dinner—this time it's Austin coming at Megan's request."

"Let me guess—she asked you to cook."

"Nope, she said she wanted to do it herself—although I offered to make a fruit salad."

"What's she burning—er—making?"

"Beef stroganoff."

"Hope you stocked up on Pepto Bismol. By the way, how are Liz and Megan? This situation has to be getting to them."

"Megan's doing pretty well, considering. She has a hard time sleeping at night, though—wakes up with nightmares."

"How are you doing in that department?" David had always shown compassion for Erica, who still suffered occasional nightmares after being locked in the dark basement closet when she was six.

"Good. I've only had one." She went back to Megan. "A lot of times Megan will get up and study, and I'll find her asleep on the couch."

"So you're not sleeping well either."

Rats. Erica hadn't wanted to worry him with that. "I'll sleep better once this is over. The one I'm worried about is Liz. She's under a lot of stress, but we're going to go to the beach next week to relax. They also have some neat lighthouses there."

"So do Megan and Liz *want* to go see lighthouses, or did you play dictator and tell them that's where you were going?"

"Maybe a little of each," Erica admitted.

"That's okay; I'm just teasing—I know you love lighthouses." Then in a wistful tone, David added, "Wish I was going with you. Who's going to rub sunblock on your back?"

"Austin's coming." There was a teasing note in her voice.

"Maybe you ought to ask Megan to do that." After Erica laughed and assured him she would, David said, "You *are* taking your gun, aren't you?"

"I don't leave the house without it," she said, gazing at Crooked House. It was odd, but the windows seemed to be watching her. Occasionally when Erica walked inside, she felt an eerie sensation. It was hard to describe, but it was almost as if the house was sinister in some way. She shook herself as David went on.

"Keep a sharp eye out while you're there."

"I could just stay home and lock myself in the bedroom."

"Sounds good to me—if I was inside with you."

* * *

Erica was chopping a yellow apple and putting the chunks in a lemon juice solution when Megan came into the kitchen.

"Hope you don't mind having dinner early," Megan said. "When I told Austin that Detective Ranquist was coming later, we decided to go to a movie and be gone before he arrived. He wanted to miss the intrigue with Frank." Megan took a piece of apple and popped it into her mouth. "Thanks for making your Tropical Fruit Salad[6]—I love that." She got out her recipe and set it on the counter. "Okay. I'm ready to make the cake. Tell me what to do."

"No mix, eh?"

"Nope, I wanted to make my grandma's spice cake. It has a great cream cheese frosting."

Erica examined the yellowed recipe card with its faded writing. "There aren't any directions."

"Why do you think I'm asking you what to do?"

Erica explained how to cream the sugar and shortening then said, "You ought to have the eggs at room temperature before creaming them into the sugar and shortening—otherwise the mixture won't emulsify properly."

"Am I supposed to know what *emulsify* means?"

"Blend. You want the mixture to *blend* together well."

Megan got out the eggs. "How long do I need to wait until they're room temperature?"

"Since you're in a hurry, just put them in a bowl of warm water for ten minutes."

"Okay. Any other bits of gourmet advice?"

Erica thought. "All I can think of right now is to put the pan in the center of the oven for better air circulation. Do you know what *circulation* means?"

"Very funny."

As Megan dipped a measuring cup into the flour, Erica asked, "You've got to sift that."

"We don't have a sifter."

Erica groaned. When Megan started to pour the cup of flour in the bowl, Erica stopped her. "Hold on!"

"What's wrong now?"

"You've got a heaping cup of flour," Erica objected. "How much did the recipe call for?"

"A cup. And it's *not* heaping. It's just up to the top."

"I have eyes, my dear—I can see the flour is above the top. You need to level it off."

Megan gave an exasperated sigh. "It's close enough."

---

6 See the appendix at the end of the book for this recipe.

"If the recipe calls for a cup, you put a cup in. No more. No less. Otherwise you won't know how things are going to turn out. The recipe is your guideline—you have to follow it."

Opening the utensil drawer, Erica got out a bread knife and handed it to Megan. "Level the flour." Then she yelped, "Don't use the *rounded* side! Use the *flat* side."

"What's the difference?" Megan groaned.

"If you use the rounded edge, the cup won't be precisely level."

Megan rolled her eyes. "What if I stab you with the knife—as long as I make sure it's perfectly level?"

"Ha, ha." Erica began peeling the kiwi fruit, keeping an eye on her protégé. "Hey, I started reading that book, *An American Tragedy.* There was a ticket stub in it for *Les Belles Soeurs.* That's the play you saw with Todd, isn't it?" When Megan nodded, Erica asked, "Did you like it?"

"Mais oui! *The Beautiful Sisters* was very good. I could tell Todd didn't really want to go, but he did just because I wanted to. Isn't that sweet?"

Erica smiled. "Mais oui! Todd sounds like a very thoughtful person." She paused. "Austin is too."

"Austin's great, but he's a complication I'd rather not have right now." Megan spoke over the hum of the mixer. "We're poles apart. I'm not sure why he even calls me."

Erica wanted to smack her forehead. Or Megan's. "Sometimes I really do think you're a fruitcake. Austin calls because he *likes* you. And for your information, two people can be different and still enjoy each other's company."

"I suppose. But in high school, I wouldn't have had anything to do with such a nerd."

Erica was shocked. "How can you call Austin a nerd? Nerds are skinny, geeky-looking, and often dull, and that's about the opposite of Austin."

"But we're so different. Austin's conservative, and I'm liberal. He's a conformist; I'm a dissenter. Plus, Austin's family has always been Republican. It's a genetic defect that's been passed down from generation to generation."

Erica laughed. "Austin is also bright, articulate, and even-tempered," she reminded her friend. "But then, what we ought to talk about is your similarities."

Megan gave her a snide look. "You're so funny, Erica."

"All I'm saying is that it doesn't matter if you're not alike. Remember, 'Love conquers all,' according to Virgil." She gave Megan a sly look. "Maybe it *is* love—"

An attractive blush came to Megan's cheeks. "I like Austin *and* Todd, but I don't intend to get serious with either one."

It was hard to stifle the laughter that threatened to burst out. Since when did love ask permission before blossoming? Megan was very young if she thought love could be staved off with willpower. Love just *happened.*

After washing the beaters, Erica began whipping the cream. "Actually, I wouldn't worry about it. David and I are dissimilar too, but we love each other and work around our differences."

"How does he cope with your OCD?"

"What's there to cope with?" Erica shrugged. "I like things clean and organized, and of course, David does too. We're alike in some ways, different in others, and because we love each other, we compromise, adjust, and at times, just give in. There are a few things I wouldn't mind changing about David, but I've learned to accept him for what he is."

Megan snorted as she poured the batter into the floured pan. "You forget I've met David. What exactly would you change? The way he calls you every day? Sends you presents in the mail? What's to change when David is a wonderful father and worships you? He's completely awesome, and it doesn't hurt that he looks a little like Brad Pitt and a lot like a younger George Clooney."

"Okay, you got me. David *is* perfect. I'll tell him you said so."

Megan set the timer for the cake. "I called Beth's parents yesterday."

"Did you tell them about the car bomb?"

"No, I didn't want to freak them out. It sounded like they were having a good time."

There was a knock at the back door. She glanced out the window and saw Austin's car. Brown eyes alive with excitement, Megan ran to open it. "Austin! You're early." She sounded delighted and chagrined at the same time. Realizing she still wore her apron, Megan whipped it off and threw it behind her back at Erica, who caught it.

"How are you doing, Erica?" Austin came over, peered into the bowl of fruit salad, and took out a piece of pineapple to eat. "I asked Megan if I could take you guys out to dinner tonight, but she wanted to cook. Too bad. I got paid a week ago and put some money aside, in case you wanted to go out. Now I'll just have to blow the money on frivolous stuff, like rent, groceries, and my electric bill." He snatched a piece of kiwi, narrowly avoiding the wooden spoon Erica used to swipe at his hand. "You'll have to be quicker than that to catch me." His eyes danced with mischief.

Nobody had a sunnier disposition than Austin, Erica thought.

He leaned his back against the counter. “I came over early to help, but I feel it only fair to warn you I’m not a very nice cook.” When Megan looked at him inquiringly, Austin went on, “I beat the eggs and whip the cream.”

Erica groaned at the ancient joke while Megan rolled her eyes.

“That’s not it,” Megan said. “Austin also pinches pennies till they scream.”

“I’m surprised you even know what a penny is,” Austin replied.

“A penny is something the government makes to annoy the crap out of people.” Megan then explained to Erica, “Austin and I have different philosophies about money.”

Erica got out the celery and a cutting board. “If you really want to help, Austin, you could cut this up for me. I need one cup.” Then she asked Megan to measure out the salad dressing.

When she was done, Megan leaned close and whispered to Erica. “Watch this.” She walked over to where Austin was slicing and, looking inside the salad dressing jar, said, “There’s only half a cup left—not worth saving.” She then tossed the jar into the garbage.

“What are you doing?” Appalled, Austin dropped his knife and dug the jar out. “Why would you throw it away when there’s so much left?” He opened the container and peered inside, as if to make sure the contents hadn’t been damaged.

Megan and Erica giggled.

“I *knew* you’d do that,” Megan said with a grin. “If I was *really* throwing it away, I wouldn’t have put the lid back on.”

“Waste not, want not.” Austin intoned the old cliché solemnly. Going back to chopping, he asked, “Is Liz home tonight?”

“She had to work,” Megan replied.

Austin said, “Megan said the police figured out that someone put a pipe bomb on Liz’s car.”

“That’s right,” Erica said, measuring out the coconut.

“Galvanized pipe and black powder, eh?”

Erica’s green eyes rested thoughtfully on the young man. “Yes. How did you know?”

“Pipe bombs are supposed to be simple to make. The hardest thing is the blasting cap.”

“Can we please change the subject?” Megan asked. “How’s your grandfather, Austin?”

"Not good. He can't get out of bed without help now. And he doesn't recognize me or Mom anymore."

Erica said, "Thank goodness you're able to have a private nurse to take care of him. They're very expensive."

"I know, but Medicare pays some, and Grandpa had insurance."

"That must be an exceptional policy."

There must have been something in her tone because Megan scowled at her. "You know, Erica, this isn't really your concern."

Erica could take a hint, especially when it had been made with a sledgehammer. She arranged apple slices on top of the salad, sprinkled on coconut, and put it in the fridge. "All done. I've got some calls to make, but if you need any more help, just holler."

* * *

Erica waited in the shadow of the towering spicebush in front of Crooked House, enjoying its pale-yellow flowers and distinctive, spicy scent. The dinner had gone well, and Megan and Austin had left by the time the Dover police car pulled up in front of Frank Stratton's house. Detective Ranquist, looking official in a neatly pressed uniform, got out, and when Erica walked over, he introduced her to Officer Hayward, a quiet, broad-shouldered man.

As they walked to Frank's front door, Erica asked, "Did you have a chance to question Todd about the ticket stub?"

"I did. He said he must have dropped it when he brought Megan home."

"The stub wasn't there before the bombing." Erica was positive. "I look at Frank's yard every time I go outside. I would have seen it."

Detective Ranquist was skeptical. "The stub was small, and it was in a bush, Erica. It could have been there for days without anyone seeing it."

"*I* would have noticed."

They stared at each other for a few moments. Erica refused to blink. Finally the detective raised and dropped his arms in a gesture of acquiescence. "Okay, so maybe you would have. But with your OCD, you're not like a normal person. Your testimony wouldn't hold up for two seconds in court."

With an inward sigh, Erica followed the officers. Officer Hayward knocked loudly.

Frank opened the door, and his rheumy blue eyes widened when he saw the uniformed officers.

"I'm Officer Hayward, and this is Detective Ranquist. We have a warrant to search your house." The policeman handed him the paper.

Frank's mouth fell open, exposing a repulsive display of yellowed teeth and amalgam fillings. After examining the warrant, which listed the items the officers were searching for, his face flushed.

"So you're looking for a gun and stuff to make a bomb with, eh? You're out of your minds." He surveyed the two men coldly then glared at Erica as if she were a Japanese beetle he'd found munching on his prized roses. "What's she doing here?"

"Special consultant," Detective Ranquist said.

Frank frowned ferociously and ran a hand through his disheveled gray hair. "Guess there's nothing I can do but have my rights trampled on. I've done nothing wrong, and you're invading my private property on nothing but that gal's word." He spoke with scalding bitterness.

The men made no reply.

Once inside they began going over the house systematically. Erica longed to straighten the rug, wind the paper towels that were drooping onto the counter, and close a cupboard door that Officer Hayward left partially open, but she forced herself to remain an observer. It was a small house, and when they were done, Frank was triumphant.

"Didn't find a thing, now, did you?" His craggy face was dark with anger. "I could have told you, but you wouldn't have believed me."

"Sir, we'd like to search the shed and grounds next," Officer Hayward said.

Frank erupted. "What? It's not enough that you violated my home; you've got to rummage through my yard too? I won't have it! You have no right, none at all!" Frank's face was mottled red and white as he told the officers in ripe terms where they could go.

Officer Hayward remained calm. "The search warrant includes curtilage—which allows us to search the outside grounds and any sheds on the premises."

Over Frank's mumblings, Officer Hayward suggested they start in the front yard and work their way to the back. Erica examined the ground along with the officers, searching for signs of recent digging. In the shed, they started by the door, going over every inch meticulously. Again, Erica had to restrain herself from straightening things, even though Frank kept the shed in excellent order. There were bins for small yard tools, while rakes and shovels hung on the wall.

A stack of heavy chains lay in a corner, and as Erica bent for a closer look, she noticed that some of the top chains weren't dusty, while links below had a thick layer of dust. She caught Detective Ranquist's eye and nodded toward the chains.

"Those chains have been moved recently," she whispered.

"What do you want with them?" Frank griped as Detective Ranquist moved the chains. Underneath were several short lengths of galvanized pipe.

"What's that?" Frank asked, acting bewildered. "Pipe? I didn't put that there."

"Looks like you've sawed off the end of this piece fairly recently," Detective Ranquist said, holding the piece of pipe up with gloved hands. The end was jagged and shiny.

"That isn't mine," Frank fumed. "Liz must have put it there. Or BJ." His eyes were hard with suspicion when he glared at Erica. "I bet it was *you*. How else would you have known where to look?" He was still sputtering as Officer Hayward placed the pipes in separate bags.

"Do you have a hacksaw, Mr. Stratton?" Detective Ranquist asked. "Or a pipe cutter?"

Frank pointed wordlessly at a pegboard. Officer Hayward retrieved the two tools and placed them in plastic bags.

As the men continued searching, Erica could help herself no longer and turned the cans of spray paint so the labels faced outward. Frank noticed. "Leave my things alone," he growled, turning them back.

Going outside, they began searching the backyard. Erica found various lengths of lumber piled against the back of the shed and called to Detective Ranquist.

When he came over, Erica pointed at a stack of small slats. "Redwood."

Expressionless, Detective Ranquist nodded, knowing—as she did—that Frank could claim the redwood particles on his saw had come from these slats and not Liz's poles.

"Building a planter?" she asked Frank, who stumped over to see what they were doing.

He glowered at her more darkly than ever. "Don't tell me *that's* against the law?"

"Just curious."

When they finished, Detective Ranquist thanked Frank, who snorted and stalked away. As Officer Hayward put the bags in the trunk of his patrol car, Detective Ranquist eyed the Stratton home, a satisfied glint in his eye.

"We'll see what the lab results are, but we may have just caught the killer."

Chapter Twelve

That night, Erica rapped lightly on Liz's bedroom door. "Mind if I come in?"

"Not at all." Although it was late, Liz was welcoming. She sat curled up in a chair by the window. "I was reading, hoping to get tired enough to sleep tonight."

Erica's heart went out to her. It seemed like none of them were able to sleep well. She sat on the side of the bed. "Can I ask you something?"

"Sure."

"How long did you date Todd?"

Liz bit her lip and thought. "Let's see—maybe six weeks."

"Didn't work out, huh?"

"At first, things were great. Todd was fun, and he's so good-looking. But the chemistry wasn't there, and he started acting possessive. Then I met someone else." Liz's voice changed—becoming emotionally charged—and she ducked her head. After a minute, Liz gained control and went on. "That's when I decided to break it off. Todd didn't take it well."

"How so?"

"He kept calling, even when I asked him not to. He'd e-mail and text. A couple of times he even showed up outside my classrooms. He also came to where I work." The distress in Liz's voice was clear.

This didn't sound good. Apparently something unsavory lay behind all that charm. "He sounds like a stalker."

Liz gave a little shiver. "I finally told Todd that if he didn't knock it off, I'd get a restraining order. He stopped, then a month later, he started dating Megan."

Erica felt a growing sense of alarm. "So he could still come around and see you?"

"That's what I thought at first," Liz admitted. "I confronted him, but Todd swore he was over me and sincerely interested in Megan. And he has kept his distance—for the most part." There was uncertainty in her voice.

"But not entirely?"

"Once in a while he'll say something suggestive, but nothing I can really call him on. It's more in his tone of voice. And sometimes, I'll notice him staring at me."

"Have you talked to Megan about this?"

"I tried to, but you know Megan—she shrugged it off."

Vintage Megan Kemp. If she didn't like what she heard, Megan would simply disregard it. But that might not be wise in this case. Erica shifted on the bed. "Besides Todd, how are you doing?"

"Knowing that some maniac is trying to kill me? Oh, I'm just peachy." Liz jumped up and moving the curtains aside a few inches, peering out the window. When she turned back, her shoulders seemed to sag with unseen weight. "I try not to think about it, but sometimes I wonder how much more I can stand." The air of good cheer Liz usually wore had disappeared.

"I thought you were taking things fairly well under the circumstances."

"That comes from my job training." Distractedly, Liz picked up a few stray pens on her dresser, tossed an old receipt into the garbage can, and rearranged her perfumes on the dresser. Her movements were restless and jerky. "It's drilled into employees never to show any frustration or get upset with customers. Put on a mask of calm even when some jerk swears at you because their child was running by the pool and fell or because the maid left six towels instead of seven."

"You've put on such a good front—I don't think I've fully understood how hard this must be for you." Erica felt like she was finally seeing the true Liz.

"No one understands. But how could they?" Liz stopped, and in a high voice that was tinged with hysteria, she cried, "How many people know what it's like to have someone trying to kill you?" Her face had a wild look. "Have you ever had anyone try to kill you?"

"Yes." Erica's reply was soft. She didn't like to think about it and didn't volunteer that it had happened more than once because her experience was far different from Liz's. It made a great deal of difference whether you put your life on the line because you chose to be a police officer or if you were an innocent person being stalked by some homicidal maniac.

With a look of shock, Liz gulped. "I'm sorry, Erica. I forgot you used to be a police officer. I'm only thinking about myself." She flung herself into the chair. "I guess my nerves are getting the best of me tonight. It's just hard to know that someone wants me dead."

Liz's low, depressed voice had an edge of desperation to it, and Erica realized she hadn't appreciated the incredible strain on Liz. It was like living in a pressure cooker, and it was inevitable that fear—if left bottled up for so long—would eventually make itself manifest. She felt nothing but sympathy for the young woman.

"You've been hiding it all so well," Erica remarked.

"I've been trying to hold on, but it's been hard. Especially because . . ." Her voice trailed off, and she raised her troubled blue eyes. "There's something else that's been upsetting me. Something you don't know about. But I don't feel like I can talk about it tonight. I'm afraid that if I do, I'd really lose it."

"Does it have anything to do with the case?"

"No. It's personal."

"All right. Take your time then, and tell me when you feel up to it."

* * *

The next morning, Erica lowered the heat on the pot of simmering chicken then turned to Liz, who was finishing her cereal. She was glad to hear that Liz had slept well—even though it was with the aid of a sleeping pill.

"I wish you didn't have to work today, Liz. You'd be much better at discussing the furniture with the appraiser than I would."

"You'll do fine." Liz was unsympathetic. "I wrote up notes on most everything. Besides, I'm not crazy about seeing a stranger drool over my things."

Megan slept in, grabbed a bagel, and zoomed out of the house soon after Liz. Erica made a few phone calls, researched the last of Liz's old roommates, and shredded the chicken for the Creamy Chicken Noodle Soup[7] she was making for lunch. Megan got off at noon on Saturday, so Erica had reminded her to come home to eat before she did her errands.

Midmorning, Erica felt restless. She went over the case in her mind, trying to see it from different angles, but without much success. Her thoughts whirled in a morass of speculation from which it was difficult to extract anything cohesive and helpful.

To clear her mind, she went jogging, which usually helped, but when she returned, Erica still felt troubled. Time for Plan B. Erica got a bucket; pulled on her yellow, heavy-duty gloves; and had scrubbed herself into a corner of the tiled kitchen by the time Megan opened the back door.

7 See the appendix at the end of the book for this recipe.

"Cross at your own risk," Erica warned. "The floor might be slippery—although the part by the stove should be dry."

"Why are you on your hands and knees?" Megan asked as she gingerly crossed to the front room. "I'll let you in on a secret—there's a new invention you might like to know about. It's called a mop. We even have one."

"I like to do it this way."

"You don't have to work this hard while you're here. Liz isn't expecting you to find a murderer *and* keep the house spotless."

"I know, but cleaning helps me think. And it soothes my nerves."

"I thought cooking did that."

"They both do."

"You are too weird. But you're welcome to stay as long as you want." Megan winked. Then she glanced at the hardwood floor under her feet. "You didn't wash in here, did you?"

"I do not have a death-wish, nor do I want to know how it feels like to be strangled." Erica tossed the scrub brush into the bucket.

A short time later, she dished up two steaming bowls of soup and cut slices of crusty French bread before calling for Megan. "Lunch is ready! Come and eat before it gets cold."

"Yes, Mother," Megan replied. After the blessing, she blew on her spoon and took a bite. Her face brightened. "Hey, this is really good!"

"Thank you," Erica said. "Although I feel a bit insulted by the surprise in your voice." She moved on to other matters. "I talked with Donna and found out a little more about Liz's family. Has Liz ever mentioned her Uncle Ron to you? Donna said he was upset when his father gave Crooked House to Liz's father."

"I thought she only had one uncle and that his name was Lee."

Apparently Liz didn't see her uncles very often. "Another thing, Donna told me that Liz loves this house, but I thought you told me Liz is always grumbling about it."

"She is, at least lately. Liz is always complaining about the small, dark rooms, how narrow the stairs are, and how there are so few closets. Liz told me she'd unload it if she could, but the house needs too many repairs for someone to buy."

"That's odd." Erica's brow furrowed. "Donna said she'd tried to get Liz to list the house, but she wouldn't because she's so attached to it."

"I've never gotten that from Liz. I bet if she had a decent offer, she'd sell. I wonder why Donna would say that? Maybe she misunderstood Liz or got the wrong idea."

For some reason, that last phrase stuck in Erica's head. It seemed significant somehow. Perhaps she had also gotten the wrong idea. If so, it was time to start thinking about things from a different angle.

After lunch, Megan went to her room to study until her date with Todd. Erica continued her research until the appraiser arrived.

Andrew Glaus was slim and wore pressed gray pants and trendy glasses with black frames. Erica went over the information Liz had left as he examined each item. Occasionally, he took pictures and typed notes on his iPad. Although Andrew took pictures of the paintings, he didn't spend as much time on them as Erica thought he might.

He caught her quizzical look and explained, "I haven't had a lot of training in paintings."

Andrew sniffed at the couch and end tables but stared in open admiration at the two chairs in the front room. There was reverence in his voice when he said, "These are Chippendale."

"How can you tell?"

"The 'S' scrolls and the claw-and-ball feet." Going closer, he pointed. "See how the center part of the chair back is woven? That's another clue. And they're made of mahogany."

Andrew also seemed excited about the small desk in the front room. Running his hand over its lacquered finish, he exclaimed, "This desk and chair are really very nice. Queen Anne, you know. You can tell by the refined, scrolled form."

Going to the mirror, Erica asked, "What about this? It looks really old."

Andrew took it off the wall and examined the back. "Do you mind if I take out one of the screws?"

"Go ahead."

Setting the mirror on the mossy-green rug, Andrew opened his bag and retrieved a screwdriver. Once he had the screw out, he murmured, "Just as I thought." He held up the screw. "See the irregular widths between the spirals? That means it's very old. And look at the veneer on the mirror—can you see how thick and irregular it is?"

She nodded. "What about the glass? Why is it so gray?"

"That's a marker of old age—as is the very thin glass."

Andrew went through the upstairs furniture fairly quickly then returned to the front room. Earlier, he'd betrayed his interest in the corner cabinet, eyeing it from time to time. Apparently Andrew had saved it to examine last. He went over it meticulously, occasionally using a magnifying glass.

After taking a number of pictures, he declared, "This could be very valuable. It's made of rosewood. And look at the brass inlay and lattice grille doors. *Very* nice." When he finished taking copious notes, Andrew shook Erica's hand. "I'll show the pictures and notes to my boss, and if there's anything that interests her, I'll be in touch."

Apparently, Andrew thought they wanted to sell something. Good thing Liz wasn't there. To make things clear, Erica explained, "I think there might have been a misunderstanding. Liz doesn't want to sell anything now, although she might in the future. What we wanted to know is if any of the furniture or paintings were valuable. Do you have any idea how much the cabinet, mirror, or desk is worth?" Erica studied the appraiser's face.

"I really can't say. Perhaps my boss will be able to give you an idea once she's seen the pictures and notes." And with that, he left.

* * *

Aha. Another one saved!

The only time Erica dared check the traps was when Megan and Liz were gone. Finding a mouse in one of the traps, Erica hurried outside, carrying the box in yellow-gloved hands. Duke came running. Smelling the treat in her pocket, he pranced around, nearly tripping her.

BJ had made good progress on the deck. New poles with metal bracketing had been set in concrete, which had been left to harden. Erica went down the cobbled path bordered by flowers in bright splashes of color, to where BJ was using a carpenter's pencil to mark a two-by-four. His sleeves were rolled up, and his arms had the tan, leathery look of someone who worked in the sun. BJ's circular saw zipped through the wood that rested on two sawhorses.

"I'm glad you bring Duke with you," Erica said as she scratched the dog around the base of his ears before giving him his doggie treat. "I miss my dogs, so it's nice to have one around."

"I like having Duke with me."

"Somebody once said, 'Dogs are not our whole life, but they make our lives whole.'"

BJ nodded approvingly. "I'm glad Liz lets me bring him. He likes it here." He glanced at the box in Erica's hand. "What's that?"

"Can you keep a secret?"

"Yeah." His lean face was solemn.

"It's a mouse. I replaced the mousetraps Liz had with humane ones that don't kill the mice. I've got a cage, and I'm going to put this mouse with the others."

BJ followed her to the back corner, where Erica had hidden a small wire cage under a bush. She opened the door, held the trap next to it, and tapped until a gray mouse scurried out.

"I thought about just letting them loose but thought they might go back to the house."

BJ hunkered over. "You've caught three of them? What are you going to do with 'em?"

It was a natural question. The only problem was that she didn't know. "You don't happen to know of anyone who would like some mice, do you?"

"I've got a friend with a snake."

"Ah, I don't think so."

He smiled and readjusted his ball cap as he straightened. As they walked back to the house, he asked, "How's Liz? I haven't seen her for a couple a days." The longing in his voice was apparent.

"She's doing all right."

"Do the police know anything yet?" She glanced at him, and when his eyes darted away, a wave of suspicion washed over her. He and Todd had asked nearly the same question. Of the two, BJ acted far more uneasy. Although Todd was smoother, Erica didn't trust him any more than she did this gangly young man. Both men were far too interested in Liz—BJ, openly, and Todd, more discreetly. Did they want to know about the investigation out of simple curiosity or for some other reason?

"They're still looking into things." It was hard to read the expression on his face. Then out of the blue, she asked, "Have you ever thought of asking Liz out?"

BJ jerked, as if he'd hit his thumb with the hammer hanging from his tool belt. He shook his head roughly.

"I know you like her, so I was wondering." Erica kept her voice calm and matter of fact. "She's really nice, isn't she?"

"Yeah." BJ's face softened, then he asked, "Is she still dating that Todd guy?"

"She hasn't dated him for a long time."

He dipped his head to pat Duke but not before Erica saw the naked hope on his face.

* * *

Early that evening, Megan and Todd came in carrying two plastic sacks, which they set on the little kitchen table.

"What have you got there?" Liz asked.

"Dinner. I texted Erica so she'd know not to start anything," Megan said. "After we played racquetball, Todd thought it would be nice to stop at the China King Restaurant and get take-out. Wasn't that thoughtful?" Megan beamed at him as he busily opened sacks and set out the white boxes.

He announced, "We have ham fried rice, chicken chow mein, sweet and sour pork, and kung pao beef. Also spring rolls. Something for everyone."

"Including MSG headaches," Erica remarked.

"It was very kind of you to get dinner, Todd, but I have a lot of studying tonight." Liz took a step toward the stairs, but with an agile move, Todd slid over and blocked her exit.

"Come on; you have to eat," he said cajolingly. Todd put an arm on her back, as if to lead her to the table, but Liz moved deftly away.

"All right. I'll get the plates."

When Megan set out the plastic-wrapped chopsticks, Todd said, "No forks allowed," then grinned, his eye lingering on Liz.

When Erica lined up the boxes, Megan quirked an eyebrow. "Let me guess—alphabetical?"

Todd started to snicker but stopped when he realized Megan wasn't joking.

"Now we don't have to guess what's in each box," Erica said.

"Yeah, it's impossible to tell by looking inside," Megan commented dryly.

During the meal, Erica kept one eye on Todd. Now that she was keeping track, it did seem Todd was paying a great deal of attention to Liz. It was disconcerting how many times his gaze went to her. Or was it just because Erica was focusing on it? Todd's smile was broad and his laughter loud whenever Liz made comments or small jokes. Yet he also laughed at Megan's comments and paid attention to Erica.

Liz took small amounts and ate quickly. When she rose, saying she had to study, Todd appeared disappointed. Then he teased, "You just don't want to help with the dishes."

"You got me." Liz smiled briefly, showing small white teeth. She thanked Todd for dinner then breezed upstairs.

"I need to study too," Megan said a little later as they were clearing the table. "I have a test Monday."

"You can study later," Todd said easily. "Let's watch a movie."

"I really can't."

"Sure you can." When Megan stood firm, he appealed to Erica. "You talk to her."

"Sorry. Megan knows best. Besides, she's on a scholarship and has to keep her grades up."

"Spoil sport." Still, Todd took it with good grace. "Guess I'll have to call it a night."

"I'll walk out with you," Erica said. "I need to get a book I left in Megan's car."

Todd gave Megan a hug and a kiss. At the bottom of the steps, he stopped and faced Erica. "What did you want to talk to me about?"

Todd McCauley was a remarkably perceptive man. Obviously there was no need to beat around the bush.

"Liz told me the two of you used to date." Todd watched her, polite interest on his face as she asked, "Did you break it off, or did she?"

In the dark, Todd's white teeth gleamed. "Liz did, as I'm sure she's already told you."

"It's nice that you've remained friends." Erica put a slight emphasis on the word *friends*.

There was a definite pause before Todd answered. "Makes things so much more civilized, don't you think?"

"You know Megan and I are old friends."

"She's mentioned that, yes." He was perfectly polite.

"I think a lot of Megan." She waited for the implications of that to sink in.

"I get it. No breaking Megan's heart. I'll put that at the top of my list of things not to do."

His flippant attempt nettled Erica, and she decided to be more blunt. "I wouldn't want you using Megan to see Liz."

A look of hostility rested on Erica for a moment then disappeared. "Liz and I are last year's news. We're friends now. That's all." He remained unflustered and imperturbable. "What I feel for Megan is very different."

"I'll hold you to that."

He acknowledged that with an upward tilt of his head. Then Todd's practiced charm took over. "Thanks for having me over. I had a great time." He made it sound as if Erica had planned the evening just for him. Todd paused before opening the door of his sports car and called up to her. "You have a good night now." Even though he nodded pleasantly before climbing inside, there was something in his tone—annoyance perhaps?

Instead of feeling relief at Todd's denial, Erica felt more anxious than before. She'd hoped to feel reassured and, instead, was still not sure if Todd was truly interested in Megan or simply using her to be near Liz.

When she went into the front room, Megan eyed her speculatively. "What were you and Todd talking about?"

"Oh, this and that. Have you got a minute? We need to talk."

"Whenever anyone says, 'We need to talk,' it means bad news."

As Erica settled beside her on the couch, Megan made a face and asked, "This isn't going to be a mother-daughter talk disguised as a friend-to-friend talk, is it?"

Erica ignored that. "I talked with Liz the other day—about Todd. Liz said that when she tried to break it off with Todd, he practically began stalking her. I'm not sure he's the kind of guy you want to get involved with."

Wearing a defiant expression, Megan said in a steely voice, "You're not my mother."

"I'm not trying to be. I'm your friend."

"Todd's a good guy, and we have a lot of fun together. You're worried about nothing."

"I'm worried because he can't keep his eyes off Liz."

"That's ridiculous." Megan's face darkened. "Is that what you were talking to him about?" Her voice went high and had anger threaded through it. "Did you accuse him of dating me to see Liz?"

"I didn't put it that way."

"*I bet.* I can't believe you did that!" Megan's eyes flashed with fire, and her hands clenched. "I know what you're thinking. A man as handsome and successful as Todd couldn't possibly be interested in *me*. There *has* to be another reason."

"That's not it at all."

Flushed, Megan stood and struck a belligerent pose with arms outstretched. "You think I'm stupid and naïve. Poor little Megan. She can't tell that a good-looking guy is just *pretending* to be interested in her. Well, let me tell you, Todd *is* interested in me! Why do you think he calls me all the time and asks me out? Why do you think he bought dinner tonight for all of us?"

Megan breathed hard, as though she had been running. "If you'll recall, Todd said he wanted to stay and watch a movie with *me*! He didn't ask Liz, and he didn't ask you! I know you still think of me as awkward and plain, but Todd *likes* me. I know it's hard to believe, but he does and I like him, so butt out!" Megan whirled and was gone, leaving Erica staring after her.

* * *

Much later, when Erica climbed the stairs, she heard sounds coming from behind Liz's door. She knocked softly and, when there was no answer, opened the door. Liz was sobbing in a chair, her feet tucked up underneath her.

Erica hurried over and knelt beside her. "What's the matter?" As Liz scrubbed at her face with a tissue, Erica murmured, "I know you must be frightened."

"It's not that." Liz shook her head and said brokenly, "I really don't care if whoever is trying to kill me succeeds. Not now."

"Why do you say that?"

"It's hard to keep going when life is meaningless." Liz was trembling even as she spoke, and her eyes were glimmering wet and bloodshot.

"Meaningless? But you're so young. You've got your whole life ahead of you."

"That's what makes me even more depressed."

"Has something happened?"

From her lap, Liz lifted a small picture frame that had been in the folds of her nightshirt. She handed it to Erica.

"His name is Joel Goldstein. We were engaged to be married, and now he's dead!"

Chapter Thirteen

A CHILL WENT THROUGH ERICA as she knelt by Liz in her bedroom. "I didn't know you are—were—engaged!"

"No one knew," Liz said, raising a tear-streaked face. "Joel and I kept it a secret."

"Joel?"

"Joel Goldstein. He was a race car driver."

"Like Todd?"

Liz's smile was slight and sad. "They were both stock car drivers, but Joel was better." Tears overflowed again. "Why did he have to die?"

Erica patted her comfortingly.

"I'm sorry," Liz apologized when she regained control. "Whenever I see Todd, I can't help but think of Joel. They were friends. Both of them raced on the NASCAR circuit."

When the tears eased, Erica sat on the bed. It was hard to take it all in. "When did you meet Joel?"

"Last year, in June, when he was in Dover for the NASCAR races. Joel and some of his friends went to the Air Mobility Command Museum. I don't know if you've heard of it, but it's at the Dover Air Force Base. I'd talked Beth into going with me, and, well, we saw these cute guys and started talking. Turns out a couple of them were race car drivers, and the others were crew members." Liz brushed back her hair and struggled to control the trembling of her lips. "Joel and a couple of his friends asked to meet me and Beth that night for dinner. We all went out as a group a few times, then Joel and I started dating."

"But didn't he have to leave to follow the NASCAR circuit?"

Liz nodded. "There are thirty-six races in the Sprint Cup series, but most of them are in the Eastern part of the country, so Joel was able to come back quite a bit. We kept in touch by phone and e-mails, and we were together a lot when he was in town last September."

"How long had you been engaged?"

"Since March—three months."

Outside the window, the moon rode high, and the earth blazed with light from it. Erica hesitated before asking what she knew would be a painful question. "How did Joel die?"

"How else?" Liz intoned sadly. "Racing. Joel went overseas to get more experience and was racing in France, at the Circuit de la Sarthe when . . . when he crashed."

"How did you find out?"

"Joel usually called me every other day. When I hadn't heard from him for a few days, I called, but there was no answer. I kept trying, and finally, a nurse answered Joel's cell phone and told me about the accident. He'd been in the hospital two days before I found out." Her voice sounded mechanical, almost rehearsed. "I asked if I could see him, but the nurse said Joel was in intensive care and that no one except family could see him. I explained we were engaged, but she still said I wouldn't be allowed in. I was going to buy a plane ticket anyway, but then a friend of Joel's called and told me he had died." Liz covered her face with her hands and wept noisily. "I never got to see Joel before he died."

"I'm *so* sorry. When was this?"

"Almost three weeks ago, on May 5." Liz's voice was barely a whisper.

"But no one even knew you were engaged. Why didn't you tell anyone?"

"We couldn't. Because of Joel's grandfather—his narrow-minded, dictatorial, tyrannical grandfather." Liz's voice was bitter. "Joel was adamant about keeping our engagement a secret. Then again, we didn't have many people to tell. Joel was an only child—like his father—and both his parents were gone." She wiped her eyes.

"But why didn't you say something when Joel died?"

"I don't know." Liz sounded weary. "Mainly because it hurt so much. I couldn't stand to talk about it." There was an aura of despair, of black hopelessness around the young woman.

"I guess it would be painful to explain that you were engaged but your fiancé had just died."

Liz nodded. "Actually, it's kind of a relief to tell someone. I felt so numb at first, and then I started having all these weird 'accidents,' and

I was scared." She paused. "But I think the biggest reason I didn't tell anyone was because if I told people, it would make Joel's death real. But if I kept it a secret—then I could pretend Joel was still alive—that he was just away racing, like he was so much of the time anyway." Looking lost, Liz took a ragged breath. "But Joel's not coming back. Not ever—" She burst out in great racking sobs.

Erica went to Liz and held her tightly.

* * *

Setting off for a Sunday afternoon walk, Erica locked the back door, then glanced toward Frank's house. A curtain twitched in a window, and Erica thought she saw the vague outline of a man behind the sheer linen.

She waved and called, "Hello," though it wasn't likely he'd hear. Erica grinned when he moved out of sight. Lately, Frank had been avoiding her. Whenever Erica went into the backyard and Frank happened to be outside, he would bolt for the house. Once he'd been pruning shrubbery and, upon seeing her, lowered himself to the ground as if he could hide behind the short bayberry hedge, causing Erica to giggle. It was a toss-up whether Frank was angry or afraid—probably both, since the search warrant had turned up evidence against him.

The budding shrubs, trees, and gentle sunshine heightened her enjoyment of the day. The lightest of May breezes refreshed Erica as she stopped to take pictures of amazing houses with Doric columns and arched windows, or others with faux turrets, cupolas, and domed roofs. She stopped for a long time in front of one house resembling a layer cake. The bottom layer had narrow, ten-foot-high windows, arched at the top. The second floor was a few feet smaller on all four sides and had more narrow windows facing the street. The third level was smaller still all the way around, with the same number of windows, only greatly reduced in size. Last of all was the petite fourth story, which looked just like a cake topper.

Her thoughts went back to Frank. He claimed the pieces of pipe had been planted by someone else, which begged the question of who could have put it there. Planting evidence to incriminate someone else was not a novel idea, and anyone who knew that Frank and Liz had an acrimonious relationship could have done it. Yet it was also possible Frank had hidden the evidence himself, never thinking the pipe would be found.

Arriving at the historic Episcopal Church on Water Street, Erica wandered the grounds, reading headstones and markers. In the background, a veritable chorus of birds—whitethroats, swallows, and chickadees—sang from the enormous trees. Sitting on a bench in the shade of a white oak, Erica pulled out her phone and called her husband. "Hi, sweetheart, did I get you at a good time?"

"Anytime you call is a good time," David replied.

Erica melted. How sweet he was. "I wish you were here. I went for a walk. Right now, I'm at the old Christ Episcopal Church."

"The way you love old churches, I knew you'd find one eventually."

"At Crooked House, I can hear bells ringing from time to time. I asked Liz about it, and she told me about this church. It has an awesome bell tower. I'd love to look inside, but I came at the wrong time; the building is locked. But get this—the church is smack in the middle of a cemetery! No kidding! It's surrounded on all four sides by graves—some of them go back to the 1700s."

"Sounds like a great place to spend Halloween."

"I'll say. The church is over 300 years old. It's got the most gorgeous stained glass windows. And the door is painted red—not sure if that means anything."

"Houses of ill repute used to have red doors."

"Oh dear. I wonder if the painter knew . . . Anyway, it's beautiful here. I'm sitting on a little bench, soaking it all up. So catch me up with what's new at home."

David proceeded to do exactly that—describing the new litter of kittens, her mother taking the kids to the library, and Kenzie spilling grape juice on her shirt. "Aby told me to soak it in that Oxy stuff you have. Which reminds me, Aby got an A on her history test."

"She told me. That's great."

"So, what else have you been up to today besides walking in graveyards?"

"Well, I went to church this morning. Going at nine is a snap when I don't have to make sure the kids get ready on time. After that, I had lunch—alone. Liz went to visit friends, and Megan left early this morning to visit Beth's parents. I hope she didn't go just because she was mad at me."

"Why would she be mad?"

Erica sighed. "Do you remember Todd—the race car driver Megan's dating? Well, I talked with Liz and started worrying that he might be dating Megan because he's still interested in Liz—"

"Don't tell me you said that to Megan?" David sounded unbelieving.

"Well, not really. But kind of. And Megan got upset and thought I was saying Todd couldn't possibly be interested in her because she's so plain—or something like that."

"Sounds like the old insecure Megan we all know and love."

"I think I understand how she feels. Megan has always lacked confidence, and she's unsure of Todd. She's told me several times that she thinks Todd might still be interested in Liz."

"So it's okay for Megan to express her misgivings, but you, her friend, are not allowed to have doubts?"

"That's about it," Erica said. "Anyway, I'll talk to her when she gets home."

"So what's on tap for tomorrow?" David asked. "Doing anything special for Memorial Day?"

"Not really, although Megan wants to drive out to visit Beth's grave in the morning. After that, I'll finish checking out Liz's roommates. Some of Pinnacle's databases didn't have the information I needed, so I'm checking a few others. I also have a lot of phone calls to make."

"Don't forget to put 'eat chocolate' at the top of your list of things to do. That way, you'll get at least one thing done."

Erica chuckled. "And I still have plenty of chocolate from what you sent. I'm rationing it. My taste buds thank you every day. And the comic books are great."

A couple strolled by, walking hand in hand. The woman's flip-flops made slapping sounds on the red brick pathway.

"Oh, I almost forgot to tell you the big news." Erica told him about Liz's engagement.

"Wow, that's really something," David said. "Do you think it could have any bearing on the case?"

"I hope so. This might be the break I've been hoping for. Liz said Joel died May 5. I checked my notes, and three days later, someone tampered with her car."

"Hmm. Interesting, although I guess it could be a coincidence."

"I don't think so." Erica had always felt there were very few coincidences in life. "What's the most common motive for murder?"

"Money. But Liz doesn't have any. We've gone over that again and again."

"Yes, but now we have a new player in the game—Joel Goldstein. What if he had a will? And what if he listed Liz as his beneficiary?"

David asked. "Did you ask Liz about that?"

"I didn't think about it until I woke up in the night. Liz was still asleep when I left for church, and when I got home, she was gone."

"Joel wouldn't be too much older than Liz, would he? Isn't that kind of young to have a will?"

"But he's a *race car driver*, sweetie. I bet Joel made a will as soon as he started driving professionally. Stock car racing is a dangerous occupation."

"That's true, but Liz and Joel weren't married. I'm not sure he'd name her as a beneficiary when they were only engaged. And you're assuming he had money to leave."

"I'll have to check into that. But Liz did say Joel was an only child and that both his parents were gone, so if he did have a will, who else would he name as his beneficiary?"

* * *

"I'm glad you're not mad at me anymore," Erica said to Megan as they sat in the gazebo that evening. Megan had made some smoothies, and she and Erica enjoyed the icy treats as they talked things through.

"Oh, I'm still mad. Good thing you didn't see what I put in your smoothie." When Erica grimaced and looked into her glass, Megan laughed. "I'm teasing. But sometime in the next day or two, you might find a frog in your bed or a spilled bottle of perfume, or discover that your Lava soap has disappeared."

Erica shrugged. "I like frogs, I'll hide my perfume, and I have more Lava in my suitcase."

"I can see ordinary measures are not going to work." Megan narrowed her eyes. "Maybe I'll have to ramp things up." A mischievous expression crossed her face. "I could leave the cap off the toothpaste or mess up the shoes you line up so carefully. Maybe I'll take your socks, undo them, and match them up wrong."

Erica was aghast. "You wouldn't dare."

"Now you've done it." Megan grinned evilly. "You know better than to dare me not to do anything."

Erica was no dummy. "I take it back."

"Wise woman." Megan leaned back, contented. Then she asked, "What do you think I ought to wear tomorrow when Todd comes for dinner? I was thinking about that new orange blouse I bought last week. Do you think Todd would like it?"

"I'm sure he'll love it." Erica wasn't about to go down the slippery slope of suggesting Todd might not be anything other than totally infatuated with Megan or her clothes. Their talk had smoothed things over, but Erica knew that underneath, Megan was still smarting and determined to prove Todd was dating her because he liked her—not because he wanted to be around Liz. Erica would make sure that from now on, Megan felt no need to prove anything.

* * *

Erica woke early Monday morning and dressed quietly in the near-dark to avoid waking Megan, who lay curled in bed with the quilt pulled up to her chin. Erica picked up her scriptures from the nightstand. Occasionally Megan read with her in the mornings, but today, Erica wanted to read early. Downstairs in the front room, she flipped on the light switch and jumped to see someone sitting in a chair.

It was Liz, wrapped up in a fluffy blue bathrobe.

"Hi, Erica."

"You're up early." Erica sat on the couch and put her scriptures aside.

"Couldn't sleep." That much was evident from Liz's tousled hair and drained expression.

"I've been thinking about what you said—that you had to keep your engagement a secret because of Joel's grandfather," Erica began. "Why was that?"

"To understand, you have to know a little about Joel's background. First of all, Joel's grandfather, Adam, was Jewish, and he was very strict in his religion. Joel went to live with him when his parents died, and Adam drilled it into Joel that he had to marry someone of their faith."

"And you aren't Jewish."

"Exactly. After we fell in love and got engaged, Joel began to worry that once his grandfather found out about us, he'd drop all financial support. You see, Joel's grandfather had been financing him, and in the racing world, you *have* to have financial backers." Words poured from Liz. "Joel was doing really well, though, and thought that if he won just a few more races, he'd be able to get enough sponsors to get along on his own."

"Without his grandfather's help."

"Right. But he hadn't quite reached that point yet. But there was another big reason we kept quiet. Joel's grandfather got cancer a year ago, and the chemo treatments were really hard on him." Liz rubbed her eyes.

"Joel felt like his grandfather was having a rough enough time without crushing him emotionally by getting engaged to someone who wasn't Jewish. Joel said it would break his grandfather's heart. With him so sick, Joel just couldn't do it."

"I can understand that."

"It was frustrating, even though I could see where Joel was coming from. He loved his grandfather and didn't want to hurt him further—not when he was already suffering so much." They sat quietly for a few moments, then Liz added, "Adam hung on longer than the doctors expected, but he passed away in April."

"April?"

"Yeah. Joel didn't want to announce our engagement on the heels of his grandfather's death, so we decided to wait a few weeks before telling anyone." Silvery tears glistened on Liz's cheek.

"Oh, Liz, I'm so sorry." It must have been terrible, Erica thought, to wait to announce your engagement, then have your fiancé pass away in the interim. After a few moments, she said, "I hate to ask, but did Joel have a will?"

"A will?" Liz blinked. "I don't know."

Inwardly, Erica groaned. A promising lead shot down—not completely, but it made Erica's head ache to think of the research it would take to find out if Joel Goldstein had a will and if he'd listed Liz Johnson as his beneficiary.

Liz stood and tightened the belt on her bathrobe. "I'm going upstairs to shower. If I stay here, I'm going to start bawling."

* * *

Later that morning, to celebrate the holiday in a small way, Erica, Liz, and Megan went out for breakfast at a unique little restaurant, the Countrie Eatery. Afterwards, they stopped to buy a large potted azalea, then drove out to the Selbyville cemetery, where they placed the plant on Beth's grave. They stayed for some time, talking quietly in the spring sunshine as a whisper of a breeze played in the branches of the oak and maple trees. Sometimes conversation faltered as they became wrapped up in her own thoughts. Seeing Liz's pale face and Megan's tears dotting the glossy black surface of the new gravestone forged a steely determination in Erica to find the truth.

When they returned to Dover, Erica got on her laptop, typed in her password, and googled Joel Goldstein. The site she looked at showed a handsome young man with a bright smile and a promising career. Then Erica typed in Adam Goldstein. She was surprised to see so many sites pop up. As she bent forward to read, her heart beat faster.

According to Liz, Adam had been wealthy, but she had either been unaware of or had underestimated his real worth. Adam Goldstein was a multimillionaire. Erica leaned back in her chair. A man as rich as Adam Goldstein would certainly have a will—and a substantial one. It seemed logical to assume Adam had left most of his estate to his only grandson, but Erica had to find out for sure.

The screen of her laptop went dark as Erica sat thinking. This could be the answer to why someone was trying to kill Liz. Maybe someone knew that Adam's great wealth had been left to Joel, who in turn had left it to Liz. But at this point, it was only conjecture.

Sounds came from the kitchen, and Erica went in to find Liz getting a glass from the cupboard. Her quick movements reminded Erica of a bird who might take off any moment. Erica practically pounced on her.

"I did some research on Adam Goldstein. You didn't tell me he was a multimillionaire."

Liz's head came up sharply. "A millionaire? Really? I knew he was wealthy, but Joel never told me that." She opened the fridge and pulled out a bottle of cranberry juice. "Awesome, someone's been grocery shopping." She turned to Erica. "Thanks for getting the juice."

"I didn't. It must have been Megan."

Liz sat at the table and poured a glass. "I guess I should have known Adam was loaded. Racing is pretty expensive, and if he was rich enough to finance Joel, it stands to reason he'd have a lot of money."

Megan came down stairs. "Oh, you bought some juice. I love cranberry."

Sliding the glass over, Liz went to get another one. "I'd buy this stuff all the time if it wasn't so expensive."

Something wasn't right, Erica thought. If Liz hadn't bought it, and Megan hadn't— "Wait a minute; don't drink that!" Erica cried, snatching the glass from Megan before she could take a sip.

"Hey!" she complained.

Liz turned startled eyes on Erica. "What's going on?"

"When you took the juice out of the fridge, had the bottle been opened?" Erica asked, sniffing Megan's glass.

"Yeah. Someone must have had some."

Erica eyed the bottle. "I don't think so. If you poured back what you have in your glasses, the container would be nearly full." She glanced at the two young women. "So neither one of you bought the juice?"

They shook their heads.

A terrible uneasiness settled on Erica. She poured the juice from the two glasses back in the bottle and screwed the cap on firmly. "Don't drink this. I'm going to take it to Detective Ranquist and have him check it out."

Liz's voice was low and troubled. "Do you really think someone poisoned it?"

"I'm not sure, but after all that's happened, I don't think we ought to chance it."

Chapter Fourteen

WHEN ERICA WALKED INTO MCDONALDS at twelve thirty, Detective Ranquist was inside, waiting for her.

"Glad you don't mind eating and talking," he told Erica as they got in line. "When you called, the only time I had free was my lunch hour."

"This works out perfectly, since I'm meeting Donna in an hour."

After they ordered, they took a booth by the window.

"So what's going on?" Detective Ranquist asked as he unwrapped his double bacon cheeseburger.

"Three things." Erica set the sack she'd been carrying on the table and pulled out the bottle of cranberry juice.

Detective Ranquist glanced around, embarrassed. "Geez, Erica. They sell drinks here."

"I don't think either one of us ought to drink this. Liz found it in the fridge this morning—opened. Yet neither Megan, Liz, nor I bought it."

The detective took the cap off and sniffed. "Can't smell anything, but that doesn't mean much. I'll take it over to the lab and have it analyzed."

"Great." Erica crunched a fry. "The second thing is that Liz gave me some interesting news. She's engaged."

"What?" he hollered. Several people turned to stare at the agitated policeman, and he lowered his voice. "Whaddaya mean Liz is engaged?"

"I should have said she *was* engaged. Her fiancé died in Europe a few weeks ago."

"*Now* she tells us. We're trying to find a psycho who wants her dead, and Liz doesn't tell us she was *engaged*?" Detective Ranquist's face was red, and he spoke through gritted teeth. "What was she thinking? It's things like this that make me wish I'd gone into another line of work—like flipping burgers."

Erica was sympathetic. It was always the same—people *would* keep details back, thinking them unimportant or unrelated, which they were most of the time. But it was those few times when they *were* important that caused so much frustration. And until details were cleared out of the way, it was impossible to get the full picture. For Liz not to mention something of this magnitude was maddening. Erica told the detective everything Liz had said.

With his initial anger defused, Detective Ranquist became more sympathetic. "That's gotta be tough on her." He picked up a bundle of fries and popped them into his mouth. "But if Joel was financially dependent upon his grandfather, that rules out the possibility that Joel left Liz a bunch of money."

"I don't think so. Adam Goldstein was more than wealthy; he was super rich. And he died *before* Joel did. So, if Joel and his grandfather were as close as Liz says, it stands to reason that Adam left Joel a big chunk of his money."

"And Liz doesn't know if Joel had a will?"

"Correct. But if he did and if he listed Liz as his beneficiary, we have a pretty big motive." Erica wiped her mouth with a napkin. "And it all ties in, because the attacks on Liz started a few days after Joel died."

Detective Ranquist seemed interested. "You've probably already started looking into it, but I'm going to put a detective on research duty—he'll be able to find out about any wills that Adam and Joel Goldstein had."

That was a huge burden off Erica. Unless the will had been filed in a local probate court, the search would most likely have been difficult and time consuming, even using Pinnacle's databases. As a law enforcement agency, the police had many more options open to them.

Erica switched subjects. "Did you find out about the pipe in Frank's garage?"

"There aren't any fingerprints—the pieces had been wiped clean. But it is the same kind of pipe that was used for the bomb."

"Well, there you go."

"Unfortunately, it's not enough, because the cut ends don't match the pipe in the bomb." Detective Ranquist took a long drink.

"What? You can tell that even after the explosion?"

"Yep. The prosecutor says we need something else that connects Frank to one of the other murder attempts before we can make an arrest. Right now it's just circumstantial evidence."

"Do you think the pipe could have been planted?" Erica asked. "A lot of people know Frank isn't one of Liz's biggest fans and that he wants her house. His shed would be an ideal place to plant evidence."

"Could be."

They ate in silence for a minute. Then Erica said, "I've been wondering about Todd McCauley. He's dating Megan now, but she's gotten the impression he might still be interested in Liz."

Detective Ranquist perked up at this news. "This is why it's good to have you working with us—inside information. So what's the story? Why did he and Liz break up?

"Liz broke up with him—said the chemistry wasn't there."

"Is Todd the jealous type? Do you think he might want to get even with Liz for dropping him?"

"Possibly. But he isn't overt in his actions toward Liz—there's just a glance here, a suggestive word there. But Liz said that after she broke up with him, he almost started stalking her. It wasn't until Liz threatened to get a restraining order that he stopped. Then, he started dating Megan."

"Oh, this just keeps getting better and better." Detective Ranquist grinned as he polished off his burger. "Todd can't date Liz, but he starts seeing her roomie to be around her. And the only reason he keeps his distance is because he's afraid of jail."

"Exactly." Erica wiped her mouth. "And there's another guy in love with Liz. BJ Casteel is head over heels."

"The handyman?" When Erica nodded, Detective Ranquist said, "I'm not sure he's got the brains to make a car bomb."

"You said it was a simple device."

"Yeah, but this guy looked like he had the IQ of an eggplant."

Erica disagreed. "He's smart enough to know how to build things."

"An eggplant savant, then." The detective dredged the last of his fries in ketchup. "You said you had three things."

"Something's going on with Donna."

"Do you think Liz's aunt is the would-be murderer?"

"I'm undecided. I told you how strange she acted when I first called her and how anxious and edgy she always seems to be when I'm around."

"A lot of people are uneasy around private eyes."

"Yeah, but whenever Donna says my name, it's in the same tone of voice she would use to say 'known criminal' or 'drug addict.'"

Detective Ranquist snorted in amusement. "Am I supposed to arrest her just because she doesn't like you?"

"I think Donna's scared and that she's hiding something. Nearly every time we talk, she's unfriendly, nervous, or combative."

"It could just be her lovely personality."

Erica considered. "Possibly. She does have a lot on her mind—her father has Alzheimer's."

"But you think it's more than that."

"I do. I've got some ideas I'm going to check out." Erica absentmindedly swept crumbs from the table onto her tray. "Right now, Donna is on my short list. Something's going on with her—I'm just not sure what."

"Keep me up-to-date."

As they took their trays to the garbage can, Erica said, "One thing is certain—the killer is going to try again. The perpetrator would only keep making attempts if he felt sure he wasn't a suspect. And that's what scares me."

Detective Ranquist held the door open for her. "I agree. This guy's going to keep trying until he's accomplished what he's set out to do—kill Liz."

* * *

The bus let Erica off near Park Place Realty. She was anxious to get Donna's thoughts on her niece's engagement—among other things. Erica had called Donna that morning. Although it was Memorial Day, she wasn't surprised when Donna said she'd be at the office for a while that afternoon catching up on work. Liz was right when she said her aunt worked long hours.

At the office, Erica saw a yellow Post-it note on the door, which made her wonder if Donna had broken their appointment. But it was from Donna, saying she had gone next door and would be back in a couple minutes. The door was unlocked, so Erica walked in and went back to Donna's office.

Erica sat down but was distracted by the scattered papers covering Donna's desk. She decided to help by straightening the various piles—a stack of survey results, a pile of area listings, and a bunch of color brochures. As she tapped them together, Erica was surprised to see a paycheck in the middle of the brochures, and she set it aside. It was dated a few days ago, and she didn't want Donna to become upset, thinking she'd lost it. Next, Erica gathered up a bunch of pink, handwritten message slips that Dolores had written and put the notes Donna had written beside them. As she did, Erica took a second look at Donna's handwriting.

When Donna came in, she stopped abruptly, staring in astonishment at Erica, who was poring over her messages.

"Just what do you think you're doing?" she asked in tones of cold fury.

As Erica stood, the messages fell like pink confetti onto the desk. "I was just, uh, straightening things up a bit."

Donna's back was stiff as she pointed at the various, neatly stacked piles on her desk with a crimson-tipped finger. "Did you do this?"

"Yes, I did," Erica admitted modestly.

Donna strode around her desk, stowing her purse underneath. "You had no business coming into my office and touching my papers." Noticing the paycheck, Donna swept it into a drawer. "I know you're a professional busybody, but this is going too far." Her voice was curt.

"I apologize. I have a thing about straightening and thought you could use some help." Erica sat in a black cushioned chair.

Donna also sat, folding her arms in a purposeful, no-nonsense manner. "It's upsetting to come into my office and find you rifling through papers."

"I understand, and I'm sorry. I shouldn't have touched your things without permission."

Her tone was sincere, and Donna took a deep breath. Putting her glasses down, she became businesslike. "What did you want to see me about?"

"Liz."

Donna's face took on a look of alarm. "Has anything happened?"

"Liz is fine. But I just found out that she was engaged."

"Engaged?" Donna's voice was high and thin. "That's impossible. She would have told me."

"She had to keep it a secret."

"Why?"

"It's kind of a long story, but when I told Liz I was coming to see you, she said it was all right if I told you."

When Erica finished explaining, Donna brought her hands to her face. "How terrible! Joel Goldstein," Donna repeated the name slowly. "I knew she was dating a race car driver months ago, but she never told me his name. I could tell she was in love, but after a while, Liz stopped talking about him. I asked if they'd broken up, but Liz said she didn't want to talk about it. She seemed really upset." Donna shot a look at Erica. "When did Joel die?"

"The first part of May. Did you know Joel's grandfather was a millionaire?"

"How would I know that?" Donna stared. "I didn't even know Liz was engaged." Donna tapped a fingernail on her desk. "You know, I hate to say this, but I'm a little skeptical about this whole thing."

This time Erica was the one staring.

"The last thing I want to do is badmouth Liz," Donna went on. "I love her, but I'd think twice about anything Liz tells you. To put it politely, she has a great imagination."

For once, Erica didn't know what to say. Donna had seemed totally sympathetic at first. Why the sudden switch? Was Donna trying to deflect Erica's attention by calling Liz's honesty into question? Finally Erica asked, "Do you have reasons for distrusting Liz?"

"She tends to exaggerate, that's all."

"I'm not sure she exaggerated her car crashing into a tree or her deck collapsing." Erica tilted her head. "The fact is that Joel's grandfather, Adam Goldstein, was a multimillionaire, which means he might have left a good part of his fortune to Joel. It's very possible Joel also had a will and left *his* money to Liz—his fiancée."

Donna's face began to flush. "I get it. And naturally, since I'm Liz's beneficiary, you think I tried to kill her, but that's crazy! I would never hurt Liz." The older woman's eyes became troubled. "I can't think why Liz didn't tell me about Joel. And to have finally found someone, only to have him die . . ." She bit her lip. "I don't know how she's managed to keep this all inside. Poor thing." She paused. "I wonder if Austin knows."

"I don't think so."

"Austin told me Liz invited him to go to the beach with you and Megan tomorrow,"

"That's right. He's been seeing a lot of Megan lately. They make a cute couple—both of them tall and good-looking."

A look of pain crossed Donna's face. "Megan is very young, of course. That must be why she thinks it's okay to date two men at the same time."

"Actually, Megan is very mature for her age."

Donna appeared unconvinced. "From what I hear, she's quite—uh—free spirited. And all that black hair." Her tone was full of disapproval. "And Megan's just a freshman, isn't she?"

"She would have been a sophomore, but she took a lot of college classes in high school, so actually she's a junior. Megan's a very bright girl."

There was suspicion in Donna's eyes. "You two are close, aren't you?"

"Yes. Her mother, Wendy, and I have been best friends since college."

Donna paused, and when she went on, her voice was cold. "I know you suspect me of trying to kill Liz, but what about Megan? Isn't she a suspect?"

"Megan is the one who asked me to look into Liz's accidents," Erica replied. "Besides, I know Megan. She isn't capable of killing anyone."

"Even if she were jealous?" When Erica didn't say anything, Donna went on. "I would have thought that since you're living with them, you would have noticed how jealous Megan is of Liz."

"I haven't seen any jealousy. Megan and Liz are good friends."

Donna made a scoffing sound. "For a private investigator, you're not very objective or observant. You're obviously letting your private feelings get in the way of seeing things as they really are. Liz has told me many times how jealous Megan is of her because men find Liz so attractive. You need to take a closer look at Megan. Or are you afraid of finding out *she's* the one trying to kill Liz?"

* * *

"I hope you've noticed I'm trying to be supportive by helping you make dinner tonight." Erica threw it out as a pitiful attempt to win points as she deftly diced a cucumber.

Megan stood beside her at the kitchen counter. "Noted and appreciated. It's nice of you to help—I spent too much time studying." Megan tossed the sliced celery into the bowl with lettuce greens then began chopping a tomato. "And it was nice of you to suggest Todd come over in the first place, since it's a holiday and he'd be alone."

While it was true Erica was making a real effort to let Megan make her own choices regarding the men she dated, she'd had an ulterior motive in suggesting Todd come over for a barbeque. It was a chance to put him under her microscope. Erica was especially eager to see his reaction to the news of Liz's engagement. She'd even gone so far as to wonder if Todd—upon learning Liz's fiancé was gone—would try to win her back.

Erica took two pieces of celery and a few bits of purple cabbage from the bowl and set them aside on a saucer.

Eying the minute amounts, Megan asked, "You on a diet?"

"That's for Hamlet."

"You're always giving him stuff."

"That's because he's a paid informant, and he prefers vegetables over hard cash."

"You're spoiling him."

"Hamsters need love too."

Megan frosted the cake while Erica cut potatoes in quarters. She then tossed the potatoes in olive oil and seasonings and put them in the oven to bake.

When Todd arrived, he gave Megan a hug and a sweet kiss on the cheek. He could certainly take your breath away with those chiseled features and intense blue eyes.

He flashed a smile at Erica. "Megan tells me you're a great cook. How is your husband managing without you?"

"David does his own share of cooking, but most of my family lives nearby. While I've been gone, he and the kids eat a lot with either my parents or my brothers and their families."

Todd pretended to roll up his sleeves. "Well, I came ready to eat. Let's get this grill on the road!" Megan chuckled and went outside with him to start the grill. When they came in to get the hamburger patties and the corn on the cob, Erica called upstairs to Liz, who'd been napping.

Megan had set up a card table inside the gazebo, and as they carried out the paper plates, potatoes, and salad, the delicious smell of barbecued burgers drifted in the air.

As they ate, Erica kept a watchful eye on Todd. He was charming, funny, and directed comments to all three women. Yet it seemed his face softened whenever Liz spoke. Was it Erica's intense scrutiny that made her think Todd's eyes flickered a little too often to Liz? She needed a piece of paper and a pencil to keep score.

Todd raved about Megan's burgers, asking her what seasonings she'd used. Then he pointed a fork at the Oven-baked Potato Wedges[8] on his plate. "These are delicious. How did you make them, Erica?"

It was a little embarrassing to admit to such a simple recipe, but Todd was highly complimentary. As he passed the bowl of potatoes to Liz, Erica noticed how Todd's eyes locked onto Liz's for a few moments. Then things were as before. Had Erica imagined that look?

Talk turned to the upcoming NASCAR races, and Erica asked Todd if he was ready.

"Just about. I always come to town early to prepare. There's a lot of fine-tuning to do, and we have to make sure the car's in top working condition. The pit crew and I also like to get in all the practices we can. Right

---

8 See the appendix at the end of the book for this recipe.

now, I'm only in the Developmental Series race on Friday—but soon I hope to qualify for the Nationwide Series."

"I've been wondering about the ads and signs I've seen for the track," Erica asked. "Sometimes they'll say the Dover International Speedway and other times, Dover Downs. Are they the same thing?"

Liz said, "That can be confusing to newcomers—a lot of people ask me about that where I work, but Dover Downs is actually the harness horse race track that's inside the speedway."

"When people talk about Dover Downs, they're talking about horse racing or the casino and hotel," Todd added.

"Austin told me the race track is nicknamed the Monster Mile." Erica broke an ear of corn in half and buttered it.

"It's that, all right," Todd said with a grim nod. "It's called that mostly because of the concrete surface. Concrete grips the tires and lets drivers race aggressively, but it's really rough on cars. Most NASCAR tracks are asphalt. Another thing about the Dover track is that it's one mile long. Technically, that means it's not a superspeedway or a short track." Todd speared a few more potatoes. "The speedway's publicity department came up with the icon of a strong, scary monster to give the track a He-Man image. The kids eat it up, and actually big guys do too."

"I'd love to see you race," Erica said.

"Come on out! I'm racing on Friday." Todd exchanged glances with Megan. "I've already asked Megan to come and cheer me on. Then on Saturday, we could all go watch the shorter Nationwide Series race or the longer one on Sunday for the Sprint Cup."

He glanced at Liz, but she remained silent, looking down at her plate.

Erica decided to bring up the subject. "Liz told me Saturday night that she was engaged to Joel Goldstein but that he died in a car race in France."

"Megan just told me about that," Todd said softly. Watching Liz, he added, "Joel didn't say anything."

Sitting very still, Liz made no response and didn't look up.

"That's right," Erica said to Todd. "You knew Joel, didn't you?"

"We were friends. In fact, I was racing in Europe with him when the accident happened. NASCAR had just sanctioned the Racecar Euro Series for stock car racing in 2012, and most of the venues were in France."

"That must have been awful," Megan said.

"It was. All the drivers were stunned."

"I'm so sorry, Liz." Megan murmured, pushing her empty plate away. "Erica said you had to keep it a secret because of Joel's grandfather. Did you ever meet him?"

Finally Liz looked up, bitterness in her eyes. "No, and I'm not sure I would have liked him even if I had. Joel said his grandfather was very strict and set in his ways." She bit her lip. "I'm sure he loved Joel, but Joel said his grandfather would go ballistic if he knew Joel was dating someone who wasn't a member of their faith."

"He sounds like a fanatic," Megan observed.

"Joel tried to explain that religion and tradition meant everything to Adam. It meant a lot to Joel too, but to a much lesser degree. Because of that, I even considered converting."

Liz brushed back her hair from her face and took a sip of lemonade. "Joel idolized his grandfather, but he was also a little afraid of him. Sometimes I'd get upset because Joel didn't want to tell his grandfather about us, but after he told me some business stories about Adam, and how harsh he could be, I understood why Joel was leery of crossing him. From what Joel said, Adam was very opinionated, close-minded, and inflexible."

"But Joel's grandfather couldn't stop Joel from marrying you," Megan said, "not when you loved each other."

"That's true, but it was complicated," Liz responded. "You see, after Joel's parents died, his grandfather took Joel in and raised him. And when Joel decided he wanted to be a race car driver, Adam backed him all the way."

Todd spoke up. "Joel told me his grandfather was his biggest sponsor. Adam gave Joel whatever he needed. Without his grandfather's financial support, Joel could never have made it as a stock car driver."

"Joel's dream was to race cars, and Adam helped him live his dream." There was a little tremor in Liz's voice, and she stopped to rub her temple as if that would help control her emotions.

"It's a tough business to get into if you don't have the right strings to pull," Todd said, giving Liz time to collect herself. "One of the hardest parts of racing is getting and keeping sponsors. That's why we have all those brand names on our cars and clothes. But if Joel wanted a better engine, a new kind of tire, or a more experienced guy in his pit crew—Adam paid for it."

"Which meant Joel was very tied to his grandfather," Erica said.

Liz agreed in a low voice. "Joel was tremendously grateful to him."

Megan waved at a wasp, which was circling the salad bowl. "I still can't believe you kept all of this a secret."

"We never meant to let it go on as long as it did. Joel and I were just about to announce our engagement when Adam got sicker. We hoped the chemo would work and the cancer would go into remission, giving him some time. But Adam's health went downhill really fast, and Joel couldn't stand the thought of upsetting him. He passed away just before Joel left for Europe."

"Why didn't you announce your engagement then?" Megan asked.

"It was a terrible time." Liz's voice was a small thing. "Joel was devastated at losing his grandfather. It was a time for remembering him and his life. We didn't want the focus to be on us. It would have seemed, I don't know, disrespectful. Besides, we thought we had plenty of time. We decided to announce it when Joel got back from Europe, but . . ." Liz's voice broke. Rising awkwardly, she mumbled, "Excuse me." She half ran to the house.

"Poor Liz," Megan said, starting to rise. "Should I go after her?"

"I think she'd prefer to be alone for a while," Erica said. "It's got to be hard on her opening up about all this. Let's give her a little time, then we'll check on her."

* * *

After cleaning up, Erica and Megan went to see Liz, who insisted she was fine. Liz apologized for the drama but said she preferred to have some time alone. When Todd took Megan out for ice cream, Erica borrowed Megan's car to go rent a movie at a cute little old video store in town—almost a relic in these days of Netflix and Redbox.

Ever since she'd seen Megan reading *An American Tragedy*, Erica had wanted to watch *A Place in the Sun*, which was based on the book. It was a beautiful evening. Driving home from the video store, she enjoyed the way the setting sun illuminated the rooftops of Dover with a film of soft yellow light. When she pulled into the driveway, the last rounded slice of the sun disappeared over the horizon.

Erica asked Liz if she wanted to watch the movie, but Liz said she was going to bed. After making popcorn, Erica went to her room and made herself comfortable in bed by propping up pillows by the headboard.

The plot was intriguing. A factory worker, played by Montgomery Cliff, found himself involved with two women: a female coworker and a beautiful socialite—Elizabeth Taylor. As she watched, Erica's thoughts strayed to Liz's unhappy situation. She felt a tug of something ominous, but it remained just out of reach.

Once Erica paused the movie so she could concentrate on the weird feeling, but nothing came of it. Something was at work in her subconscious, but it refused to rise to the surface. After a while, Erica decided her uneasy feelings must have something to do with the theme of the movie. Or it could have been just the title of the book, *An American Tragedy*, which pretty much summed up what had happened to Beth and Liz.

Chapter Fifteen

The Overfalls Lightship and the two lighthouses—the Harbor of Refuge and the Delaware Breakwater—were all close to Lewes, Delaware, only thirty miles from Dover. Erica was excited to see the lightship—she'd never heard of such a thing. Liz explained that lightships were put into operation where a lighthouse was needed but it wasn't possible to build one. They decided to tour the lighthouses in the morning, go to Lewes beach for a picnic lunch and to play in the water, then to see the Overfalls Lightship in the afternoon.

There was free parking in the Foot Passenger lot, so they left Austin's Jeep there and went to the long-stretching finger pier behind the Cape May–Lewes Ferry Terminal. The air over the shimmering water was clear and bright, and the waves hit the pier with a rhythmic slap as the group walked across the faded boards.

After handing over their tickets, they joined the other passengers on board. One of the crew members, a man with a face bronzed and wrinkled from sun and wind, handed out life jackets.

Megan had pulled her hair back into a shining ponytail at the back of her head, and she flipped her hair up and over her life jacket. Then she elbowed Erica to take a look at the captain, who was talking with an elderly couple. The captain's beard was long and thick enough to hide a couple of herons, and under his cap, his wiry brown hair looked like a mat of seaweed drying on the beach.

Launches crossed to and fro as the four of them gathered at the railing and watched the sun reflect off the ruffled water of Delaware Bay in quicksilver flashes.

Liz seemed in high spirits as the boat puttered across Lewes Harbor and headed for the Delaware Breakwater Lighthouse. "Before we left, I felt a little guilty playing hooky from my classes, but this is too good to miss. I'm so glad we came."

"Me too," Erica said as the lighthouse drew near. "I'm glad you could come with us, Austin. How's school going for you?"

"A little hectic right now. I'll be glad to wrap it up in June."

Liz spoke up. "He'll be one of the privileged few to get his master's degree."

"He even has a job lined up," Megan added.

Erica was impressed. "Did you have a hard time finding a job?"

"Not really. Accounting and finance are fields with a lot of good job opportunities."

"Unlike a liberal arts degree," Liz said with a wink at Megan, who bristled with indignation.

"A liberal arts degree gives me a good, all-around education and prepares me for a number of interesting careers. Isn't that the purpose of education?"

"*Some* people think the purpose of a higher education is to get a job," Liz replied.

"I'll be able to get a job." Megan moved back from the railing as water splashed up the side of the boat. "Come on, Erica, back me up here. You understand the benefits of having a liberal arts major, don't you?"

"Yes, I do. It makes for a more rounded education. Albert Einstein once said, 'All religions, arts, and sciences are branches of the same tree.'"

With a haughty lift of her eyebrows, Megan put on a supercilious expression as she glared at Liz. "See?"

Liz only smirked. "Have you heard that joke about people with different degrees?"

"No, and I don't want to," Megan replied.

"It goes like this," Liz said without missing a beat. "A graduate with a science degree asks, 'Why does it work?' A graduate with an accounting degree asks, 'How much does it cost?' A graduate with an engineering degree asks, 'How does it work?' And a graduate with a liberal arts degree asks, 'Do you want fries with that?'"

"Ha ha ha." Megan rolled her eyes. "I wouldn't talk if I were you—not with you majoring in retail management. I've got a joke for you, Liz. How do you get a graduate with a degree in retail management off your porch?" She paused then said, "Pay her for the pizza."

Austin laughed loudly. "I haven't heard that one before."

The boat drew near the red lighthouse, which had a white band at the bottom and was nestled on rocky ground. Erica imagined how the lighthouse would look at night, with its great light shooting out through the circle of windows at the top.

Erica felt the in-board motor thrum through the soles of her sandals as the tour guide spoke into a microphone. "The Delaware Breakwater East End Lighthouse is the oldest in the United States. Lighthouse keepers lived here from 1885 until 1950, when the light was automated. The keepers kept a nightly vigil in the light's watch room to ensure the light was burning bright to protect mariners from dangerous rocky shoals."

The captain throttled back on the engine and pulled alongside a dock. A volunteer directed the passengers to gather for a short lecture. Afterward, they clambered up the winding stairs into the cool interior of the lighthouse. The top level was the lantern room, where a 125-year-old, fourth-order Fresnel lens was still in place, though it was no longer used.

Someone in the group asked what a fourth-order lens was, and the guide replied, "There are seven sizes of lenses. First-order lenses are the largest, but fourth-order lenses are quite common along the Eastern seaboard."

After the tour, they sailed to where Delaware Bay joined the Atlantic Ocean then on to the historic Harbor of Refuge Light Station. Erica snapped a few shots of the squat white lighthouse, which rested on a tall, black, iron caisson that had been built into the breakwater. The guide informed them that the seventy-six-foot Harbor of Refuge Light was one of the most exposed lighthouses on the Atlantic coast and was occasionally pounded with waves so tall they washed over the black tower at the top.

As they disembarked, gulls and cormorants bickered back and forth in the air before swooping down to perch on nearby rocks. At the lighthouse, a different volunteer opened the door, which creaked uneasily, revealing a cavernous darkness inside. The guide flipped the light switch, and they crowded inside. The tour guide informed them that Harbor of Refuge had been built in 1926 to replace a lighthouse that had been damaged by a storm. Like the Delaware Breakwater, it had been originally equipped with a fourth-order Fresnel lens. Now the lighthouse was operated by solar power.

When the tour was over, Austin and Megan perused pictures on the walls, while Erica and Liz went back up the circular stairs and outside onto the catwalk. They had an unbelievable view. The sky overhead was the pale-washed blue of May, and the wakes of pleasure crafts made crisscrossing patterns on the sparkling water.

"I've been thinking," Liz said as she held onto the iron railing. "Do you remember when you asked me if Joel had a will?" When Erica nodded, Liz said, "I went back and reread a bunch of Joel's emails."

"Find anything?"

"I'm not sure. In one, Joel said that if anything happened, I'd be taken care of. When I first read it, I thought Joel was talking in some kind of spiritual way. You know—that he would watch over me like an angel. I never thought about a will."

"You said Joel and his grandfather were close, so it's likely that Adam would have left Joel part—if not all—of his money. So if Joel *did* have a will and you were his beneficiary, you could be a very wealthy woman."

Liz's blue eyes went wide. "But if Joel had put me as his beneficiary, wouldn't I have been contacted by his lawyer or something?"

"I imagine that with a man as wealthy as Adam Goldstein, it would take time for the executor to see that the terms of the will were carried out. And Joel's death would further complicate matters."

Several couples came out onto the catwalk, and Liz and Erica went inside to the lantern room. They paused to examine the glass slabs that made up the great beehive-shaped lens.

"I talked with Detective Ranquist. He's having someone look into Adam Goldstein's will and finding out if Joel had one." As they started down the circular iron stairs, Erica asked, "I know you said Joel was an only child, but what happened to his parents?"

"They were killed in an airplane crash. Joel's father loved to fly and had his own plane."

"Did Joel have any other living relatives?"

"None that he ever mentioned. Adam was the youngest in his family. I know he had a sister and brother, but both of them passed away years ago."

They found Austin and Megan and returned to the boat. Waves slapped against the hull as passengers climbed aboard. Austin and Megan stood at the rail, holding hands, while Liz and Erica sat on seats in the middle.

Talking loudly to be heard above the noisy throb of the motor, Erica asked, "How is your aunt doing? Donna always seems kind of stressed and jittery when I see her."

"It's the same whenever I see her. I've asked Austin about it, but he claims she's fine. I've asked him and Donna if there's anything I can do to help, but both of them clam up." The boat began to plow forward, leaving a tumbling wake of white water behind. "I know Aunt Donna has been working really long hours the past few months, and she's worried sick about Grandpa. It could be she's worried about money—I know things are pretty tight for her right now."

And yet there had been an uncashed paycheck lying on Donna's desk. Erica had done a lot of thinking and had started to develop several hypotheses that could explain what was going on. But she still had a lot of questions. Perhaps the biggest one was that if Donna was indeed in dire financial straits, how far would she go to rectify that situation? And second, was Austin involved?

"Austin seems a little stressed at times too," Erica commented mildly.

"I've noticed that," Liz said. "He's got a lot going on with finals and finishing up his degree. And he's worried about his mom and Grandpa."

Appearing drowsy, Liz closed her eyes, and after a few minutes, Erica did the same. There were the sounds of people talking, seagulls squawking, and the motor humming. Yet something nibbled at Erica's brain. What was it? Something had been stirred by their little chat. She tried to sort through their conversation to figure out what was bothering her. Erica felt it had something to do with Donna's paycheck. But why? Erica went over her last visit with Donna carefully, recalling how she'd straightened Donna's desk—the brochures, the stack of Dolores's messages, and the smaller pile of notes Donna had written. A warning buzz went off in her mind, and Erica's eyes flew open.

The piles on the desk. Donna's handwritten notes. The check. The handwriting. One by one, all those items clicked and slid into place. The handwriting—it was the same. Too bad she hadn't noticed it that day. The vague suspicions Erica had voiced to Detective Ranquist were justified. Erica glanced over at Liz, who was still dozing. If Erica was right, this would explain a lot of things about Donna—from her strange rudeness and anxiety to the expensive nurse she'd hired. However, Erica liked to confirm things and decided to check one source. There were a few minor, unexplained points with Donna, but the main picture was now clear.

* * *

After docking at Cape May-Lewes Ferry Terminal, they returned to the Jeep. Austin carried the cooler while Megan, Erica, and Liz brought a shade tent, chairs, and tote bags. They needed to tie the tent because of the breeze, so Erica brought out her Leatherman tool and cut pieces of rope to fasten the tent to pegs driven into the sand.

Megan opened a bag Erica had packed and showed it to Austin. Sun block, mosquito repellent, aloe vera, lotion, first-aid kit, and a multitude of other items. Megan turned to Erica, "You're always organized, aren't you?"

"Mais oui!"

Megan laughed then said, "I'm surprised you didn't bring a life raft in case the tour boat capsized."

"I thought *you* were bringing that." Erica took off her sandals, enjoying the feel of her bare feet on the warm sand. She brought out a jug of water and Lava soap for washing as Liz began setting out the sandwiches.

When Erica unwrapped the deviled eggs she'd made, Austin popped one in his mouth. "Hey, these are good!"

"They taste even better if you let them linger in your mouth at least half a second."

"Good idea. I'll try that."

When Austin took another, Liz slapped at his hand. "Leave some for us." She picked up an egg. "What did you put in them, Erica? They don't look like the usual kind."

"They're Bacon-Cheddar Deviled Eggs."[9]

She ate one. "Yum! They *are* delicious."

"I can vouch for that," Austin said, getting into the cooler. "Now I need something to wash them down."

"Soda pop is on the left, and water is on the right," Erica told him.

When all that remained of the sandwiches were crumbs, Austin contentedly stretched out his long legs. Gazing at Megan, he recited, "'A jug of wine, a loaf of bread—and thou, beside me singing in the wilderness.' Omar Khayyam."

"Oh my gosh." Megan sounded a bit horrified. "That is so weird. Erica and David come up with all sorts of quotes too. You'd think they majored in English lit instead of criminal justice."

"If you like it, I can get a book of quotes and find a few more." His grin, as always, was boyish and attractive.

"No—one's enough." They all laughed, and then with a buoyant lightness, Megan took Austin's hand and pulled him up. There seemed to be a glow around the two. "Come on, let's walk along the beach."

Austin winked at Liz and Erica and went off happily, holding Megan's hand as they walked along the shoreline. The water lapped at their feet;

9 See the appendix at the end of the book for this recipe.

then Megan bent to splash Austin. When he retaliated, she ran a short distance and splashed him again. Austin did the same, and as they twisted and twirled, it was as though they were doing some intricate dance.

"It seems like Austin has found someone he really cares about," Liz remarked, going to the cooler and grabbing two icy cans of lemonade. She handed one to Erica. It was peaceful sitting in the shade, relaxing and enjoying the brilliant blue water. The sound of Megan's laughter, clear as a bell, floated back to them.

"I never thought those two would get together." The light breeze blew Liz's light-brown hair as she continued watching the pair. "Austin has always been such a straight arrow, and Megan is such a free spirit."

"Megan's had to find her own way," Erica remarked. "She's had a rough life—growing up with an emotionally abusive father. And when he wasn't abusive, he showed zero interest in her. Her parents finally divorced, but she's close to her mother. I'm glad Megan's found someone like Austin, but then again, I know she also likes Todd."

"Both of them are great, but my vote's for Austin."

"That's because he's your cousin."

"Nah, I'd say that even if we weren't related. He's a great guy."

Erica hoped that was the case. First of all, she didn't want Megan to get hurt, and second, she had to suspect everyone until Beth's killer was in custody. Also, there was this other matter with his mother. Was Austin involved in that? She hoped to find out tomorrow.

When Austin and Megan changed into their swimsuits and continued frolicking in the water, it looked like so much fun that Liz and Erica joined them. They tossed a beach ball around in the water. Once, Erica reached too far for the ball and fell backwards, gulping a mouthful or two of water while the others laughed. Afterwards, they walked over to the beach shower building then returned to the shade tent.

"I called Beth's parents a few days ago," Megan said as she ran a comb through her hair.

Erica spread her towel out to dry and sat in one of the sling chairs. "Didn't they go see their son and his family?"

"Yeah. They're still in Illinois, but Brenda gave me her cell number. She sounded a little better. I think it's been good for them to visit family."

"Are they still going to church?" Erica squirted some lotion on her legs then passed the bottle to Liz.

"Yep. The missionaries challenged them to be baptized, but they said they want to learn more about the Church first. Also, since Beth told them she wanted to be baptized, Brenda and Gary want that done for her." Megan went on. "I told them I could be proxy for Beth, but Brenda said she'd like to do it—if she joins the Church."

"Do you think they'll want all of Beth's ordinance work done?" Austin asked as he passed around bottles of water then sat beside Megan.

"I didn't ask, but what if she and her husband don't get baptized?" Megan seemed worried. "If they decide not to, could I go ahead and do the work for Beth? I hate to think of her in heaven waiting and waiting."

"I think you'd need to get permission from her parents," Austin told her, "but it sounds like they'd let you. Say, do you remember a couple years ago, when a group of Jews got upset when they found out Mormons were baptizing Jews who died in the Holocaust? They felt it was disrespectful and asked Church leaders to put a stop to it."

Perplexed, Megan asked, "What does it matter? The baptism isn't binding unless the person chooses to accept it. And isn't doing temple work for the dead one of the main missions of the Church?"

"Yes, but our primary duty is to see that the work is done for our own families," Erica said. "Religion is a very personal thing, and people have strong feelings about it."

"A lot of people were upset when they found out that—contrary to Church policy—prominent people like Anne Frank and Gandhi were being baptized," Austin added.

Liz, who had been content to quietly listen, now spoke up. "I can see why Jews would be upset. They have a long, rich history, and it seems a bit arrogant for another religion to come along and baptize their ancestors without permission."

On the beach, some children threw bread out to a screaming committee of seagulls that dove at the crumbs, squawking loudly. Nearby, a snowy white egret stood on a rocky outcropping.

Looking serious, Austin agreed. "That's why Mormon leaders agreed to remove Jewish Holocaust victims from the list of candidates for baptism unless they were related to living Church members. They also asked Church members to only do ordinance work for their own families, but some members kept doing it anyway."

"I remember that," Erica said. "I heard the Church developed a new computer system that had a firewall in the genealogical database to block anyone who attempted to access the names of celebrities or Jewish victims of the Holocaust."

Austin added, "Also, President Monson sent a letter condemning proxy baptism for Holocaust victims, Catholic saints, and celebrities. He said people needed to stop the misguided practice of submitting those names for baptism. If they didn't, they would have their access to the Church's genealogical database cut off and could lose their good standing—unless they could prove a legitimate family connection."[10]

"That's good to hear," Liz said. "I guess I have a different perspective since I'm not LDS, but I can see where people would be upset if their ancestors were baptized without permission."

"I can too," Austin said. "Now, I suggest we leave this fascinating subject and move on to politics." Liz, Megan, and Erica groaned loudly, and he went on. "Just kidding. How about heading over to the Overfalls Lightship? All in favor, say aye."

A chorus of ayes echoed across the beach.

* * *

"Most of you are probably wondering about lightships," the guide said as the tour began on deck. "A light vessel or a lightship is used in water that is too deep or otherwise unsuitable for constructing a regular lighthouse. Of the 179 lightships that were built from 1820 to 1952, the Overfalls Lightship is one of only 17 that remain." The tour guide led them below. They bunched together, with Megan fidgeting beside Erica. "Overfalls' dual electric lanterns flash every three seconds from dusk until dawn and can be seen up to twelve miles away. All of them are equipped with a foghorn and a radio beacon that has a range of twenty-five miles."

Megan rolled her eyes. She whispered to Erica, "Who cares? This is boring. And it's stuffy down here. I'm going up."

Erica went with her. They climbed the metal stairs and strolled around the deck of the red ship. *Overfalls* was painted on the side in large white letters.

"I didn't know a lightship was just a lighthouse on a boat," Megan said. "If you'd asked me before we came, I'd have said a lightship was something on *Star Trek*." Erica laughed, and Megan went on. "Did I tell you Todd asked me *again* if he could come with us today?"

Erica shook her head.

"I asked Liz if I should invite him, and she said, 'No way.' So that's what I told him. Not in those exact words, though."

---

10 See *The Salt Lake Tribune*, March 8, 2012.

Thank goodness, Erica thought as they walked on. Alongside the dock was a forest of bare masts—ships at permanent mooring. She and Megan meandered toward the prow, enjoying the late-afternoon sun.

"I don't want to hear 'I told you so,'" Megan said, "but I'm still getting vibes that Todd is interested in Liz."

It was an amazing admission, and Erica had no intention of touching that remark with a ten-foot pole. Instead, she looked over the brilliant blue sea as it rolled with a gentle swell. "Todd seems like a nice guy."

"Yeah, he is. And he's a lot of fun."

"It's been fun having Austin around today."

A soft expression came over Megan's face. "Yeah, it's weird, but we really have a good time together."

Erica was puzzled. "Why is that weird?"

"Because we're so different. Austin likes to play it safe, but he's flexible too. And me—I like to do whatever I want, whenever I want, and I can be rigid. How can two people who are so different get along so well?" Megan glanced around to make sure Liz and Austin were still below. "But I get the feeling he's getting *serious*."

"Oh no! That *would* be awful!" Erica said in mock horror. Then her voice returned to normal. "Do you want to know what I think?"

"Not really." Megan rolled her eyes again—she was a master at it. "Oh, go ahead."

"I think you're a little more cautious in your relationships than most women. I know it was hard when your father walked out on you, Brandon, and your mom. I think that's made you fearful of serious relationships. Don't overthink your relationship with Austin—just have fun and enjoy. Let your heart guide you. Pray sincerely, and you won't go wrong. Of all the decisions I've made in life, marrying David was the best one. But before I decided to say yes, I worried a lot and held back. I thought the timing was all wrong because I was still in college."

A pair of gulls mewled and wheeled overhead as Erica went on. "I finally stopped fighting my feelings and accepted that David loved me and I loved him. It wasn't the timing I had planned on, but it was God's timing. He was watching out for me. I'm glad David and I went ahead. I'm not saying it was easy—I got pregnant and had Aby during my senior year—but it worked out. And you know why?"

For once Megan had no teasing retort. "Because you loved each other."

"Exactly. David and I are different, but we're right for each other. You can overcome a lot of differences if you have love to smooth the way."

* * *

The light was seeping out of the day, and the shadows were long and blue as the four of them made their way to the Jeep. Seagulls were making their last circles over the bay, and in a few hours, beacons from the lightship and lighthouses would begin shooting across the water.

Ensconced in the backseat, Erica called David, and they talked about the pictures she'd sent him of the lighthouses and lightship. They talked quietly, and at the end, he gave the phone to Aby, Ryan, and Kenzie.

They arrived home safely. When Erica got out of the shower, Megan told her someone had called on her cell. Erica unplugged her phone from the charger and touched the screen.

"It was Detective Ranquist," Erica said, looking at Megan.

"It's kind of late," Megan said apprehensively. "What do you think he wants?"

"I don't know, but it can't be good if he's calling at night."

Chapter Sixteen

Detective Ranquist's deep voice sounded solemn. "Liz Johnson ought to give you a great big hug. She's alive today because of you."

Megan had summoned Liz, and Erica sat on the bed, sandwiched between the two of them. Erica had her phone on speaker so they could all hear.

There was a collective gasp, and Erica inhaled sharply. "So the juice *was* poisoned."

"Someone put Norflex in it—very powerful stuff. Norflex is used for muscle pain. If Liz had taken a drink, she'd have started having blurred vision, weakness, vomiting, and headache—among other symptoms—after about half an hour." Detective Ranquist went on. "Another three to six hours, and she would have either died from heart failure or been in a coma. Powerful stuff. Oh, the lab also said Norflex has a bitter taste."

"Which would have gone undetected in the cranberry juice," Erica said.

"Most likely. Sorry for calling so late, but I thought you should know."

"Thanks." Erica laid the phone on the bedside table.

Liz gazed at her out of great, fear-darkened eyes. "I—I don't understand how the juice could have been poisoned." Unconsciously, a hand went to her throat. "And I just about drank it. And Megan almost did too."

"Did either of you see anyone come to the house that day or the night before?" Erica asked. Liz and Megan shook their heads.

"Who could have gotten in and put juice in the fridge?" Megan's voice was loud and upset. "We're the only ones who have keys to the house!"

"BJ has a key," Liz said quietly. When Megan turned to her in astonishment, Liz defended herself. "I'm not always here when BJ's working—he's got to be able to use the bathroom."

"Does anyone else have a key?" Erica asked. "What about Donna?"

"Well, sure she has one." Liz paused. "Frank does too."

Megan screeched, "You gave a key to *Frank*?"

"It was when he first moved in," Liz said defensively, "before I knew he was a crackpot. I had to leave for a couple of weeks, and Frank offered to take care of the place while I was gone."

"Did you ever ask for the key back?" Erica wanted to know.

"I didn't think about it."

"Oh, Liz." Erica was reproachful. "Anyone else?"

"Well, Joel had one, but—"

"Is there any chance he could have given it to Todd?"

"Of course not." Liz said. "I mean, why would he?"

* * *

Another one saved!

Hunkered down on the floor by the kitchen sink, Erica murmured soothingly to the little gray mouse in the trap. "I know you're scared, but don't worry. I'm not going to hurt you. You'll soon be with friends."

"Who are you talking to?" Megan asked as she came down the stairs.

Erica swung round, adroitly sliding the box behind her. "To myself."

"I know you're cracked, but I didn't think OCD extended to talking to yourself." Megan went toward the fridge, and as she did, Erica turned, keeping her right arm behind her back.

One of Megan's eyebrows lifted. "What have you got behind you? And why are you wearing your extra-thick gloves?" She bent to the right, trying to see behind Erica, who twisted and blocked her view. Megan put her hands on her hips.

"Okay, what are you hiding?"

It was no use. With a sigh, Erica brought out the small box.

Warily, Megan took a step back. "What's that?"

"I replaced those awful mousetraps Liz had with humane ones—traps that catch but don't kill poor little mice."

"There's a mouse in that? I know you've always been a softhearted pushover for any kind of animal in trouble, but how can you stand being around mice when you have OCD out the wazoo?"

"What does OCD have to do with saving innocent little mice?"

"Says the woman wearing heavy-duty yellow gloves."

"I'm just taking reasonable precautions. And what's wrong with mice, anyway?" Erica stood and asked accusingly—as if Megan was racist. "You like Hamlet, and he's a first cousin to a mouse."

Megan eyed the trap. "What are you going to do with it?"

"It's going to a safe house."

"I vote for the outside garbage can. Make sure the lid's on tight."

Erica put on her most winning expression. "What about having him stay with Hamlet? Wouldn't that be nice? They could be friends and hang out together."

"No way!" Megan grimaced at the thought. "That mouse might have some horrible disease."

Looking into the box, Erica saw shiny black eyes peering back at her. She held the box out toward Megan. "See those eyes? Clear and bright. You can tell a lot about a person's health by their eyes."

"*It's a stinkin' mouse!* Vermin! A pestilence-carrying rodent!"

Erica peered inside. "Its coat is shiny and smooth. That means it's healthy."

"It's probably carrying the bubonic plague. Or that hantavirus thing."

"Only deer mice carry hantavirus. The mice around here are as healthy as you and I."

Megan's eyes narrowed. "You just said *mice*, plural. Don't tell me you have more of these things?"

"Just three."

Megan looked around wildly, as if expecting a mouse attack. "Where are they?"

"Don't freak out. They're in the backyard. But they'd love to come inside and be roomies with Hamlet."

"Over my dead body." Megan pressed her lips together. She appeared to think hard. "Look, Erica, you can't put a wild mouse in with a domesticated hamster. They'd have nothing in common. What would they talk about?"

"What do you and Austin talk about?"

"Shut up, and get that thing out of here."

* * *

Following an afternoon jog under cloudy skies, Erica showered and was towel-drying her long hair when she heard a noise from downstairs. She tilted her head to listen, knowing Liz and Megan were at work. The floor creaked, and there was the sound of water running in the kitchen.

Someone was in the house.

Setting the towel on the counter, Erica moved quietly into her bedroom. Opening her drawer slowly, Erica pulled her gun out of its holster then crept to the top of the stairs. The water had stopped, but there were other sounds. Barefoot, Erica went down the steps one at a time, arms outstretched, her revolver pointed and ready to shoot.

Taking aim, Erica barked, "I have a gun. Turn around slowly, and put your hands up!"

BJ turned. Seeing the gun, he dropped the cup of water, which crashed to the floor. Water splashed his jeans, and he raised his hands even as Erica lowered her gun.

"BJ! What are you doing in here?"

"Getting a drink of water. I didn't know you were home." A little color came up in BJ's tanned face, and he blinked. "You've got a gun."

"That's right. And you have a key to the house."

He gulped. "Do you want it back?"

BJ sounded so plaintive, she was tempted to smile. Instead, Erica said, "That would probably be a good idea."

"Here it is." He handed it over. His voice sounded mild enough, but for just a moment, Erica fancied a different expression showed itself in BJ's pale blue eyes. Then it was gone.

"Good thing you had a plastic glass," Erica said as she grabbed a towel.

After helping mop up the water, BJ straightened. "Did you catch the person that's after Liz?"

"Not yet."

"When Liz came home for lunch today, she told me she had a good time at the beach, but I can tell she's still scared." BJ scratched his stubbly chin. "Is there anything I can do?"

"Maybe. Tell me about Frank. What do you think of him?"

"Frank? He's okay."

"Did you know Frank wants this house?"

BJ nodded. "Liz told me Frank is trying to get it condemned. But Liz and I have done a lot of work on the yard. It looks a lot better than it used to."

"It's nice of you to help Liz." Erica looked at the handyman curiously. "Has Frank ever talked to you about Crooked House?"

"Sometimes. Mostly, he asks me what the house is like on the inside—you know—the plumbing and electrical and other stuff." BJ tugged at his ear like he was nervous. "I told him everything was fine."

"You've worked for Frank and know him better than I do. Do you think he'd hurt Liz in order to get the house?"

"I don't think so," he said slowly, considerable doubt in his voice. Then BJ's voice changed, becoming grim and determined. "If I thought he wanted to hurt Liz, I'd stop him."

"Has Frank ever made any kind of comment about Liz that sounded like a threat?"

"No." BJ shook his head emphatically. "If he had, I would have told the police."

After BJ left, Erica paced the front room while she worked out exactly what she planned to say that evening. That is, as long as her visit to the nurse that afternoon went as expected. Earlier, Erica had called Park Place Realty and spoken to Dolores. No, Donna was not there but would be later. Yes, she would tell Donna that Erica needed to talk and would be over later.

The back door opened, and Erica turned to see Megan slam it shut. Then she flung her backpack to the kitchen floor, where it skittered across and hit the wall with a soft thud. Her black hair was disheveled from the blustery wind.

Erica came to stand in the doorway. "What's going on?"

"I should have known—*I should have known!*" Megan clamped her arms across her chest as if physically trying to hold herself together. "He always did seem too good to be true. Now I know why." Her eyes were overly bright.

"What happened?"

"I found out someone was not the person I thought he was."

"This is no time to be metaphysical. Define 'he.'"

"Austin, of course."

Erica felt a sinking in her stomach. "What did he do?"

"He lied to me. *Lied!*" Megan's face was anguished. "I knew Austin was too nice to be true. It's not possible for someone to be as nice as I thought he was."

Erica sat at the kitchen table. "Sit down, and tell me what happened."

Megan rubbed her eyes with her fists—like a child. Then she pulled a chair out and sat across from Erica.

"I asked Austin about going to lunch today, and he said he couldn't—that he was busy. Okay, no big deal." Megan gave a slight shrug. "I grabbed a sandwich in the student center then went to the Dover Mall. I wanted to look for a pair of pants. Afterwards, I went to get a pretzel at Auntie Anne's, and guess who I saw at the Dairy Queen?" Megan didn't wait for

Erica to hazard a guess but answered in glacial tones, "Austin—*and* he had company."

Rats.

"He was having lunch with a beautiful blonde! So much for being too 'busy' to have lunch with me." Megan jumped restlessly to her feet and strode to the sink.

"But you're not going steady with him," Erica pointed out. "You're seeing Todd too."

"I knew you wouldn't understand." Megan said bitterly, without turning around.

It was amazing how much Megan sounded like Erica's teenage daughter, Aby. She would try to reason with Megan, even though that hadn't yet worked with Aby. "Let me see if I've got this straight. It's okay for you to date Todd, but Austin can't date anyone else."

"That's different," Megan snapped. "I *tell* Austin whenever I go out with Todd."

"Oh, that's got to make him feel good."

Megan ignored the sarcasm. "But Austin didn't tell me he was going out with someone else."

"Maybe it's someone he works with."

"It isn't. I know everyone at Park Place Realty." Megan's eyes were shining with unshed tears.

"It could be someone interested in buying a home."

"Right. A beautiful blonde with no husband in sight." Megan gulped. "Stop trying to find excuses for him—it makes me want to strangle you. Besides, you're missing the point, which is that Austin lied! He should have told me he couldn't have lunch because he had a date with some other girl."

"But Austin did tell you he was busy. I not sure that not telling you *what* he was doing qualifies as a lie."

"Okay then, but Austin *did* deceive me." Megan's voice was pure ice. "What's the difference? I'm just glad to know what kind of a person he is now, before things got too serious."

Before they got serious? If Erica had read the signs right, Austin and Megan's relationship was already serious. Hadn't they just talked about that yesterday? Erica tried to think of what she could say. Perhaps a little dose of honesty. It was one thing to be overly dramatic when you were Aby's age, but another when you were in your twenties.

"Megan, you need to get a hold of yourself," Erica said sternly. "I know you're upset, but you have to calm down, think things through, and not jump to conclusions. Besides, I'm sure there's a simple explanation. Austin really cares about you—I've seen how his face lights up when you're with him. Talk to him, and find out what's going on."

"I intend to." Megan ran up the stairs. A few seconds later, her bedroom door slammed shut.

* * *

The pungent smell of an orange filled the air as Erica peeled one at the kitchen table. She always tried to keep the peel in one long strip. *Oops—not today.* The strip broke as Liz, who had been studying in the front room, came in.

"I'm going to change. I work this afternoon."

"You do? I hoped you could show me that e-mail from Joel you told me about."

"Come on up. I can show it to you now."

Giving Liz part of the orange, Erica rinsed her hands. Upstairs in her bedroom, Liz opened the bottom drawer in her dresser and pulled out a thick folder.

"Wow, you printed them all out," Erica commented as Liz thumbed through the stack of paper. "And they're in chronological order—very nice."

Liz smiled. "I'm glad you approve." There was an occasional postcard between the printed pages, and she held one up. "Joel always sent me postcards from where he was racing." She paused and, in a sad voice, said, "I was going to make a scrapbook."

Erica picked up a postcard of the Eiffel Tower and turned it over. It was addressed to Miss Angel Johnson.

Liz said softly, "That was his nickname for me—Angel."

"Do you still have the e-mails on your computer?"

"Oh yes, I couldn't delete them."

There was quite a stack. Liz ruffled through the file, reading snippets here and there. Then she pulled one out and handed it to Erica. "This is the one I told you about."

Dearest Angel,

I wish you were here with me. It seems like I've been away from you forever. Hope school is going good. Can't wait until we're back together. I've been thinking about our future. I'll be glad when we're married so you can travel with me.

I know you worry about me racing, but don't. I'm a good driver, and my pit crew is the best. They make sure my car is in perfect condition.

You may have heard there was an accident at the track today. A backmarker got lapped. He tried too hard to catch up and lost control. Fortunately, he went into the catch fence and didn't take anyone out with him. He's fine. But it made me think about you.

It's funny—I know you worry about me, but I worry just as much about you and what you would do if anything happened to me. I've taken steps and made sure that if anything should happen, you'll be taken care of.

It's late, and I've got to get some sleep.

Love, Joel

Erica asked, "What's a backmarker?"

"A driver who's behind all the other racers."

"I see." Erica glanced at the paper again. "Well, after reading this, I think it's pretty clear Joel was saying you'd be taken care of financially if something happened to him. Joel probably wasn't more explicit because he didn't want to worry you."

* * *

After Liz left for work, Erica took advantage of the quiet house to call home and talk with her children. Then she spoke to David. As they talked about the confrontation she planned to have with Donna, there was a rumble, and Erica went to look out the front room window. The clouds that had threatened all day were finally making good on their promise. Rain pelted the windows, making trails as gravity pulled the droplets down.

"Are you sure you want to get involved in this, Erica?" David sounded uncertain. "It really doesn't have anything to do with you. Why don't you just go to the police?"

It was tempting. "I guess I could, but I'm not sure the police can do anything. Because of that, it might be better for everyone if this was handled as quietly as possible. Of course, the police might still have to get involved, but I won't know for sure until I talk with Donna. All I know is that this has to stop before it goes any further."

"And you're sure about what's been going on?"

"As much as I can be. The identical handwriting clinched it. I'm going to stop at Donna's house and talk to the nurse before I go to Park Place Realty. Hopefully she'll verify my suspicions."

"All right. Good luck, and let me know how it turns out."

Rummaging in the closet, Erica found an umbrella and walked to the bus stop.

On Donna's front porch, Erica flapped the water off her umbrella and rang the doorbell. The nurse, a friendly, capable-looking young woman with a soft mass of blonde hair, invited her inside when Erica explained who she was and that she was staying with Donna's niece, Liz.

Erica told the woman she had a friend who was interested in becoming an RN but wanted to take care of patients at their home. She wanted to know more about it, if the nurse wouldn't mind talking with her. Erica had a way of putting people at ease, and seeming pleased to help, the nurse answered all sorts of questions about private care nursing, past and present patients, her schedule, and even her salary, which was considerable.

In the end, Erica felt satisfied that her suspicions were correct, although she was by no means happy about it.

* * *

Dolores eyed Erica as she wiped her shoes on the rug. Glancing around to see if anyone was within earshot, Dolores leaned over and confided in a conspiratorial whisper, "Donna's not in a very good mood. You might want to talk with her another time."

"It can't wait, but thanks for the warning."

Donna's door was shut, so Erica knocked.

"Come in." When Erica stepped in, the older woman's face was hard. "What kind of game are you playing? Dolores told me you called and wanted to talk to me but that you wouldn't leave a message."

"It's rather involved—I thought it would be better to talk with you in person."

After a pointed glance at the clock on the wall, Donna said, "It's late, and I need to get home. Can this wait until tomorrow?"

"Tonight would be better." Erica leaned her damp umbrella by the door. "Since all the other employees have gone home."

Donna drew back—a nervous, irritable creature at bay. Her eyes were darkly intent and questioning. "Why does that matter?"

"What I have to say would be best said in private."

The door opened, and Austin peeked in. "Hi, Erica. I didn't know you were here." Then he saw his mother's face. "Is something wrong?"

"I need to get home, but Erica says she has to talk to me." Donna picked up her purse and stood. Her hands were trembling.

"I'd really like to talk with you tonight," Erica said to Donna. "But if you can't make the time, I can go talk to your boss instead."

"Mr. Rochford?" Austin looked in confusion from Erica to his mother, who appeared as though she had been doused in ice water. "Why would you need to talk to him?"

"Ask your mother." Although Erica spoke gently, there was a warning in her tone as she addressed Donna. "You've been hiding something for quite a while, and it's time you came out with it. You can talk to me, or I can go to Mr. Rochford or even to the police. It's your choice."

Chapter Seventeen

Donna went to the door, and for a moment, Erica thought she would walk out. But she merely shut the door. Coming back to her desk, Donna sat abruptly. It was if the strength had suddenly left her legs.

"Mom, what's going on?" Alarmed, Austin pulled around a chair to sit close.

One of the questions still in Erica's mind was if Austin had played any part in it. She spoke directly to Donna. "First of all, I need to know if Austin knew what you were doing."

"No. He had nothing to do with it." Donna's fingers clasped the arm of her chair, and although her voice sounded hollow, it was firm.

"Why are you talking about me as if I weren't here?" Austin sounded irritated. "What is this about?"

"Would you like to tell him?" There was no threat in Erica's voice—only a matter-of-fact calmness. Their eyes locked, and it was clear Donna understood—either she told Austin, or Erica would. Something passed over Donna's features like the shadow of a bird flying across water. An expression of anguish twisted her face. Austin reached for her hand, but she drew away.

"You're probably wondering how much I know," Erica told Donna. "Let me say it's enough. I just left your house, where I had a long talk with the nurse you hired for your father. That confirmed my suspicions."

"Suspicions about *what*?" Austin spoke up impatiently. "Why would you talk with the nurse? Is this about her salary? You've asked how we could afford a private nurse, and I told you my grandfather had insurance. But I don't see what business that is of yours."

"Your mother may have told you he had insurance, but that's not quite the truth. Is it, Donna?"

Mother and son exchanged glances, and Donna's eyes fell before Austin's searching look. Then Donna said, "My dad talked about getting long-term care insurance, but he never got around to it."

"What?" Austin was astonished. "But you told me Grandpa had insurance."

"I didn't want you to worry." Donna's face was gray and pinched. It looked bloodless.

"What about his Social Security and Medicare?"

"Medicare only provides nursing care if it's necessary after a hospital stay and the patient is getting better. Social Security helps, but it doesn't make a dent in what it costs for a nurse." Donna sounded like this was something she had gone over time and again. She rubbed her face tiredly. "Dad had some money, but it didn't last long. It's been a lot more expensive than I thought it would be to keep him at home."

"So this is why you've been so stressed," Austin said as enlightenment dawned. "I wish you'd told me what was going on. I thought maybe something else was wrong with Grandpa, so I had lunch with the nurse to find out."

Ah, so *that* explained the lunch date Megan was so upset about. But now was not the time to get into that. Erica stared pointedly at Donna, who appeared close to tears.

"I can't do it," Donna whispered with a shake of her head. "Go ahead and tell him."

There really was no easy way to say it, Erica knew, so keeping it short, she said bluntly, "Your mother has been embezzling from Park Place Realty."

Austin's eyes were circles of incredulity. "I don't believe it." The young man's voice was uncomprehending, even though the truth was written there on his mother's ravaged face.

"I wasn't going to keep the money," Donna cried out, her voice bleak. "I just needed to borrow it for a while. I always meant to put it back."

"Why don't you tell us the truth," Erica said. "And keep it short. I don't want either one of us getting dizzy from too much unadulterated honesty."

It was a verbal slap, but Donna didn't react. Instead, her face and voice became oddly toneless. "An old friend of mine told me he had a sure investment deal—very short term. It was too good to pass up, especially since I needed to hire a nurse, so I borrowed money from the firm and invested it. Three weeks later, I put all the money back, having made enough to pay a nurse for a full month." A note of defensiveness crept into her voice. "It didn't hurt anyone."

"So you did it again." It wasn't a question Erica was asking.

"Yes." Donna sounded bitter. "My friend came and talked to me again. I didn't want to do it, but he caught me at a bad time."

"You needed the money for your father."

"You've got to understand," Donna pleaded with Erica. "My father was terrified when he found out he had Alzheimer's. He made me promise I wouldn't put him in a home. At first, it wasn't too bad. I went over to his house every morning and every night to make sure he ate and to give him his meds. When his health began to fail, I hired a neighbor to help him during the day." A few tears spilled and ran down Donna's cheeks. Erica felt sorry for her but had to wonder, were they tears of remorse or tears because she'd got caught?

Donna went on. "His health got so bad I had to hire an aide. Later, I moved him to my home, but shortly after, Dad needed a full-time nurse." The grayness of disappointment and anxiety was clear in Donna's voice—the blackness of no hope.

"I know this has been hard on you and that you've done all you can to take care of him," Erica said. "But even though your father didn't want to go to a nursing home, would he have resisted if he knew keeping that promise would bankrupt you?"

"But I promised!" This came out as a keening wail as Donna bent forward and covered her face with her hands.

Austin had appeared dazed, trying to take everything in, but now he spoke up in a choked voice. "Mom, Grandpa doesn't even realize where he is—and hasn't for months. He doesn't even know who we are. You don't need to feel bad about putting him in a home. If Grandpa was lucid even part of the time, it would be different."

Donna uncovered her face and asked Erica wretchedly, "How did you find out?"

"It was a long process, but I'd say it started the first time I talked to you. Do you remember? I told you I was a private investigator, and you said you knew why I was calling."

"I thought for sure my boss had hired you."

"I can see now why you would think that. Yet even after you knew I was here on Liz's account, you still seemed unfriendly and nervous. Then you lied and said you were showing a house when Liz was pushed into traffic."

Donna looked aggrieved. "I had to talk to my bank manager that day about some bounced checks, but I didn't want to tell you that."

"It would have been better if you had." Erica shifted in her chair. "All along, I wondered how you could afford a private nurse on your salary and real estate commissions." When Donna started to interrupt, Erica raised her hand lightly in a gesture that was not so much a *request* to let her continue speaking as a signal indicating she was *going* to continue.

"When I talked with your nurse this afternoon, she let it slip that you paid her in cash. One of the first things I learned working on white-collar crime is that the biggest tip-off to embezzlement is when an employee seems to have unlimited amounts of cash. The second is when a person has been in the same position for a long time and has the trust of their employer, making it easy to siphon money away from the business. You fit both."

"But you have no real proof," Donna said, earning a glance of reproach from her son.

"I got evidence when I found that paycheck you wrote to yourself."

Donna's face went white. "You saw it. I thought you might have when I saw you snooping in my desk." Her voice was like acid.

"Technically, *on* your desk," Erica corrected. "And I'm a private eye—so sue me. And I was straightening your desk because—let's face it—it was a mess. When I saw your paycheck, I noticed the date. Later, I remembered Austin saying payday was on the seventeenth, but your check had been written a week later."

Erica went on. "I also saw some notes on your desk that you'd written to yourself. The writing seemed familiar, but it took me a while to realize it was because the check was in the same handwriting—even the signature."

Austin stared at his mother. "You *forged* Mr. Rochford's signature?"

"Your mother didn't even try to imitate his writing," Erica said, "because no one was ever going to see the check."

Donna ran her hands through her short hair as if she wanted to pull it out.

Facing Austin, Erica continued. "Your mother had authority to write checks—so she wrote checks to herself then cashed them."

She turned to Donna. "I thought about going to Mr. Rochford, but I didn't because I know the main reason you embezzled was to take care of your father. Your one saving grace is that you weren't motivated by greed but by need. So I'm giving you a chance to confess. If you do, Mr. Rochford might be more lenient than if I told him. But I expect you to tell him tonight."

Knowing she was beaten, Donna agreed to do so.

"Now, besides writing unauthorized checks, were there any other ways you embezzled?"

After a few moments, Donna confessed, "I created a false vendor account to bill Park Place for fictitious services and cashed the checks myself." Her voice was flat. When Austin looked sick, his mother blurted, "I really thought I could just borrow the money, invest it, and put it back—having made enough to pay for my dad's care. But the investments didn't do as well as the first time. I was always short and needed more money. At the time, it seemed to be the only thing I could do, but I know taking money from the company was the most foolish thing I've ever done."

Austin had been watching his mother in troubled perplexity. In a strangled voice, he asked, "How much did you take?"

His mother was so quiet that Erica wondered if she would answer. Shooting an uneasy glance at Erica, Donna said, "I kept a ledger so I could pay it back. It's around $30,000."

"That's enough to be a felony," Erica informed her grimly. "And, attempted murder is also a felony."

Donna's wide, terrified eyes fixed themselves on Erica. "I never tried to kill Liz."

Erica wasn't so sure. There might be more to this embezzlement than what met the eye, and she wasn't convinced Donna had told the full story. "Desperate people do desperate things."

"It's the truth, Erica," Donna spoke with sudden fierce energy. "You've got to believe me. I'm not the one who's been trying to kill Liz."

"I have a hard time believing someone who's been cheating their employer for months."

* * *

The early morning air was clean and fresh with the scent of yesterday's rain and of growing things. Everything had a rinsed, fresh look under the lemony sunlight as Erica strolled the backyard of Crooked House. David had worked an extra shift last night, so Erica was just now telling him about her encounter with Donna.

"Donna was acting so strangely that something had to be going on," David said. "Financial hardship is what most often pushes people to commit white-collar crime. The majority of people who embezzle see taking money as a short-term loan. They need it for rent or bills or, like Donna, for unexpected medical expenses. Medical care is so expensive nowadays that it's a real hardship on people—but don't get me started on health care in the US."

"Anything but that," Erica begged. She sat on a bench beside a three-foot-tall sundial, and a butterfly flitted past. She and her husband both agreed health care desperately needed an overhaul but differed substantially on how it should be done.

"Have you heard from Donna on how it went with her boss last night?"

"Not yet, but I'm dying to know. Austin was going to go with her."

"Do you think her boss will report it to the police?"

"He might, because Donna did commit a crime. But the police usually don't have the resources to investigate white-collar crime—not unless the employer can prove the money went across state lines, and that didn't happen here. Regardless, I thought I'd call Detective Ranquist and let him know what happened."

"Good idea. And you know Donna is going to zoom to the top of his list of suspects. I bet she knew Adam was a millionaire and that Liz was going to inherit his fortune. Either that or she wanted to get her hands on Crooked House. Even needing repairs, the house would bring in big bucks if it were sold."

Erica had to admit it was possible. A Steller's jay, with its cheeky little topknot, hopped along the cobbled pathway, and Erica held still so as not to frighten it as David went on.

"Think about it. Donna was desperate for money—that's a given because of her embezzling—and if Liz were eliminated, Donna would get all the money she needed to take care of her father *and* pay back her boss. In her mind, she probably saw it as having two choices: either kill Liz, or go to jail for embezzlement."

Erica wasn't totally convinced. "Donna does have a good motive, but I still have questions."

"Such as?"

"Right now I'm working on some ideas, but they're not very clear yet." Her thoughts were so indefinable and ambiguous, there was no way Erica could put them into words. She felt like she was missing something, and until she could catch onto it and put it in a comprehensible form, nothing would make sense.

Her husband sighed then asked, "Did the appraiser ever get back with you?"

"I finally got a hold of him yesterday. For all the good it did. He said his boss hasn't had time to go over his pictures or notes yet."

"I had no idea appraisers were such busy people," David said.

"I think this is a classic case of getting what you pay for. If I'd been a paying customer, I bet Andrew's boss would have been on the phone to me days ago."

"Perhaps Liz ought to pay to have that desk and the cabinet appraised." He paused then teased, "Or you could ask Frank to come over and examine them. He sounds like an expert."

"And have another murder if Liz finds him in the house? No thanks."

* * *

"Erica!" Megan's voice floated up the stairs.

"Be right there." There was something in Megan's tone that made Erica hurry. She hurried down to the front room and found Megan pacing back and forth on the green rug. Her arms were folded tightly across her chest. Not a good sign.

"You told me to talk to Austin. Said I should ask him *calmly* about his little lunch with that blonde." Megan took a hiccup of a breath and hurried on. "So I go to Park Place Realty, and Dolores tells me Austin just left a few minutes ago. I asked her where he went, and she said Austin went to a pawn shop."

"A pawn shop?"

"Yeah. I asked her which one, and Dolores said Austin had her look up the address for Arrow Pawn shop. It was only a few blocks away, so I walked over."

Oh boy, Erica thought as she slumped onto the couch. This had all the earmarks of a real disaster.

"I went inside, and Austin's at the counter, talking with the clerk. I hid behind a display so he couldn't see me."

Spying on Austin. This was getting worse and worse.

"He and the clerk were looking at a bunch of necklaces and rings and stuff." Full of indignation, Megan's voice rose, and her eyes had a knife-edge glitter. "Austin was pawning a bunch of jewelry!"

"Where'd he get it?"

"That's what I'd like to know. When he started to leave, I popped out and he nearly jumped out of his skin." Megan made a face. "He asked me what I was doing there, and I told him I was looking for an iPhone. Then I asked him what *he* was doing there. He turned red and said he was just looking at stuff. Ha! Austin's a terrible liar."

Erica waited for the next installment.

"I told Austin I'd seen him with a bunch of jewelry, and I asked him what he was doing. He said he couldn't talk about it. But he seemed upset." Megan's eyes flashed fire. "I told him if he had to keep secrets, there was no sense in us talking about *anything*. And I walked off."

"Oh, Megan," Erica said sorrowfully.

"It's all right." Although her face was ravaged, Megan had control of her voice. "Like I said before, Austin did always seem too good to be true. Now I know he was."

"I'm sure there's a reasonable explanation." Erica wanted so badly to tell Megan that Austin was probably pawning his mother's jewelry to get her debt down. But she couldn't, not without revealing what Donna had done.

"Right. He's a thief. A thief who likes to keep secrets. Now I know how different we really are. And then Austin had the gall to be upset with *me*!"

"Come on, Megan." Erica tried to stay calm even though she felt Megan was being entirely too judgmental. "You don't know his reasons, you haven't listened to his side of the story, so stop judging him. You used to do this when you were a kid, and you're doing it now." Erica took a deep breath. "And it doesn't matter how different two people are if you love each other. There aren't any guarantees in life or marriage. If that's what you're looking for, you'd better go live with a car battery. By the way, Erma Bombeck said that."

"But you *have* to be honest." Megan stood in front of the fireplace, her face red and upset. "Austin called me later, and when I asked him again to tell me the truth, he said he couldn't. So I hung up." When Erica groaned, Megan shot back, "If Austin can't tell me the truth, I don't want anything to do with him. He's the most obstinate person I've ever seen."

Erica stood up. Taking Megan by the shoulders, she guided Megan to the gilt-framed mirror. "No, *this* is the most obstinate person I've ever seen."

Megan's mouth began to tremble, and without warning, she took a few steps and crumpled onto the couch, crying as if her heart would break.

Erica went to hold Megan until the storm subsided. Then she handed the girl a box of tissues, went to the kitchen, and returned with a bar of chocolate, which she handed over. "Cheaper than therapy, right?"

Megan gave her a watery smile. Then, with a small twinkle in her eyes, she looked at the chocolate bar. "Do you have any with nuts?"

"Are you kidding? David knows better than to send me something like that. Nuts just take up the space where chocolate ought to be." Erica smiled warmly then turned serious. "Try again to talk with Austin. As it happens, I found out all about his lunch, and it's not what you think." When Megan began to sputter and shoot out half-formed questions, Erica cut her off. "And no, I'm not saying a word. This is something you and Austin need to work out." Erica brought her legs up on the couch. "Now, there's something else I need to tell you, and it's very important. I've got a gut feeling that things are coming to a head and that whoever is after Liz is getting desperate, so I'm putting a gag order on you and Liz. I don't want either one of you talking to *anyone* about the case—*not even each other*, and certainly not Todd, Austin, Donna, or any of your friends."

Puzzled, Megan looked at her out of red, swollen eyes. "Why can't I talk to Liz?"

"Liz is so open she might let something slip that could put her or you in danger. And I'm going to tell her the same thing—she isn't to talk to *anyone*—including you."

What Erica didn't say—but hoped Megan understood—was her fear that the murderer wouldn't hesitate to kill anyone who got in his way. A shadow lay over Crooked House, and Erica was unable to shake the feeling that some dreadful calamity was about to occur. Erica had known ever since the car bomb that Megan was in nearly as much danger as Liz. The murderer was ruthless, and Megan had to understand this.

"I mean it," Erica stressed. "You cannot say *one word* to anyone. Even if you overhear me talking to Detective Ranquist, you are not to say anything to Liz. The best way to protect her is to say nothing."

Chapter Eighteen

THE NEXT MORNING WHEN ERICA left Crooked House, Frank was snipping old blooms off his roses. She waved and, in return, received a glare before he returned to his work. Erica climbed in Megan's car and drove to Donna's cream brick house.

When she knocked, Austin opened the door. He looked worn out. He hadn't shaved, and beard stubble showed dark on his face. *Not a good sign*, Erica thought. Donna must not be doing well if her son was here. Austin showed her into the simply furnished front room then went to get his mother.

Wearing a wrinkled blouse and blue jeans, Donna walked in slowly—as if it took a real effort. She sat on the couch with Erica. She wore no makeup, and her face was drawn and tired-looking. Austin sat in a nearby chair.

"How did it go with your boss?" Erica asked, though it was evident from the slump of Donna's shoulders and the dark circles under her eyes that it hadn't gone well.

"Horrible." Donna said succinctly. "George felt betrayed, and rightly so. I told him I'd pay him back—every penny—but he was so angry he called the police. I've never been so scared in my life."

"The policeman told him that if he didn't have an airtight case and solid proof, the case would never make it to court," Austin said. "That made Mr. Rochford even more angry, and he kept arguing."

Donna sat still—it was as if she had no energy to move. "When he got off the phone, George said the policeman had told him that these kind of cases take years to prosecute but that he didn't care—he was going to get a lawyer and pursue it." She bowed her head. "I've never seen him so angry."

"Mr. Rochford cooled down eventually, mostly because we reassured him he'd get his money back," Austin said.

Donna bit her lip. "George, Austin, and I talked for hours and finally worked out a deal. I'm going to give him a small lump sum now—as much as I can scrape together—and I'll also sign over my final paycheck. He agreed to take monthly payments for the balance of what I took. George will also work up a termination document that outlines terms of confidentiality and restitution. If we follow those terms, George said he wouldn't prosecute."

"I've got a little money saved, and I'll give that to him," Austin said. Donna began to protest, but he told her, "No. We've been through this. I'm going to do it."

"I'm glad Mr. Rochford decided to be lenient," Erica said.

"I am too—very relieved," Donna whispered.

Then Erica turned to Austin. "Did you go to Arrow Pawn Shop?"

Austin frowned. "I see you've been talking to Megan."

"You went to Arrow Pawn?" Donna leaned forward, hands on knees and sounding upset.

"Easy, Mom," Austin said. "Remember when I had to move your car the other day? When I got your keys, I found a pawn ticket in your purse. I went to Arrow Pawn to see what you'd taken in. The clerk showed me a whole bunch of your necklaces, bracelets, and rings."

"Why didn't you just ask me?"

"And get the same answer I've gotten the past six months?" Austin's impatient tone showed his annoyance. "Every time I've tried to talk to you, you brush me off. You were always telling me everything was fine when I knew that wasn't true."

Leaning back, Donna closed her eyes a moment, looking contrite. "I'm sorry. I didn't want you to worry. And I didn't want you to know I'd pawned my jewelry to pay the nurse."

"I don't imagine you got much for it," Erica said.

"No, I didn't," Donna admitted frankly, massaging her temples. "But it was enough to pay her for last month." She turned to Erica. "I called the nurse this morning and said I couldn't afford her anymore. She was really nice about it and told me about an assisted living facility that takes really good care of their patients. I'm going to call and see if they have an opening." Donna rose slowly, as if her body ached. "I've got a splitting headache, so if you don't mind, I'm going to take something for it and go sit with my father."

Austin watched her shuffle down the hallway. Then in a low voice, he confided, "I still can't believe Mom took money from Park Place. I knew she was worried, but she'd never talk to me about it. She still thinks I'm twelve years old, I guess." He sighed deeply. "I just want you to know, Erica, that this is really out of character for her. Last night when we got home, Mom said she knew taking the money was wrong but that she was just trying to keep her promise to Grandpa. Then she fell apart and couldn't stop crying. I finally gave her a sleeping pill." His eyes watched Erica intently, as if gauging her thoughts and feelings.

"Sometimes people can get caught up in circumstances and do something wrong for the right reason. They think the end justifies the means, and now your mom is realizing that isn't so. I'm sorry for your mom, I really am. I know how much it hurts to have a loved one decline. It was hard to watch my grandmother when she got Alzheimer's and didn't know who I was. I loved her and wanted to do everything I could for her. It must be even harder when it's your own parent who's slipping away."

They sat for a time in silence, each with their own thoughts. Then Austin said. "I know you think Mom might be the one trying to kill Liz, but she wouldn't do that."

"Of course not." Erica hadn't meant to sound sarcastic, but that's how it came out. She changed the subject. "Did you know that when Megan saw you, she thought you were pawning that jewelry?"

"*Pawning it?*" Austin was astonished. "Just where does she think I got it?" He stared at Erica. "No, don't tell me—she probably thinks I stole it. Well, it's nice to know Megan has such a high opinion of me."

Now, that was sarcastic.

* * *

When Megan came downstairs after a prolonged study session, she leaned against the counter, where Erica was busily chopping an onion on a wooden cutting board. "I'm sick and tired of studying. I'm so glad school will be over next week. Two more finals, and I'm done." Stretching her neck, she peered into the front room. "Where's Liz?"

"At work. I told her I was going to make Beef Casserole,[11] something easy to heat up for dinner." Erica scraped the onion into the frying pan along with hamburger that was beginning to sizzle. "Make yourself useful," Erica said, handing Megan a block of cheese. "Grate a cup, will you?"

---

11 See the appendix at the end of the book for this recipe.

Megan unwrapped the cheese and asked, "Do you still want to go to the NASCAR races with me and Todd? We're going Saturday."

"I'd love to, but I thought you were going with Austin."

"Not anymore. He can go with his new girlfriend."

"You haven't talked with him yet?" Erica's brow furrowed. "How can you be jealous when you don't even know what that lunch was about?"

"Austin can do what he wants. I don't care."

Erica shook her head in disgust. Sometimes Megan could be soooo exasperating. She yanked off some paper towels and blotted the fat off the hamburger. "For your information, I know what Austin was doing at lunch and also at the pawn shop, and it's not what you're thinking."

Megan turned sharply. "What *was* he doing?"

"If you really want to know, you can start acting like a reasonable, mature human being and talk to Austin. Stop being a brat and hanging up on him."

"I only did that once. Now I'm just not taking his calls."

"You're being childish. Push Austin too far, and he'll stop calling."

Megan stood very still.

"Come on, Megan, I know you're upset, but you're not being fair. Talk to him," Erica urged. "You're so unhappy."

"I'm fine."

"Sure you are. If your face was any longer you'd be tripping on it." Erica rapped a round package of refrigerated biscuits sharply on the edge of the countertop. When it split open, it sounded like a gun going off.

"So do you want to come with me and Todd or not?"

"I'd like to, but three is a crowd."

"Not in this case. Liz and Donna are coming too." Megan measured the cheese, and when she saw there was too much, she took a pinch and ate it. "And just for *your* information, I talked with Todd. I told him that while I liked him, we weren't going anywhere—relationship wise—and asked if we could just be friends."

Holding a spoon in midair, Erica stared. "Wow. So you dropped him. Just like Liz. What did he say?"

"Todd said he really liked me but would respect my decision. Then, if you can believe it, he asked me if Liz could go with us to the races." Megan made a face. "What a jerk. Oh well, what do I care? So there will be five of us going."

"Six, if I invite Austin." Erica put the last of the biscuits on the casserole, covered it with foil, and put it in the fridge.

"You wouldn't dare."

"I just might." Erica stared calmly at Megan.

"I'll never speak to you again."

"All the more reason."

* * *

When Erica stopped by Park Place Realty that afternoon, Austin was talking to Dolores at the front desk. He looked up. "Why, hello, Erica, what can I do for you?"

"I wondered if I could talk to you a minute."

"Sure, come on back."

As Erica took a seat, she eyed the pencils on his desk, standing upright in their round container. They were all of varying lengths. The effect was highly disturbing.

Austin slid some papers over and sat on the edge of his desk. "How's Megan?"

"Sad and hurting, but determined not to show it."

"She is so stubborn! I've tried calling her, but she won't pick up." Austin looked glum.

To butt in or not to butt in—that was the question. But then, wasn't that why she had come? Erica decided to come straight out with it. "Megan saw you having lunch with the nurse—the same day you'd told Megan you were too busy to eat with her."

"Oh, great." Austin grimaced and ruffled up his hair between his fingers until it stood up all over his head. "Did you tell her why?"

"Nope. Tattling to you is as far as I'll go. I told Megan to talk with you about it. But since I'm blabbing, I will say Megan's pretty upset you weren't straight with her about lunch."

"Yeah, that was a mistake."

Unwillingly, Erica's green eyes were drawn back to the pencils. "I know I'm jumping around, but hadn't you two planned on going to the NASCAR races?"

"That's off now," Austin said bitterly. "Mom said Megan invited her and Liz to go on Saturday and that Todd's going. I thought he'd be racing, but apparently he's only racing on Friday."

"Megan asked me to go, and I told her I was going to ask you to come."

Austin's face showed nothing. "What did she say?"

"Um . . . she became emotional."

He asked Erica doubtfully. "Is that good or bad?"

Erica wasn't about to explain. Her eyes strayed again to the pencils. Unable to resist any longer, Erica grabbed the longest five. "You don't mind if I sharpen these, do you?"

He peered at them. "They're not dull."

"No, but they're longer than the others."

Austin roared with laughter. "Be my guest."

Over the grinding of the electrical pencil sharpener, Erica asked, "So will you come?"

"Gee—it sounds like a lot of fun to tag along on a date with Megan and her boyfriend, but I could have just as much fun staying home and hitting my thumb with a hammer." Austin rolled his eyes and dropped the sarcasm. "I'll pass. I'd probably end up punching Todd. The only way I'd go is if they had tickets on the Monster Bridge."

"What's that?"

"The Monster Bridge sits over turn three on the race track. The seats are thirty feet above the track. Great views but very pricey."

"That sounds awesome, but I doubt they have tickets for that. But you really ought to come." Erica spoke cajolingly. "You might be able to finagle some alone time with Megan. Besides, she isn't serious about Todd."

"She's not?" There was a hopeful note in Austin's voice.

"I shouldn't be telling you this, but Megan had the 'let's be friends' talk with Todd. So come on and go with us. Megan, Liz, and I are going over to the track tomorrow around noon, and your mom is going to drive over later, so why don't you come with her? It might help smooth things over between you and Megan." When he appeared skeptical, Erica added, "At least it'll give you a fighting chance."

Austin thought for a minute. Then he nodded. "All right. I'll be there."

* * *

That night, Liz praised Erica's casserole and even took a second helping. Then after reading for a while, Liz went to bed early. Megan had gone to meet with a study group, so it was a perfect night for Erica to watch an old movie—one of her favorite things to do. She made popcorn, settled in bed, and clicked the remote. It was a windy night, and an errant draft from the closed windows stirred the curtains ever so slightly, making Erica glad she was wearing her fleece pajamas. The only light came from the TV and a lamp on her bedside table.

Erica munched away happily, watching *Cat on a Hot Tin Roof*. She loved Elizabeth Taylor and was only slightly annoyed when the movie action was stopped now and then by lengthy plugs asking viewers to support public broadcasting. Fortunately, the promotions weren't a complete loss, as they gave interesting tidbits about Elizabeth Taylor and Paul Newman.

When she heard a car, Erica thought Megan had come home, but when the girl didn't appear, Erica climbed out of bed. Light from the flickering TV cast long shadows around the room as she went to the window, where the wind was whispering eerily through the cracks. She pushed the draperies aside. Megan's car wasn't in the driveway. The sound must have come from one of the neighbors. Suddenly a light flickered around the storage shed. Erica gripped the windowsill, peering into the night. It stopped then flickered again.

Someone was out there.

Rats.

She'd have to go out there. After another long look into the darkness, Erica took a deep breath. *Don't remember the past. Don't.*

Erica grabbed a belt, cinched it around her waist, then strapped on her holstered gun. Slipping on her shoes, she hurried down the stairs and opened the side door. The night was dark, with only faint, intermittent light showing as clouds raced across the moon. The hedge between Crooked House and Frank's yard tossed in the wind as Erica opened the door. A light beading of sweat was already covering her forehead when she stepped out into the darkness.

Chapter Nineteen

A BREAK IN THE CLOUDS allowed moonlight to brush the persimmon trees with the sheen of rippling silver foil. When Erica slipped around the corner of the house, the wind hit her with full force. She stayed in the deepest shadows as she crept toward the newly completed deck. Seeing nothing, Erica crouched and followed the pathway of pale stone wedges in the lawn. When she stepped on an uneven stone, Erica stumbled and gasped involuntarily as she fought to regain her balance.

There was a faint scuff of footsteps off to the left, in the direction of Frank's yard. Erica twisted, jerking her head to get her long hair out of her eyes while straining to see. Her heart beat wildly as old, unbidden memories played across her mind. Alone. In a dark closet. Her throat sore from screaming.

A dark shadow appeared against the shed then disappeared around the corner. Had it been a play of moonlight and clouds or a human shadow?

The night air had grown cool, and Erica felt a chill as she inched toward the hedge that separated Liz's yard from Frank's. The wind twisted the trees in black silhouettes, and except for the rustling of leaves and branches overhead, there was no sound. Still crouching, Erica moved toward the shed. Clouds again covered the moon, and the night became a black entity, encasing the house and yard.

Reaching the shed, Erica pressed her back against the rough wood. She drew her gun, held it in front of her, and inhaled a gulp of air. After peering around the corner and seeing nothing, she went around it. Moving along, Erica rounded the next corner, stopping when she heard a noise. Taking a deep breath, Erica peered around the final corner.

No one was there.

With a slight frown, Erica straightened, lowered her Glock, and surveyed what she could see, which wasn't much. She sensed someone was close, but was it just her imagination telling her someone was near?

No, there was a sound—albeit a faint one—which left her sweating and cold. This time, it seemed to come from the direction of the gazebo. Erica moved carefully toward it in the thick, dusty shadows, trusting the darkness to keep her hidden.

A noise to her left caused Erica to spin round, and she moved stealthily toward it, moving as silently as possible and ignoring the shrubbery that slapped at her legs. Her foot crunched on a rock, and she bent near the ground, making herself small and holding very still.

Shredded clouds blew past the moon, allowing its light to touch the ground. With every touch of the wind, tree branches cast shadows like spidery fingers along the ground. Despite the noise she'd made, inadvertently announcing her presence, no one came at her, and there was no further sound. Erica crept again toward the gazebo.

Once again, there was an indeterminate noise. This time, it sounded like it had come from someplace near the house—possibly by the deck or from Frank's yard. Clouds blew across the face of the three-quarters moon, but they were so thin and gauzy, the night remained brightly lit.

As Erica gazed at Crooked House, a sudden strong gust caused the old house to groan faintly, and she felt again as though some dark presence abided there. What was this odd sense of evil she sensed about the house from time to time?

Again she had to consciously push old, childhood memories back. She picked her way through the dark garden, past the fountain, and on to the house. Her pajamas were damp with sweat.

Grass deadened the sound of her steps, and the black forms of bushes and trees stood as sentinels. Erica moved in the direction of the gloomy, towering house with its ghostly tilting turrets. She felt a coldness, as though some unknown terror was creeping up on her. Erica cast a glance at the sky, where the moon's silver beam etched a cloud. In a minute or two, the clouds would have sailed past, allowing the moonlight to shine down once again. The darkness made it difficult to see, but if she couldn't see, neither could she be seen.

Then, with a sudden chill, Erica remembered she hadn't locked the door. She shivered, and her eyes searched the outer brick walls of the darkened house. Surely the intruder wouldn't go into the house.

Or would he?

She considered. Erica had made enough noise to alert the trespasser to her presence. There had been no sound for some time. Surely he or she had fled in the night. Erica moved along the pathway, gun in hand, checking left and right to confirm no one was on either side as she approached the house.

No one was visible on the porch either. An intruder would have been silhouetted there. But could someone have gone inside already? An upward glance showed wind-driven clouds still covering the moon's face. She could wait a few seconds until they blew raggedly away, giving her more light to see—but no, she couldn't wait. Liz was in the house—asleep and utterly defenseless. She made her decision.

The wind tore at Erica as she ran for the house—buffeting her as though trying to beat her back, as though there was a purpose in its thrust. She reached the steps and, with shock, saw that the door was ajar. Erica was sure she'd shut it when she came out. Her heart was racing as she swung the door open. The kitchen light had been on when she left. Now, all was dark.

Standing utterly still and listening, Erica held her gun ready. An old house talks to itself at night and more so when the wind blows. Erica reached out to feel along the wall for the switch.

When the overhead light blazed, it revealed nothing out of the ordinary. Staying close to the wall, Erica peeked into the front room and flipped that switch. The room came to life, but the corners were dim. Cautiously, Erica checked it out. Nothing. Hearing a creaking sound, Erica turned abruptly. The sound had come from upstairs.

Erica went up as silently as possible. Passing her room, Erica noted her door was now open, but her concern was for Liz, and she went on. She took a quick breath, flung Liz's door open, and flipped the light switch. Liz stirred then groggily opened her eyes.

When she saw Erica roving through her bedroom, holding her gun, Liz sat upright. "What are you doing?" she asked in a low, fearful voice.

Erica held a finger to her lips then checked the closet. Nothing.

As the wind whistled in the chimney, Erica crossed to Liz and whispered, "Someone's in the house. I'm going to check the other rooms. Lock your door after I go out."

"Don't go," Liz cried. Slipping out of bed, she held onto the bedpost a moment, as if trying to get her bearings, then reached for her cell phone on the bedside table. "I'll call the police."

"Lock your door first." Erica went into the hallway. She waited for the click of the lock behind her before approaching Beth's room. Turning on the light, Erica sprang inside. But that room was also empty.

She paused before her door, fighting a sense of evil that seemed loosed upon the night. In spite of her gun, Erica was fearful as she peered inside. The lamp beside her bed was off, and as she flipped the switch, the room appeared in all its shocking turmoil. Bedspreads and blankets had been yanked off her and Megan's beds. Clothes pulled from drawers had been tossed on the floor. It was as if the intruder had been searching for something.

Erica went down the stairs cautiously since it seemed that the intruder had gone down while she'd been checking the rooms. In the distance came the faint sound of a car door shutting, but whether it was the intruder or a neighbor, Erica had no way of knowing. There was no one in the kitchen, and she checked the front room again before returning to the kitchen. There, she turned off the light so she could see outside better. The clouds were thicker now, and Erica could see no shadowy figures.

After another check of the main and upper levels, she told Liz the house was clear except for the basement.

It was the last place on earth Erica wanted to go. But she had to.

Liz grabbed at Erica's hand as they stood in the kitchen, eyeing the wooden door leading to the basement. "You're not going down there, are you?"

"We'll never feel safe unless I do." Erica tried to swallow past the dryness in her throat.

"Let the police do it."

Actually, it would be better to wait for backup. She would be exposed going down the wooden steps, and if something happened to her, Liz would truly be defenseless. Or was she rationalizing? Erica hoped not. "All right," she said slowly. "I'll wait for the police."

* * *

With the worst timing in the world, Megan came home seconds before the police arrived. The officers surrounded her, shouting commands with drawn guns, their faces shining in the flashing red, white, and blue lights. Erica hurried outside to explain, and Megan fled inside the house.

A light rain began whispering at the window panes as the police searched the house and yard. Erica, Liz, and Megan talked quietly in the front room.

"I'm so sorry," Erica apologized to Liz. "I never should have gone out and left the door unlocked."

"I would have done the same thing," Liz replied, her eyes dark. Then she shivered. "Actually, I *wouldn't* have done the same thing. No way would I have gone outside at night if I thought someone was out there." She looked at Erica in admiration. "You're a braver man than I am, Gunga Din."

Megan's eyes searched out and locked onto Erica's. "I don't know how you did it," Megan said softly, knowing about the terrifying childhood prank Erica's cousin had played, locking her in a basement closet and leaving her with a dread of the dark.

When the police suggested the intruder might have stolen something, Liz went through the house to check, while Erica and Megan looked though their bedroom. Nothing was missing. Even Erica's laptop—an easy item to snatch—was still in the front room. Why, then, had the intruder gone into her bedroom and thrown her and Megan's clothes all over the floor? Had he been searching for something? And if so, what?

She couldn't stand clothes being strewn all over, so while Megan stayed with Liz, Erica folded and put things away. Once again, she wondered if Liz knew something that posed a danger to someone. Perhaps it was something Liz wasn't even aware of knowing but which was so important that someone was willing to kill Liz before she could let it slip. But this explanation was less than satisfactory because if that were the case, surely the intruder's goal would have been to get Liz. Why, then, would he or she take time to come into this room and throw clothes around?

Perhaps he was after something in the house. But what? Erica folded a pair of pants and laid them in a drawer. Matters were intensifying, speeding up. She glanced out the window at the trees swaying in the wind. Once again, as she had earlier, Erica had the sinking feeling that some malevolent person was on the loose.

* * *

Detective Ranquist called early the next morning. "Sounds like you had quite the night. I read the incident report. So you didn't actually see anyone?"

"That's right. And nothing was taken from the house."

"At least whoever it was didn't get to Liz."

"Fortunately." Erica was still upset at herself for not locking the door and thought it kind of the detective not to mention it.

"It's interesting that Megan was away at the same time an unknown intruder shows up."

The suspicious undertones in his voice were something Erica hadn't expected. She was about to say that Megan couldn't possibly be the killer, but what was that based on? A lifelong friendship? She doubted Detective Ranquist would be swayed by the fact that Erica had known Megan nearly all her life. Policemen went by facts—not emotions. And actually, what grounds did Erica have other than a personal belief that Megan *wasn't* the killer? He waited patiently for her response, and it was a weak one, since Erica merely related what Megan had told the police. "Megan was with a study group."

"And so she was. And after the group left, Megan stayed to study. Alone."

So, he'd already questioned her. This was not good. Erica hated hearing the suspicion in Detective Ranquist's voice. Megan had no alibi. But then again, she had no motive either, at least that Erica could see.

"There's no *reason* I can see for Megan to want Liz dead. There's zero motive."

Detective Ranquist countered, "Just because we haven't discovered her motive doesn't mean there isn't one."

Feeling restless, Erica began putting away dishes from the drainer as he went on grimly.

"Even with last night's incident, we're not any further along. Other than knowing the killer is taking more chances and becoming more daring."

That was undeniably true. Yet at the same time, Erica felt sure they were getting close—even though she just couldn't explain why. All that was missing was some key bit of information that would make sense of everything. Very soon now, the ground had to either become solid or fall out from beneath them.

Detective Ranquist broke into her thoughts. "What *are* those clinking noises?"

"Sorry. I'm in the kitchen, putting glasses away in the cupboard."

"For a minute I wondered if you were at a bar."

"It's too early. I don't usually go until happy hour."

He chuckled. They'd talked once about her 'weird' religious restrictions.

Then Erica became serious. "I meant to tell you something and forgot, but the other day, I was upstairs and heard a noise. When I came down, I found BJ in the kitchen."

"He broke in?"

"Liz had given him a key. And he's not the only one." Erica explained there were at least three other people who had keys to the house.

The detective snorted. "Geez, why doesn't Liz make a few more copies and pass them out in front of Walmart?"

That made Erica smile. "Oh, and Liz showed me the e-mail I told you about—the one that indicated Joel planned to take care of Liz financially if he died. My guess is that he had a will."

"My guy's still working to find Joel's will, but he did turn up Adam Goldstein's. You were right—he left a sizeable chunk of his fortune to his grandson."

It was nice to have that confirmed. "Liz also showed me a bunch of other e-mails Joel had sent her."

"Anything interesting?"

"Actually, it's what *isn't* in them that's bothering me."

"Something's missing, huh?"

"Yeah. Also, I woke up early this morning, thinking about the case and going over each of the murder attempts."

"And?"

Erica hesitated. "Has anything in particular struck you about these attempts?"

Detective Ranquist's radio crackled in the background. He listened to it then said, "Sorry, I've got to go, but did you come up with anything?"

"Just a little idea. I'll tell you about it later."

* * *

When David called, he asked if there was anything new on the intruder then asked when she was going to the races.

"Around noon. I'm going to run a few errands this morning. Liz is getting off work early, and Megan took the day off."

"NASCAR races are great. I wish I was going with you." He gave an enormous sigh.

"Me too," Erica said, buttering a piece of toast. "I talked Austin into going. He and Donna are going to meet us at the race track between one and two."

"I'm surprised Austin's going if Todd's going to be there."

"I hope it works out. Megan wasn't too happy when I told her Austin was coming."

"Say, how did Todd do in his race yesterday?"

"He finished sixth. Megan went out to watch him and said that was a pretty good finish for someone as young as he is."

"I've been thinking about Donna," David said. "Do you think she branched out from embezzlement to murder?"

"Once I thought there was a good chance of that, but now I'm not so sure."

"The woman was desperate for money—so desperate she committed a crime."

"That's true, and money *is* a powerful motive."

"Does Liz know Donna embezzled from Park Place Realty?"

"I haven't told her, and since Liz hasn't mentioned it, I don't think Donna has. But Liz did seem on edge this morning. I think someone coming into the house last night really scared her. She told me that if I wasn't going to the races today, she wouldn't even think about going."

"Just be careful. There'll be a lot of people there, making it easy for a killer to hide."

"I'll be careful."

* * *

The distinctive aroma of bayberry was in the air as Erica crunched down the gravel driveway on her way to the bus stop. When she saw Frank wheeling his trash can toward the road, she called, "Good morning!"

He grunted noncommittally, and Erica stopped to wait for him. He glanced at her warily, positioning his can by the curb.

She asked, "Did you happen to see anyone in your backyard last night?"

Frank shot her a look. "Is that why the police were all over the place?"

"I thought I saw someone."

His faded eyes darted away. "Probably a stray dog."

"You spend a lot of time watching Liz's house, don't you?"

"Why do you say that?" Frank's massive eyebrows drew together. There was hostility in the look and something else. Fear?

"I see you watching from your window whenever I leave the house or come back."

"What of it?" Frank said belligerently. "It's a free country, ain't it?" He wheeled round and stomped off, his face red and wrathful.

* * *

Erica was in the checkout line at Walmart when her cell phone rang, but she let the call go to voicemail. She took the bus to the bank and stopped at another store. It wasn't until Erica was nearly home that she remembered to check the phone message. It was from Megan.

"Erica, listen—I just found a letter from Joel, but it was written to Beth. It was in that book of Beth's that I've been reading. Joel said he loved *her*!" Megan sounded upset and confused. "I can't understand it, but it sounds like Joel was two-timing Liz. Give me a call when you can."

This was going to upset Liz dreadfully. Hadn't she been through enough? Erica had to talk to Megan about this, but it had to be in person. The bus was late, frustrating Erica. It was agonizing to pull over at each bus stop along the way. When the bus finally pulled up at her stop, Erica was the first one off. She hurried down the road, up the driveway, and flung the door open.

"Megan?" She threw her sacks on the kitchen table.

No answer. Erica took the stairs two at a time. Megan wasn't in her bedroom, and Liz wasn't in hers. Feeling increasingly apprehensive, Erica came downstairs. Then she noticed the note on the fridge:

Change of plans. Austin came early and picked up me and Liz. I wanted to wait for you, but they insisted. Donna will pick you up. See you at the race track. Megan

Erica studied the note as if it were written in hieroglyphics. Why the change? She fought feelings of annoyance and impatience. What was Liz thinking to leave without her? Would she never get it into her head that she was in danger? She probably thought it was safe enough going with Austin and Megan, but she was too trusting. A shiver ran down Erica's back, and she called Donna.

"Why the sudden change in plans?" she asked when Donna picked up.

"I didn't know anything about it," Donna complained, "until Austin told me he'd decided to go over early to get Megan and Liz. I tried to talk him out of it, but he wouldn't listen."

"What time are you leaving?"

"Actually, I wish I wasn't. But Austin made me promise I wouldn't stay home." Donna sounded depressed. "A neighbor is coming over to stay with my father. When she gets here, I'll come and pick you up."

Going into the front room, Erica threw herself into a chair across from the fireplace. So Joel had written to Beth. And according to Megan, it appeared to be a love letter. Had it been written before or after his engagement to Liz?

Something in the fireplace caught Erica's fastidious eye. A light sprinkling of soot was the one incongruous touch in a room that was usually ultra neat and tidy. And yet—the appearance of soot seemed unusual for the beginning of June. Seeing it gave Erica a weird sense of déjà vu. This had happened before—but when? She tried to remember as she went for a broom and dustpan. As she knelt in front of the fireplace, something stirred in her consciousness.

Now she remembered. It had been after Beth had been killed. Erica had planned to clean the front room the day before the funeral because she'd noticed soot in the fireplace, even though it had been warm, with no need for a fire. But when she went to clean the fireplace, the soot was gone. It had already been cleaned. She'd shrugged and gone on to the rest of the room. Yet here it was again. Soot in the fireplace.

Erica eyed the stone fireplace with the fascinated gaze of a bird watching a snake. The soot suggested various possibilities. There had to be a reason for it. A raccoon in the chimney? A bird? Erica pulled a pair of gloves out of her pocket, knelt before the hearth, and carefully felt the stones—pushing and pulling any that protruded.

What Erica expected to find, she hardly knew, but all the same, she went on poking and prodding with dogged perseverance. When Erica felt a brick that was loose, she pulled out her Leatherman tool and used the flat screwdriver to feel between the bricks. No mortar. She pried the brick out, then another, and another, stacking them neatly on the hearth. Behind them was another row of loose bricks. Once those had been removed, Erica found a metal cubbyhole, which she opened to find a metal box. Erica set the box on the hearth and opened it.

Empty.

And yet, surely it had held something recently. The removal of the box was the only thing that would explain the soot. The metal was cool in her hands as she turned it over. What could have been inside?

A queer, nebulous idea began to take shape. After stripping off her gloves, Erica sat on the hearth and deliberately went over the case from the very beginning—carefully going over every detail and considering every actor in this peculiar drama.

Most recent was the letter Megan had found in Beth's book, *An American Tragedy*. Erica thought back to the movie she'd watched based on that book—*A Place in the Sun*. Something had struck Erica then, but it had never come clear. And just a few nights ago, Erica had watched another movie starring Elizabeth Taylor, *Cat on a Hot Tin Roof*.

Erica's mind leapt here and there, and she recalled the long commentary breaks in between the last movie. Something shifted in her mind, and Erica caught her breath. Could it be? Liz Taylor. Elizabeth. Beth. Her feeling of intuition surged from a trickle to a roaring river. This was it—the missing piece. In that instant, suspicion crystallized and became a near certainty.

Erica pulled out her cell phone and called Donna.

"What is it now?" The old, impatient Donna was back.

"How soon can you get here?"

"My friend just came. I'll come as soon as I go over things with her."

Not good enough. "I need to get to the race track as soon as possible," Erica said tersely.

"Why, is something wrong?"

"Yes, very wrong. You see, I just found an empty metal box."

Chapter Twenty

After talking with Donna, Erica hurried upstairs and changed clothes, putting on an oversized, lightweight denim jacket that hid her holstered gun. She was waiting outside when Donna pulled up. She had her towelettes ready, so she hurriedly wiped her seat and hopped in. "Okay, let's go!"

Donna floored it then darted a nervous look at Erica. "What was that about an empty box?"

"I'll explain later. It's best I don't get into it now. Sorry."

At a stop light, Donna glanced over. The side of Erica's jacket had fallen open. "You—you have a gun!"

Erica pulled the jacket together and did up the middle button.

"What's happened? Is Liz in danger?"

"I need to get to the race track as soon as we can. When we get there, please don't say anything about me being in a hurry or anything about the gun—not even to Austin or Liz. That's very important. Understand?"

"Austin's not involved, is he?" Donna's voice was anxious, but Erica's concern was for the red brake lights directly in front of them.

"Watch out!" Erica hollered, putting her hand on the dashboard as Donna braked hard.

"Sorry." Donna turned into the massive parking lot west of the track. "Austin wouldn't do anything to hurt Liz. I know he wouldn't."

While Donna searched for a parking spot, Erica called Megan. Making her voice sound as light and normal as possible, she said, "Hey, Donna and I just got here. Is Liz with you?"

"Yeah."

"Good. And Austin and Todd?"

"They're right here."

"Okay, where can we meet?"

"Just come up to where we're sitting," Megan replied, sounding a little puzzled. "Donna has your tickets, doesn't she?"

"Yes, but could you come down and meet us? I get turned around so easily."

"You?" Megan was shocked. "You've got a GPS programmed into that OCD brain of yours."

"Megan, honey—would you be a sweetie and meet me? I'd *really* appreciate it." Erica was anxious to ask her privately about the letter. There was an outside chance Megan had brought it with her.

"Well, all right." Her tone was less than gracious.

"Good. Donna and I will meet you just past the ticket-takers."

It was a relief to see Megan, who wore a baseball cap and a striped bag hung over her shoulder, but Erica was less than happy to see she wasn't alone. Todd and Austin walked along on either side of her. Although Todd was dressed casually in a NASCAR polo shirt and jeans, he drew a lot of second looks from passersby, especially women.

Rats. So much for talking to Megan privately. Erica nailed a smile to her face. "Hi, everyone!"

"The guys insisted on coming," Megan said a bit apologetically. "Guess they thought I'd get lost."

Going up the stairs, Erica asked Austin, "Why the sudden change in plans? I thought I was going with Liz and Megan and you were coming later with your mom."

He looked sheepish. "Liz called and said Megan wanted to talk and asked if I could come early. But I haven't had any time alone with Megan."

That made two of them.

In the stands, Erica tried to sit by Megan, but Todd took one side and Austin slipped into the other. They settled back to watch the race, with Todd providing informed commentary. Although he talked most often to Megan, Erica noticed that his eyes often went to Liz. Once, when Todd was answering a question from Donna, Austin casually tried to take Megan's hand, but no dice. Megan shot Austin a look that would have dropped a grizzly bear.

As 135,000 fans screamed for their favorites, Erica decided on a plan to get Megan alone. Standing, she announced, "I think I'll go get something to eat. Megan, do you want to come with me? We can bring back hot dogs for everyone."

Liz jumped up. "I'd better come and help you carry them." Erica sighed when Donna tagged along as well. At the concession stand, Erica pulled out her wallet to pay, but Liz beat her to it, digging into the pocket of her yellow cotton blazer and producing her credit card.

At the condiment stand, Erica yanked out several napkins and wiped splotches of ketchup and mustard off the counter. "I'm surprised they don't hire someone to clean up here."

"Why should they?" Megan asked. "They knew you were coming."

Back at their seats, Erica passed out the wipes, and Liz the food.

When they were done eating, Todd leaned over to Megan. "Would you like to go down and see my car?"

"Oh, I'd love that!"

Austin scowled, and Liz spoke up. "I'd love to come too, if that's all right."

"Me too," Erica said, popping up.

Todd hesitated. "I'd like to take everyone, but security is pretty tight. I'm not sure how many people they'll allow in."

"Well, let's try," Liz said brightly. "Come on, Aunt Donna."

Not surprisingly, Austin elected to stay behind. The rest of them went down to where signs warned, No Entrance Beyond This Point.

A husky security guard with mirrored sunglasses folded his arms as they approached. Speaking wearily, as if he'd said it a thousand times that day—which he probably had—the guard said, "I'm sorry. Spectators are not allowed beyond this point."

Todd took hold of Megan's hand and stepped forward. "I'm a driver and wanted to show her my car."

"Sorry. No one can enter without clearance."

Todd held up the tag around his neck, but the guard was not impressed. "You can come through but no one else." As Todd began to argue, the guard said, "Try the racer's entrance. They might let your group in. You know where that is?"

His face flushed with annoyance, Todd turned away.

Megan took his hand. "Don't worry about it."

They were headed back when Erica got a new idea on how to talk to Megan alone. "I'd like to stop at the restroom. What about you, Megan?"

"Sure."

"I think I'll come too," Liz said. And once again, Donna joined them. It was if they were all joined at the hip, Erica thought as they went inside.

When she came out of the bathroom stall, Donna was washing her hands at the sink.

Glancing around, Erica pulled out her bar of Lava in its Ziplock bag. "Have Liz and Megan come out?"

"Yeah. They didn't want to wait—said they'd meet us at our seats."

Oh, great, Erica thought, groaning inside. After a speedy wash, Erica hurried out and scanned the crowd, feeling a flutter of fear.

"Why are you walking so fast?" Donna complained, trying to keep up.

"Just want to catch up with them." Erica caught a glimpse of Megan's black hair and ball cap a short distance ahead. Liz was beside her.

Just then Todd came up to them. "Where are Liz and Megan?"

"Up there." Erica pointed. "Come on."

They hurried along, but it was intermission, and huge crowds poured out of the stands, heading for restrooms and concession booths. The three of them paused near a set of stairs. Erica glanced up then down, trying to spot Megan. She frowned. "I'm not sure which way they went. Donna, you go down the stairs; Todd, you go up. I'll go straight."

"Why don't we just go back to our seats and wait for them?" Todd asked, reasonably enough.

"Oh, I'd just like to stay with them," Erica said, aware of how lame she sounded. They parted, and Erica hustled forward, brushing past people and dodging around others. Then she caught another glimpse of Megan. She hurried faster. Now there were only two men between her and the girls.

It was now or never.

Erica maneuvered around the men and stepped sideways so she was behind the two women. Using a karate kick, Erica struck the back of Liz's right leg behind the knee. Liz cried out as her leg buckled and she fell.

Grabbing Megan's hand, Erica pulled her away. "Come on."

Megan tore her hand away, glancing back at Liz in concern. "*Are you crazy?*" Megan was a big girl, and there was no way Erica could force her to come if she didn't want to.

Erica began to plead. "Megan, I'll explain, but right now, you've *got* to trust me. We've got to get out of here *now*!" Erica's anxiety must have shown on her face because unexpectedly Megan gave in. They ducked and darted through the crowd. There was no time to look back.

Finally they slowed to a fast walk. Breathlessly, Erica asked, "Did you bring the letter?"

"Yeah, I did."

Now for the important question. "Did you tell Liz about it?"

"Well . . ."

Erica stared at her in despair. "You didn't!"

"It's not what you think," Megan flashed as she nearly ran over a little boy who had darted in front of her. The mother glared at them as they hurried on. "Liz overheard me when I left that message for you. She asked me about the letter on the way over here."

"Please tell me you didn't give it to her."

"She wanted to see it, but I remembered what you said about not talking to anyone, so I told her I needed to show it to you first. Just now, Liz asked me for it again. Anyway, why did you trip her? What's the matter with you?"

Seeing a restroom, Erica pulled Megan inside and pushed her into a stall. Then she crowded in after her. There was barely room to stand without touching.

"Ugh," Megan groaned. "What are you doing?"

"Liz wants that letter so she can destroy it. It's evidence against her."

"Against Liz? What are you talking about?" Megan made a move toward the door. "Let me out of here; you're freaking me out."

Erica blocked the door. "Give me the letter."

With difficulty, Megan unzipped her bag and handed it over.

Dear Angel,

I wanted to leave you a little note to read while I'm gone. I'll miss you and can't wait until we're together again. I'm excited to go overseas and race because it'll give me more experience, but I wish you were coming with me. As soon as this trip is done, I'll be home and we can be together. And soon, you'll graduate and have your teaching certificate, and we can start our life together.

I wish I could have met your parents before I left, but you're right, Beth—it would have been hard to keep our engagement a secret. But soon we can tell everyone. I feel bad Grandpa died without knowing about us and that we were going to be married. But maybe that was for the best, although I hate thinking about it that way. I wish I'd done things differently. I have a lot of regrets. The biggest one is that I didn't stand up to Grandpa and tell him that I'd found the girl of my dreams.

Love, Joel

This was it. The proof she needed. Erica tapped the letter with her finger. "Joel wrote this to Beth, his fiancée."

"But he was engaged to Liz."

"The only girl Joel was ever engaged to was Beth."

"How could that be?" Megan was aghast.

"Liz has been lying all along. Everything she told us was a mixture of fact and fiction. The fiction is that Liz was engaged to Joel. The fact is Beth was the one engaged to him. The only true part about her engagement story is that it needed to stay a secret because Joel's grandfather would go ballistic if he knew Joel was going to marry someone outside his religion."

Megan's jaw dropped. "But Liz showed me the ring Joel gave her. And what about the letters and the postcards Joel sent her?"

"Liz probably picked the ring up at a pawn shop. And Joel sent those letters and postcards to Beth. There were time gaps in the e-mails Liz showed me, so I figure she only kept the ones addressed to 'Angel Johnson' and destroyed any that were addressed personally to Beth."

Megan squirmed uncomfortably in the tight space as Erica went on. "Unfortunately, the only person Beth told about her engagement was Liz. It all started when Liz found out that Joel had made Beth his beneficiary."

"Why would that matter?"

"Because that's what made Liz decide to kill Beth. She wanted to get Joel's money by pretending *she* was the one engaged to him."

Megan was still mystified. "That doesn't even begin to make sense. If Joel's will said his money would go to Beth, how would Liz be able to claim it?"

"The will states the money will go to Elizabeth Johnson. And Liz and Beth are both Elizabeth Johnson."

For the first time, the light of comprehension dawned in Megan's eyes.

"Joel inherited a fortune when his grandfather died. When Joel died in France, Liz knew Beth would inherit millions from Adam's estate. Since no one else knew about Beth's engagement, all Liz had to do was to convince people *she* was engaged to Joel. There was just one thing standing in the way—Beth."

Megan's hand flew to her mouth.

"Liz figured if she got rid of Beth, no one would ever know. After all, she and Beth had both dated Joel, even if it was in a group. There were plenty of witnesses to that. It wasn't until Beth and Joel became serious that they started hiding the fact that they were dating."

"But what about all those murder attempts on Liz?"

"I'll explain that later." Erica pulled out her phone. "Rats, no service. It's all this reinforced concrete in here. I'll have to call Detective Ranquist when I get outside." Her nerves felt as tight as racket strings.

"We're going to trade," Erica said, taking off her jacket. "Take off your T-shirt and put on my jacket."

"Do I get your gun too?"

"I think I'll keep that. Now, hand me your baseball cap." Erica twisted her long hair and stuffed it under the cap. Now, give me your purse." Erica slung it over her shoulder.

"When we go out, I want you to go as fast as you can to the entrance. Liz has a gun, so keep an eye out for her. If you happen to see a security guard, stop and tell him what's going on. Otherwise, don't stop until you get to the gate. They'll have security there. Tell them Liz is after you and that she has a gun."

Megan turned a white, despairing face upon her. "But Erica, I can't leave you."

"You can, and you will." Erica slid back the bolt on the stall door and peeked out. "All clear." They went to the entrance to the restroom, and Erica checked again. "It's okay. Now run!"

Megan ran.

Chapter Twenty-One

ONCE MEGAN WAS OUT OF sight, Erica breathed a little easier. Leaving the restroom, she ducked behind a pillar to call Detective Ranquist. Initially, he was upset Erica hadn't called earlier but said he'd be there soon. Then she headed for the exit.

As Erica made her way through the crowds, someone jolted her from behind. She turned to see Liz, who thrust a hard piece of metal into Erica's side. Liz's hand was hidden, as was the gun, in the pocket of her cotton blazer.

"Smart of you to switch clothes," Liz said. When Erica slowed, Liz ordered, "Keep walking, and don't even try reaching for your gun." Liz directed her off to the side, and when they stopped, her eyes went to Megan's striped purse. "Give me the letter."

"Megan has it."

Keeping her right hand on the gun, Liz unzipped the purse and felt inside, tossing gum, lip gloss, and lotion to the ground. Color rose in her cheeks when she didn't find the letter.

"Let's go find Megan." There was a ring of steel in Liz's voice.

"I told her to go to the entrance and alert security. She's safe now."

A slow, self-satisfied smile spread across Liz's face as she peered over Erica's shoulder. "Is that so?"

Erica turned to see Megan's tall figure thirty feet away, talking earnestly to Todd.

"Come on, Erica, let's join them."

When they got close, Megan made as if to run. Liz called out, "Don't, Megan. Not unless you want something to happen to Erica." A number of people stared at them curiously as they stepped off to the side, out of the main stream of traffic.

Todd looked at Liz with narrowed eyes. "Megan was telling me quite a story. A lot of it had to do with you, Liz."

"It's all true," Erica said urgently.

"Keep quiet, Todd. I have a gun on Erica." Liz pressed the gun against her pocket so Todd could see its outline. His eyes widened in surprise, and Liz went on. "Erica has a letter I want, but it's not in her bag. Go through her pockets."

It took an effort for Erica to breathe evenly. "I threw the letter away."

"I don't believe you." Liz's eyes were hard.

When Todd checked Erica's pockets, he saw her holstered gun and looked at Liz in alarm.

"Take the gun, and put it in my pocket," Liz said, glancing at the masses of people walking by. "But don't let anyone see."

Todd did as he was told, taking Erica's Glock and putting it gingerly in Liz's pocket. Then he went through Erica's pockets, pulling out her Leatherman tool, packet of wipes, and disposable gloves.

Todd was about to throw them in a nearby garbage can when Erica cried, "Don't do that! I need those!"

Liz confiscated the Leatherman and allowed Todd to hand back the gloves and wipes. There was no letter.

"Now, check Megan," Liz commanded. But Todd found nothing. Liz was practically grinding her teeth when she turned to Erica. "Where did you hide the letter?"

"Where you'll never find it."

Liz stepped over to Megan, who gasped as Liz pressed the gun into her side. "Want to tell me now, Erica?"

Megan was very white now—white to the lips—as she stared helplessly at Erica.

Barely breathing, Erica remained silent. She didn't think Liz would shoot. Not with so many people around. Still, her heart began to thump.

"Enough of this," Liz snapped impatiently. "Todd, you and Erica walk ahead of us. Head for the parking lot. And remember—my finger is on the trigger." The cold menace in her voice chilled Erica.

As they made their way through the masses of people, Erica tried to formulate a plan. She didn't dare call out to a security guard. If she did, Liz would certainly shoot Megan. Erica itched to turn and do a roundhouse kick, but again—it was too risky. With Liz's finger on the trigger, Megan would certainly be shot.

As they headed down the stairs, Erica prayed that somehow, some way, something would happen to give her a chance to grab Liz's gun or her own. But time was running out. In vain, Erica tried to catch the eye of one of the security men on the main level, but the one who did look at her directly merely drew his eyebrows together, apparently puzzled by her intense expression.

They exited, going down the wide sidewalk toward the far end of the parking lot. Pigeons stirred and gave muffled croons as the entourage walked near the underside of the bleachers. The back of the parking lot was deserted. In the distance, the crowd roared and engines revved as cars raced around the track. Erica fought the panic that threatened to overwhelm her. A person who was backed into a corner and had already killed one person wouldn't hesitate to kill again.

At the end of the sidewalk, Liz motioned them toward the outermost cars and trucks, which would block them from the view of any stragglers who might venture near this isolated section of the parking lot.

There was a shout from behind, and Erica turned to see Austin in the distance, hurrying toward them. Megan also turned, but as she did, she stumbled. Trying to catch her balance, she flung her arms out wildly, and Liz fired.

Screaming, Megan fell, clutching her leg. Erica whipped around and aimed her roundhouse kick high at Liz. She connected, causing Liz to fall back against a Saturn and then to the ground. Erica pounced, scrambling to reach Liz's gun. Liz twisted away, but before she could raise her gun, Erica headbutted her. Pain flashed like a red flame, and she blinked before bringing up a knee and striking Liz in the head. The gun Liz held clattered to the asphalt.

Todd bent and grabbed the weapon.

"Help me, Todd," Erica cried as she scrabbled in Liz's pocket for her own gun. When he didn't make a move, she glanced up.

Todd was pointing the gun at Erica.

"Get away from Liz." Todd's voice was smooth but had unfamiliar, hard edges. There was a aggressive look in his eyes.

Erica felt her heart turn over as he gestured for her to move away. Breathing heavily, she did as she was bidden. Groaning, Liz pulled herself up, supporting herself by leaning on the Saturn.

"Farther," Todd told Erica, his face flushed and his forehead beaded with sweat.

Erica backed off another step as Liz straightened and steadied herself. Then Liz smiled—a crooked little smile. For a moment, the mask slipped, and Erica saw Liz for what she was—an evil doll mimicking humanity. Everything about Liz was shiny and smiling and false.

"What are you doing, Todd?" Erica cried hoarsely, a horrible fear creeping over her. There was a cold malignity about him that froze her to the marrow.

When Todd glanced over his shoulder, Erica knew he was watching for Austin, who had to be getting close. Megan sat off to the side, crying and holding her leg. Blood had soaked through her Capris and was dripping onto the asphalt.

Liz also looked around wildly. Pulling Erica's gun out of her pocket, she said to Todd. "We've got to get out of here. Now."

Before they could make a move, something hit the window of the car next to Todd with a loud thunk. As he and Liz turned, Austin jumped from behind a car and launched himself at Todd. Both men fell. Knocked out of Todd's hand, the gun skittered along the asphalt, ending up partway under a car.

Erica threw herself at Liz before the girl could recover and raise her gun. They tumbled and rolled. Erica's breath was shallow and thin as they grappled. She managed to grab Liz's forearm, holding it so Liz couldn't aim and shoot. Slowly, Erica worked her hand down Liz's arm and toward the gun, inch by inch. Liz's finger was on the trigger, and suddenly it went off, causing Megan to scream in fear.

Stretching a bit further, Erica managed to wrench the gun away. Time was of the essence. One glance at the men told her the fight was going badly for Austin, who continued to wrestle with Todd. With a push, Erica separated herself from Liz then aimed the gun at her chest. Liz raised her hands in surrender.

"Todd, I have the gun!" Erica shouted. "Kneel, and put your hands behind your head." When he didn't comply, Erica added, "*I said kneel!* I used to be a police officer and have no problem shooting people."

Todd did as he was told.

Breathing heavily, Austin went to Megan, who was crying.

"Liz, you too," Erica barked. "Kneel and put your hands behind your head."

There was a new look in Liz's eyes as she obeyed—a thin hardness like lacquer. "I almost got away with it." She spat the words defiantly. "I would have had a fortune."

"'Almost' being the operative word," Erica replied, holding the weapon in front of her. An almost savage expression showed on Liz's face. There was no sorrow for killing Beth—or for nearly killing Megan. Nor was there any compassion. No, the clearest emotion shining from those blue eyes was hate and anger, the anger of a baffled egoist whose plans had come to an end and hatred for the person who had stopped her.

Liz ground out, "If Beth hadn't put that letter in her book, you never would have guessed."

"Perhaps not, but there were other clues. Although I have to admit you had me fooled. You should have been an actress."

"I was. All the time you've been here."

* * *

The paramedics—on call at the race track—were there quickly. Holding Megan's hand, Austin tested the paramedics' patience until they finally ordered him to back off. As they loaded Megan into the ambulance, Austin asked Erica if she would get his mother and meet him at the hospital. He then ran for his Jeep.

Detective Ranquist arrived as the ambulance exited the parking lot with lights flashing. His lean face was sober. "Let's go over to my squad car, Erica, and you can fill me in."

Although the incident had left her feeling drained, Erica still fished out her wipes and went over her seat before climbing inside. Detective Ranquist watched with tolerant amusement. Then Erica went over everything she'd told Megan, as well as what occurred in the parking lot—including the revelation that Todd was in on it with Liz.

The detective shook his head in admiration. "You're remarkable, Erica—to be so calm after a knock-down, drag-out fight."

"If you must know, I'm hanging on by a thread."

"So Liz was the one behind it all." Detective Ranquist's mouth pressed into a hard, thin line.

"I think after Liz overhead Megan leaving me a message about the letter, she decided to arrange for Megan to have an 'accident' here at the race track."

"Liz probably figured it would be easy to make us think—once again—that she was the intended target and that Megan's death was just another unfortunate case of mistaken identity."

Erica nodded. "But Donna and I got here sooner than Liz expected. I called Megan as soon as we pulled in, to get her away from Liz and to get the letter."

"Where did you hide it?"

"In the restroom. I opened the metal box of paper towels and set it on top."

"And all those murder attempts were fakes—to make it appear as though someone was trying to kill Liz." Detective Ranquist wore a look of grudging admiration. "Very clever." Then he said, "You asked me the other day if anything in particular had struck me about those attempts. Did you know then that they were fakes?"

"No, but it did occur to me that there were no witnesses to any of them."

"Except for the man who pulled Liz out of the road after someone pushed her." Detective Ranquist stopped. "Of course—Liz made up a 'pretend' rescuer. But what about the deck collapsing? Beth was there and saw it happen."

"Beth didn't actually see it fall. She was in the shower when it happened. I'm thinking that once Beth got in the shower, Liz slipped outside. I noticed there was a rope tied to one of the poles. My guess is she pulled on it to make the deck collapse. She'd already sawed partway through two of the poles. When the deck fell, Liz ran back inside the house. Beth never even knew Liz had been outside."

She went on. "One thing I wondered about was the hose, which was new and extra long. Liz may have tried to weaken the deck by letting the water wash away dirt from around the poles, and when it didn't work, she used the saw on them."

Detective Ranquist asked, "What about the redwood sawdust in Frank's shed? Did Liz use Frank's saw to cut the pole?"

"Possibly. Frank did have redwood on his property, but there was so much sawdust that I wonder now if Liz just took some over to his shed and sprinkled it around in hopes the police would search there."

Erica's cell phone rang. It was a frantic Donna, who had called Austin when no one had returned to their seats. "I'll meet you at your car in ten minutes and explain," Erica told her.

Detective Ranquist went on as if there had been no interruption. "What about the brake tampering? I guess since Todd knows all about cars, he probably helped her with that."

"I think you're right. Liz was never in any real danger. She planned it well, making sure she was headed uphill and could go across grass and bushes to slow the car. I wouldn't be surprised if she or Todd even banged up the front of the car afterwards with a bat."

"And Todd is the more likely culprit in regards to the pipe bomb—again, because he knows cars inside and out," Detective Ranquist said. "I should know more after I question them. But how did Liz know someone was going to borrow her car?"

"Megan was always taking it because the battery in her car had died. She probably asked Liz ahead of time if she could borrow the car to go to the concert with Austin."

"And if the car bomb was made and ready to go, all Todd and Liz had to do was put it under the hood, which wouldn't take long."

"And like the other attempts, there were no witnesses. No one actually *saw* the bomb being planted—they only saw the *aftermath*—the explosion. The same for when Beth was shot. No one saw anyone pointing a gun."

Detective Ranquist agreed. "And it was child's play for Liz to poison the juice and pretend someone else had done it."

"Do you remember, after Beth was shot, when I said that something seemed wrong but I couldn't think what it was?"

The detective thought back. "Yeah I do."

"Today I remembered what it was. Soot in the fireplace. Today, while I was waiting for Donna to pick me up, I noticed there was soot in the fireplace—again. That's when I remembered there was also soot there the day after Beth was shot. When I looked in the chimney, I found the cubbyhole and the metal box where Liz had hidden her gun."

"I never thought I'd say this, but thank heavens for your OCD."

* * *

It took a while for Erica to go back inside and retrieve the letter, causing Donna to call her again. Then, by the time they arrived at the hospital, Erica had only half finished explaining everything because of all of Donna's questions and interruptions.

When she went back to the cubicle, Austin was standing beside Megan, holding her hand. "The nurse just left," he said. "She gave Megan a shot for the pain and set up an IV. The doctor should be here soon."

Megan's black hair framed her face, which was still and white. But her spirit was irrepressible as she lightly chided her friend. "I was getting a little nervous back there, Erica."

"I bet you were. Thank goodness Austin had the presence of mind to throw his wallet at the car window to distract Todd and Liz."

"Is Liz the one who killed Beth?" Megan asked.

"We can talk about that later. You need to take it easy."

"I have to know." Megan's eyes brimmed with fresh tears. Austin found a tissue and wiped her face. "I know you've got it figured out, Erica." Her words were choked. "Tell me."

"As long as you realize that some of this is conjecture on my part."

Megan gave a slight nod.

"On the night of Donna's barbecue, I think Liz spilled food on Beth deliberately so Beth would put on her sweater. It wasn't like Liz to be so clumsy, and her sweater was a distinctive lime-green color. Liz wanted the police to think that the killer had mistaken Beth for her. If you remember, Todd encouraged Beth to put on Liz's sweater. Liz wore the same color pants as Beth, and I think she also cut her hair short so she'd look more like Beth."

Erica stopped as Megan began crying softly. The curtain swished as a doctor and nurse came in and politely asked Erica and Austin to step out while they took care of the wound. As they were leaving, Megan asked Erica to call her mother.

In the waiting room, Austin sat with his mother while Erica stepped outside to call her best friend. As expected, Wendy immediately became hysterical. Erica understood. She would have lost it if someone called to say Aby had been shot. It took a long time to calm Wendy down and reassure her that Megan would be fine. Then it was back to the waiting room to Donna, who struggled with the idea that her niece could have planned and carried out a murder.

"But how could Liz have left the party without anyone noticing she was gone?" Donna cried in confusion.

"It didn't take all that long," Erica said. "Liz told Megan she had to use the bathroom—that was to cover her absence. Liz slipped outside, ran next door, and shot Beth. Then she came back and hid the gun. The police only did a cursory search of the house because the shot came from next door. Liz came back for the gun later."

Donna thought then asked, "When you called me, what did you mean when you said you were afraid because you'd found an empty box?"

Erica explained about finding the cubbyhole. "Once I found that, I knew where Liz had hidden her gun. And since the box was empty, it could only mean that Liz had taken the gun with her to the race track."

It was hours before Megan was ready to leave the hospital, and she and Austin had a long time to talk. When they arrived at Crooked House, Austin carried Megan upstairs to her bedroom. He laid her down gently, but before he could draw back, Megan put her arms around his neck and kissed him. He glanced back at Erica, looking both embarrassed and happy.

"I'm sorry for being such a jerk," Megan whispered. When Austin looked puzzled, she explained, "When I got angry about you having lunch with that woman and about the pawn shop and didn't let you explain."

"Well, you didn't know—"

Megan interrupted him. "Just let me get it out. I know I acted stupid. Erica let me have it a couple of times—told me I was acting like a child and that I needed to grow up." She glanced over at Erica. "I never told you, but I thought about that a lot."

She looked back at Austin. "Anyway, I'm sorry. I'm going to try hard to do better, and if I'm upset about something, I'll try to talk *calmly* with you to find out what's going on."

Tenderly, Austin caressed Megan's face. Then he kissed her lightly. "You get some sleep now. I'll be back in the morning."

He moved back as Erica came to the side of Megan's bed and clasped her friend's hand. "Can I get you anything?"

Megan's eyelids were heavy. "Thanks, but all I want to do now is sleep."

* * *

Bees hummed industriously among the flowers, whose scent drifted across the yard as Erica strolled outside to stretch her legs and call David. As the sun set, it spread a rich golden light that cast deeply slanting shadows over the yard. She'd called her husband while at the hospital but wanted to hear his voice again.

"How is Megan doing?" David asked.

"She's sleeping. The pain medication knocked her out."

"She has my sympathies. Getting shot is no fun. Guess I'll have to stop making jokes about her—at least for a while." He paused. "I can't believe it was Liz all along. What made you suspect her?"

"I didn't at first. It wasn't until later that I began to get suspicious. That's why I told Megan not to talk about the case with her. From the moment I first got here, there were a lot of little things that puzzled me about Liz. Individually they didn't mean much, but over time they began adding up."

"Such as?"

"Well, Liz said she'd talked Beth into visiting the museum at the air force base, but Beth was much more likely to suggest it, since her father had been in the air force. It was a small lie, but when a person lies about small things, it's a safe bet they'll lie about bigger things."

Erica watched a butterfly dance above the flowers as she talked. It was relaxing there, with the large green trees towering overhead.

"Liz said Joel sent her postcards from the cities he visited, yet when I looked through them, a lot of cities were missing. I wondered if Liz had held some back and, if so, why. Then I decided it could have been because Joel had addressed those particular ones to Beth. I noticed that none of cards or e-mails were addressed to 'Liz' Johnson—they were all to 'Angel' Johnson. But what really didn't make sense is that Joel never asked about how Liz was doing, even though when I first arrived, Liz told me she'd cut her arm so badly she'd had to be rushed to the emergency room."

"Aha. Smart of you to pick up on that."

"I only wish I'd been quicker to make the connection between 'Liz' and 'Elizabeth.' It was right there in front of me when I watched *A Place in the Sun.*"

Apparently she'd confused David, because he asked, "Can you explain that again—this time with clarity?"

She giggled. "Sorry. Lately, I've watched a couple of old Elizabeth Taylor movies. The first was *A Place in the Sun,* and the second was *Cat on a Hot Tin Roof.* While I was waiting for Donna to pick me up today, I started thinking about the night I saw someone in the backyard—that's when I watched *Cat on a Hot Tin Roof.* Anyway, it was on public television, and they kept breaking in to ask for donations and to talk about the movie. I remembered that they referred to Elizabeth Taylor as Liz. That must have been sitting at the back of my mind all along, and I suddenly realized that was the puzzle piece that had evaded me for so long—Liz and Beth not only had the same last name, they also had the same first name—Elizabeth."

"Wow." David sounded impressed. "I don't think anyone else on the planet would have gotten that."

"If I'd been paying more attention, I might have realized it that night, but I got sidetracked by the intruder."

"You told me about the fake murder attempts, but why did Liz keep pretending someone was trying to kill her after she shot Beth?"

"Because if the attempts had stopped after Beth died, someone might have realized Beth was the actual target. Having a few more attempts proved someone was trying to kill Liz and that Beth's death was an accident."

"That makes sense. Well, you did it again, Erica. Case solved. I'm sure glad you're coming home."

"Me too, sweetheart."

Chapter Twenty-Two

"SHE'S STILL ASLEEP," ERICA TOLD Donna and Austin when they came to visit Megan. It was twelve thirty, and she assumed they had come straight from church since they were still wearing their Sunday clothes. Austin had stopped by earlier that morning to check on a sleepy Megan but had only stayed a few minutes.

Donna carried a pair of crutches. "I thought these might make it easier for her to get around."

"Have you got a vase?" Austin asked, holding a huge flower bouquet. "I got this for Megan when we picked up the crutches last night."

"Oh, she'll love these," Erica said. She found a vase and filled it with water before stirring in the packet of flower preservative. She cut a few inches off the stems and arranged the flower in the vase.

"Thanks, Erica." Austin took the vase and headed for the stairs. "I'll take them up and sit with Megan till she wakes up."

Donna eyed the mixing bowl on the counter. "What are you making?"

"A special dessert—Coconut-Walnut Carrot Cake.[12] I thought Megan might like it."

"Sounds wonderful, but I don't know how you can bake—not after everything that's happened." Donna's face was strained. "I feel jittery just thinking about Liz and what she did."

"Cooking helps calm my nerves," Erica explained as she measured out the cinnamon. "I find it relaxing."

For a moment, Donna looked skeptical. Then her expression turned to one of interest. "Maybe I ought to help you then."

"Great. Want to chop some walnuts? I need two cups since I'm making two cakes."

---

12 See the appendix at the end of the book for this recipe.

"Two?"

"I thought I'd take a cake over to Frank." Erica opened a drawer, pulled out an apron with a zebra print, and handed it to Donna, who cringed.

"I can't wear that. I gave it to Liz." There were deep lines on Donna's face as she set the apron aside. "I still can't believe Liz killed Beth. My own niece—I thought I knew her."

"And yet you were the one who told me it was possible Liz was putting on an act and that she had always been strong-willed and got what she wanted."

"I said all of that?" Donna was bemused.

"Maybe you knew Liz better than you realized, but you didn't like acknowledging certain parts of her personality. Plus, Liz had the chance to get a fortune, and money can do things to people."

If Donna saw the irony in Erica's words, she said nothing. Erica handed the older woman a knife and a cutting board. "Liz had two sides. Most of the time you saw the good side—the charming Liz that she showed to most people. But she had another side that was quite different—and evil."

As Erica peeled the carrots, slivers of orange rained down into the sink. "I was a little confused when you told me Liz loved the house because Megan insisted she didn't."

"Oh, but she did." Donna's knife systematically thumped against the cutting board as she chopped the nuts. "Liz took pride in the fact that Crooked House had always been in her family. Her father and grandfather were born here. Since Liz didn't have a lot of close relatives—except for me and Austin—this house *became* her family. It was the only place she felt secure. It gave her a sense of belonging—made her feel like she had roots."

Erica spoke above the whirring of the hand mixer. "It was clear in so many ways that Liz loved this house. She kept the inside spotless, had people take off their shoes, and was nervous just thinking that BJ and Austin might scuff the wall when they moved a dresser. And she acted like Austin wanted to desecrate a sacred place when he suggested knocking some walls out."

"I can imagine," Donna said, shaking her head as she handed the nuts to Erica to fold into the batter. "Liz cared about Crooked House like it was a person. It almost physically hurt her not to have the money to restore it or make necessary repairs. Liz hated Frank because she was afraid he might succeed in having the house condemned. Once Frank started down that path, Liz was ready to fight with her last breath for the house."

"It's possible that part of the reason Liz killed Beth was to get the money to repair and restore Crooked House." Erica poured the batter into the cake pans.

"I think you're right." Donna's voice was grim.

"Mom, Erica," Austin called from upstairs. "Megan's awake."

It was perfect timing, Erica thought. She slid the cakes in the oven and went upstairs with Donna.

* * *

Smells of baking filled the air as Erica set the cakes on a rack to cool. The phone rang, and she peeled off her oven mitts. It was Detective Ranquist.

"I thought you'd like to know that we served a warrant on the condo Todd was renting. They found pieces of pipe under the couch and traces of gun powder. Faced with that evidence and our offer to go easy on him if he told us the truth, Todd started singing like a bird, saying the whole thing was Liz's idea."

"Did he admit making the bomb?"

"Not only that, but he gave Liz a few pieces of pipe to plant in Frank's shed. We confiscated Todd's laptop, and I'm sure our techies will find he's been on websites with instructions on how to make bombs." He sounded satisfied. "You told me Liz showed you a bunch of Joel's e-mails. How did she get a hold of them if Joel sent them to Beth?"

"That's another job for your computer guys—they'll have to check out Beth's and Liz's laptops," Erica said. "One thing I do know is that Liz is a snoop—I once caught her going through Donna's files. I'm sure she also somehow managed to get Beth's password and read Joel's e-mails. Either that or she forwarded the emails to herself, then altered them before printing so they looked like they were sent directly to her."

"If so, Liz probably deleted the originals. Still, our guys might be able to recover them, even if she thought to empty the recycle bin."

They talked a little longer, with the detective filling her in. Then he said, "Todd also told me a few other things you and Megan might be interested to hear, but I'd rather tell you about that in person. How is she doing, by the way?"

"Pretty good. Why don't you stop by later?"

"I'll do that."

* * *

Erica slid the square of softened cream cheese into a bowl with butter and vanilla. As she began to cream it for the frosting, Donna came down the stairs. She sat at the kitchen table and idly began folding the foil from the cream cheese into a tiny, neat square.

Without looking up, Donna said quietly, "You're probably wondering how I could go to church this morning after what I'd done."

It *had* crossed Erica's mind, but she'd pushed such thoughts aside and tried to think only of how plucky Donna was to attend. In a matter-of-fact voice, Erica said, "No better place to be."

"I talked with my bishop and confessed," Donna admitted. "He said the matter would be reviewed by the high council but that most likely, I'd only be disfellowshipped. I was relieved because I thought I'd be excommunicated. Still, I have a lot of repenting to do." She watched Erica ease the cakes out of their pans and onto separate plates. "I told the bishop I thought I ought to stay away from church until I was worthy enough to be there, but he said one of the conditions of coming back into full fellowship is to continue to attend meetings."

"Good advice." Erica tasted the frosting then began spreading it on the cakes. She was glad Donna felt safe talking with her, even if she was a little surprised—given their past relationship. But all of the nervous anxiety that had made Donna so irritable and defensive had disappeared. Besides, Erica thought, there were probably very few people Donna *could* talk to—so Erica listened sympathetically.

"I'm just so ashamed. I kept making excuses for myself—telling myself it wasn't really stealing because I was going to put the money back—but the truth is that there was no excuse for what I did." Donna's voice was full of remorse.

"I know you were very worried about your father."

Donna acknowledged this with a nod. "I just went along blindly, never really thinking about it." She looked up. "Anyway, enough of that. I called the assisted living center the nurse told me about. They had an opening and agreed to take my father."

"That's good news."

"I'll have him transported there the day after tomorrow. Then I'll start searching for a new job, although it's going to be hard explaining why I don't have a reference from my previous employer."

As Erica washed out the frosting bowl, she saw Frank raking his side lawn. Picking up one of the cakes, she told Donna, "Frank's out in his yard. I'm going over, but if I'm not back in five minutes, call the SWAT team."

She hurried out the door and started across the driveway. Frank saw her coming, but before he could sidle away, Erica held out the coconut-walnut cake. "Hi, Frank, I made you a cake."

He eyed it warily. "What kind of poison did you use?"

She smiled. "Frank, Frank, Frank. It's a peace offering. The case is closed. We caught the person who killed Beth."

He stared at her then said impatiently, "Well—are you going to tell me who did it?"

"It was Liz."

Frank's grizzled eyebrows rose as high as they could go. "Are you serious, or are you just trying to make me feel good?"

"It's true. Liz faked all those so-called murder attempts."

"I *told* you that girl was nuts. No person in their right mind would let a historic house go to rack and ruin like she did." In his mind, the two were inextricably linked. He gave her a sharp look. "Bet you're sorry you got that search warrant now, aren't you?"

"Not really." Erica was casual. "At the time we thought it was necessary."

"What about that pipe you found in my shed? Bet that crazy girl put it there."

"Actually, she did."

"I knew it, but you wouldn't listen to me." His bleary eyes rested on Crooked House. "What's going to happen to the house now?"

"You know, that's a good question."

* * *

Megan couldn't bear being cooped up in her room any longer, so when Detective Ranquist arrived, she asked Austin to help her down the stairs. Instead, he scooped her up and carried her to the front room.

"You're going to hurt your back," Megan protested.

"Ha! You're a featherweight."

Megan's river of black hair fell back as Austin gently placed her on the loveseat. He moved the ottoman so she could prop up her leg then sat close beside her. Megan watched him, her hazel eyes shining softly.

While Erica sliced the cake, cutting an extra-large slice for Detective Ranquist, Donna poured glasses of milk. The women went into the front room and passed out the saucers. Erica sat next to the detective, near the fireplace. When Detective Ranquist took a bite, a rapt expression came to his face.

Unable to wait any longer, Megan asked the detective. "So what else did Todd tell you?"

Detective Ranquist chewed and swallowed. "Todd went over the whole story—back to when he and Joel first met Liz and Beth at the Air Force Museum. Apparently, both of the girls liked Joel, but Joel was more interested in Beth. So Todd and Liz started dating and fell in love."

Megan's eyes narrowed. "I knew it."

"So why did Todd keep asking Megan out?" Austin was confused.

"I bet it was to cover their tracks," Erica guessed. "They didn't want anyone to know they were in on this together."

"Have you talked with Liz?" Megan asked grimly.

"I have," Detective Ranquist said, "but she won't say a word without talking to a lawyer. It's too bad that of all the people Beth could have told about her engagement, she picked Liz. According to Todd, Liz was beside herself with envy when she found out Joel had a rich, ailing grandfather who had less than a year to live and nobody but Joel to leave his fortune to."

Sharp anger shook Erica as she remembered gentle Beth. Liz was as cold-hearted and calculating as a person could be, her evilness masked by a pretty face and an agreeable outward demeanor.

"Liz must have been planning this for a long time," Donna said, then corrected herself. "No wait, she couldn't have. I suppose Liz came up with the idea after Joel was killed in that car crash in Europe."

"And that leads to the final twist," Erica said, having been informed earlier by the detective. She sat back and waited for him to explain.

Detective Ranquist took a drink of milk and wiped his mouth with his napkin. "Erica and I both thought it was an odd twist of fate that Joel would be killed a few short weeks after his grandfather passed away. Turns out it wasn't a coincidence."

"What do you mean?" Austin asked.

"Again, this is the gospel according to Todd, but he claims Liz came up with a plan to get rid of Beth *and* Joel."

"But Joel died during a race," Megan said slowly.

"With a little help," Detective Ranquist said. "You see, Todd and Joel knew each other quite well since they drove the same NASCAR circuits. Liz's plan was for Todd to sabotage Joel's car, but he had to wait until

Adam Goldstein passed away. That way, Joel would inherit a fortune. Todd chatted up Joel, making sure he had updated his will and life insurance policy and named Beth as his beneficiary. Then after Adam died, Todd sabotaged Joel's car."

Erica spoke up. "Liz's part in this was to stage her 'accidents' and to kill Beth as soon as Joel was dead. She had to move quickly because Beth probably wouldn't have kept quiet about her engagement once Joel was gone. When he died, Liz persuaded Beth to remain quiet just a little longer."

"And of course, Beth agreed," Megan said bitterly. "She always did what other people told her to do."

Detective Ranquist's face was somber. "Todd said Beth was going to skip Donna's party and go home to tell her parents. But Liz said she needed Beth's help and persuaded her to stay."

Erica felt sick. If only Beth hadn't given in to Liz's pleadings. What a complex patchwork of emotions must have ruled Liz—jealousy because Beth had been the one to win Joel's heart; covetousness for the money Liz knew Beth would eventually receive; hatred toward Frank; love for Crooked House and all it represented; and last of all, opportunism, for Liz had acted quickly once she'd discovered Beth was about to inherit a fortune. Liz had seized the opportunity, turning it to her own benefit.

Megan must have been thinking along the same lines, for she said in disgust, "Liz was as mean as she was crooked."

"Just like her house," Erica added.

Chapter Twenty-Three

After packing, Erica dusted and vacuumed the bedroom. She then went outside into the fine, sunny morning, carrying a small cage. BJ, wearing his familiar checked shirt, was trimming bushes by the gazebo. He pushed his safety goggles onto his head when he saw her.

"I guess you heard about what happened," Erica began.

"Yeah," he replied simply. BJ's eyes had the dumb, glazed look of an animal in pain. The hedge trimmers seemed to weigh a ton as they drooped toward the ground.

"I'm a little surprised to see you working here. I'm not sure you'll get paid," Erica said delicately.

He shrugged. "Doesn't matter. Liz would worry if things weren't kept up." He glanced at Erica. "Can she have visitors?"

"I think so."

He was quiet a moment. "I wanted to tell you something. Remember that night you came into the backyard when it was late?"

Erica stared. "Was that you?"

"I left my circular saw here and needed it for a job I had the next day, so I came to get it."

"Why didn't you tell me it was you?" Erica's exasperation showed in her voice.

BJ stared as if Erica had mush for brains. "You were waving that gun all around. Thought you were gonna shoot me. I just got out as fast as I could."

"Did you go into the house?"

BJ blinked. "No."

It must have been Liz, Erica thought. Liz must have heard her go outside, peeked out the window, and saw her looking around. Then Liz scattered the clothes to make it look as if someone had gone inside.

Erica said her good-byes to BJ then went to the back corner, where she transferred the mice to a smaller cage. Leaving it in the shade by the driveway, she went inside and cut two tiny chunks of carrot for Hamlet as a good-bye present. Her phone rang as she carried her bags down.

"Hi, sweetheart!" David's voice was warm and happy. "Are you on the way to the airport?"

"Not yet. Austin took Megan over to talk with one of her professors about making up a final. They should be back any minute." Erica stepped outside to stroll around the backyard one last time.

"That's awesome that you were able to solve the case."

"With a lot of help from Detective Ranquist—"

"I hate to disagree with my beautiful wife, but you'd have solved it with or without his help. I told my boss about the case and how you noticed the soot, found the box, and figured out the name thing. Tom thought it was terrific—he wants to hire someone with OCD to help solve cases around here."

Erica knew Tom Brown, and though they were good friends, his favorite pastime was teasing Erica and cracking jokes about her passion for cleanliness and organization. "I hate to disagree with my handsome husband, but your chief thinks I'm a weirdo."

"No, honestly. He thinks you're a great detective—smart and capable, with many humanoid characteristics."

"David!"

"I'm just kidding." Her husband chuckled. "You're very observant and seem to have a special radar that tells you when anything's out of place. That's part of what makes you such a brilliant detective. You're also sensitive to atmosphere—you felt from the beginning that there was something evil about Crooked House."

"It did make me uneasy at times," Erica admitted. "But of course, a house can't be bad. It's the people who live there that make it feel that way. Some people might call what I felt a premonition, but when I think back, most of those uneasy feelings came when I was around Liz. She certainly had me fooled—I can't count the number of lies she told."

"'False words are not only evil in themselves, but they infect the soul with evil.' Socrates."

Erica said admiringly, "What a memory you have!"

"I'm sure glad you'll be home soon. Your brother said he was able to get you on a good flight today. We're lucky Chris works for an airline."

"That's for sure. I can't wait to be back with you and the kids."

"They're pretty excited. You should see the house. They're putting up crepe paper all over—in your favorite colors, lavender and yellow. They've even put together a show for you tonight—a musical program."

"How sweet. And what about you?" Erica asked demurely. "Have *you* made any plans for tonight?"

"You bet."

"Rose petals on the bed again?"

"Anything you want."

"I want you."

"Ditto." His voice was husky.

"Say, while I have you in a good mood, there is one thing I ought to mention—but you have to promise that if I tell you, you'll still pick me up at the airport."

"Uh-oh." David's voice held a note of alarm. "That doesn't sound good. What's going on?"

"Um, I won't be alone when I come home."

"Is Megan coming?"

"No. Think a little smaller."

Long pause. "You're not going to bring home a kitten like last time, are you?"

"A little smaller than that."

Longer pause. "Smaller than a kitten? Wait a minute. This isn't about those mice you caught—even *you* wouldn't do that."

"Are you sure?"

"Erica!"

"I've got it all planned out—"

"No mice!" David was firm. "You are *not* bringing mice home!"

"Not to our home exactly—I'm going to take them to my *parents'* place."

"Oh, great. And this is how you repay them for giving birth to you and changing your diapers?" He paused again—possibly to wipe specks of foam from his mouth. "Have you cleared this with them?"

"Not yet, but I will."

"I see; it's easier to apologize than ask permission, right?" David took a deep breath. "Why not let them loose there? Did they want to see Utah before they end up as cat food?"

"The cats aren't going to get them," Erica replied indignantly. "And I can't let them loose here because they'd just get back into Crooked House or somebody else's house. My parents have forty-seven acres. I'll take them to the very back before I let them go. The cats don't go that far afield."

David grunted. "And just how do you plan to smuggle the rodents onto the plane? Don't tell me you stuffed them in your suitcase."

"I called the airline and asked if pets could travel. They said it was fine as long as the cage fit underneath the seat and they weren't noisy. And if they happen to look inside, I'll say they're valuable research mice."

* * *

Even though Megan appeared tired, she insisted on going with Erica to the airport. She and Austin had stopped on their way to Crooked House to pick up Donna, who had asked to come along. Megan leaned against the Jeep as Austin stowed her crutches and Erica's suitcases in the back. Megan wore a sardonic expression as Erica wiped the seats, but for the first time, she had no sarcastic comment.

When finished, Erica glanced up, pleasantly surprised.

Megan grinned. "My going-away present."

Once on the freeway, Austin reached out and held Megan's hand as they talked quietly. In the back, Donna leaned toward Erica. Then, tilting her head toward Austin and Megan, she whispered, "I worried at first because they're so different, but what do I know?"

"Their lives may never be calm, but they do seem to love each other." Erica then quoted, "'Love that is not madness is not love.' Pedro Calderon de la Barca."

Austin overheard. Talking over his shoulder, he said, "Speaking of quotes, Erica, I have a good one for you and your mouse friends. 'You can judge the heart of a man by his treatment of animals.' Immanual Kant. And you, Erica, have a good heart."

"Oh, how sweet! Thank you. I'll have to use that one on David."

Megan turned around. "So what's going to happen to Todd and Liz? Have you talked with Detective Ranquist?"

"I did. Because Beth's murder was premeditated, Liz will be charged with capital murder. Todd will also be charged with capital murder for Joel's death—a charge that will most likely be reduced or even dropped because there's no real evidence he sabotaged Joel's car. However, Todd will also be charged with attempted murder for planting the pipe bomb on Liz's car, and Liz will be named as a coconspirator. However, they'll go easier on Todd since he cooperated."

Erica faced Donna. "What's going to happen to Crooked House?"

"I'm going to see if Liz will deed the house to me and Austin. We're the beneficiaries anyway, and she knows the house will fall down if something isn't done soon. I'd like to sell it to the Dover Historical Society." Donna smiled. "Actually, Frank has already called me about that."

"Wow, he didn't waste any time."

"Well, the society has had many discussions about buying a historical home and restoring it. Hopefully this time they'll move forward with their plans."

"I thought repairs were going to be very costly. Can the society afford to buy and renovate it?"

"We have some money set aside. Once repairs are made and the house is architecturally sound, we could use it as a museum and a meeting place. We'll open it to the public for tours and charge admission. We've even talked about the possibility of renting it out for weddings."

"Or you could just sell it. You'd be able to get a good price for it since it's in historic Dover," Erica said. A flicker passed over Donna's face, and Erica wondered if she was thinking about the money she and Austin could make by selling Crooked House.

"That's true, although the price would have to be reduced because of needed repairs. But Austin and I have talked, and we'd rather sell it to the historical society. We'd also like to give them a substantial discount, since it's for a worthy cause. A good portion of the money from the sale of the house will go to pay Liz's lawyers, and I'll set some aside for Liz's needs. Austin and I will split the rest, and I'll put whatever I get toward the debt I owe Mr. Rochford."

Erica called up to the young man. "Do you have any plans with the money you'll get, Austin?"

He grinned and shot a glance toward Megan. "I have a couple of ideas. I might want to invest in a bit of jewelry—specifically a diamond. And I might use some of the money as a down payment on a house."

Erica had to look twice to be sure, but it was true—Megan was blushing. The young woman's smile was like sunshine breaking through mountain fog.

"At least I don't have to compete with Todd anymore," Austin added with another sly glance at Megan.

They arrived at the airport, and Austin signaled to get into the correct lane for departures.

"You never did," Megan replied stoutly. "Not really. Oh, I was flattered that Todd seemed interested in me, but the chemistry wasn't there. I was surprised Todd kept asking me out, even after I realized he was interested in Liz."

"The man was a fruitcake," Erica said.

Megan laughed. "And I was too—for continuing to go out with him. I think I just wanted to prove to *some* people"—she directed a look at Erica—"that Todd *did* like me—plain old Megan."

Austin pulled up at the curb and turned off the engine. "*Plain Megan?* Now that's just nuts. Since you don't know how beautiful you are, I'll have to keep telling you every day until you believe me." He kissed her.

Erica climbed out and removed the crutches as Austin carefully helped Megan out of the Jeep. There was something about the young man that caught the attention—a kind of goodness. As Megan struggled a moment getting her balance, Austin reached out to steady her. He then stroked her face, tracing it with his fingers. When Erica handed Megan her crutches, Austin's face was beaming with the satisfied look of a man who has everything he wants.

"I meant to tell you that BJ came over and worked for a while in the backyard this morning," Erica told Megan.

Megan's mouth fell open. "Does he know what Liz did?"

"Yep. Despite that, he asked if Liz could have visitors."

"You've *got* to be kidding. BJ still cares about her?"

"I guess Todd's not the only fruitcake." Erica grinned.

Megan threw her arms around Erica. "I'll miss you, Erica."

"I would think you'd be glad to have a little peace and quiet."

"Well, yes. That will be nice. And I'll be glad to get out of Crooked House." Austin pulled out Erica's suitcase and put it on the curb by his mother. "Austin and Donna are going to help me move today." Donna had offered to let Megan stay in her house for a while. Megan told Erica that Donna had laughed after offering her a room, saying she did it so Austin would stop by to visit more often.

"If things work out," Megan continued, "I might even stay and rent a room from Donna instead of finding an apartment. It'd help both of us out financially. But it'll be lonely without you."

"You can't believe that," Erica said with a grin. "Not with Austin by your side every minute."

Austin paid the skycap. As Donna walked over, Megan asked her, "Did I tell you Austin and I have reached an understanding?"

Donna's eyes widened. "Um, no you didn't. And what exactly is this understanding?"

"He won't try and change my wild Democratic ways if I forgive him for his stodgy Republican ways."

Megan laughed at the look of relief on Donna's face.

"Thanks, Erica," Austin said, coming over and giving her a hug. "You've been awesome."

Megan's eyes misted as she gave Erica another hug. "You know I love you, don't you?"

"Mais oui!"

They chuckled. Then Megan added, "I don't know what I would have done without you."

"I'm glad I could help. I just wish I could stay and see Wendy." Megan's mother was flying in that night.

"That's all right. Mom understands how anxious you are to get home."

Erica shouldered her purse and, carrying the small cage, crossed the taxi and bus lanes. As the glass doors slid open, she turned, gave a wide smile and a wave, and stepped into the terminal.

Appendix: Recipes

Jen's Rosemary Ranch Chicken

½ cup olive oil
½ cup ranch dressing
3 Tbsp. Worcestershire sauce
1 Tbsp. dried rosemary
2 tsp. salt
1 tsp. lemon juice
1 tsp. white vinegar
¼ tsp. black pepper
1 Tbsp. sugar
4 skinless, boneless chicken breast halves

Directions

1. Mix all ingredients except chicken. Let stand 5 minutes
2. Cut chicken breast in half, and pound to ½″ thickness.
3. Coat chicken with marinade, and refrigerate for 8 hours.
4. Grill chicken for 8–12 minutes, or until chicken is no longer pink in center and juices run clear.

Cranberry Walnut Bread

1 cup sugar
3 cups flour
¼ tsp. baking soda
1 Tbsp. baking powder
2 tsp. orange peel (finely grated)
½ tsp. salt
1 egg (beaten)
1⅔ cups milk
¼ cup butter or margarine, melted and cooled
1½ cups chopped, frozen cranberries
1 cup chopped walnuts

Directions

1. Preheat oven to 350 degrees.
2. In a large bowl, mix together sugar, flour, baking powder, baking soda, orange peel, and salt.
3. In a separate bowl, mix together beaten egg, butter or margarine, and milk.
4. Add egg mixture to flour mixture, and blend well.
5. Stir in cranberries and nuts.
6. Pour batter into a greased, regular-size loaf pan.
7. Bake for 60–70 minutes. Use a toothpick in the center to determine if done.
8. Cool in pan for about 10 minutes. Remove, and cool on a wire rack.

Lemon Poppy Seed Belgian Waffles

2 cups Bisquick or other all-purpose baking mix
1–2 Tbsp. poppy seeds
1 Tbsp. lemon zest
1¼ cup cold Sprite (or other lemon-lime soda)
1 large egg, lightly beaten
¼ cup butter, melted

Directions

1. Stir together baking mix, poppy seeds, and lemon zest.
2. In a separate bowl, whisk Sprite, egg, and butter.
3. Gently whisk egg mixture into poppy seed mixture. Let stand 3 minutes.
4. Cook batter in a preheated, oiled Belgian-style waffle iron until golden. About ¾–1 cup batter per waffle. Note: A traditional waffle iron can be used as well.

Blackberry Maple Syrup

½ cup maple syrup
1 (12 oz.) package frozen blackberries, thawed and slightly mashed
1 tsp. lemon zest
2 tsp. lemon juice

Directions

Combine all ingredients, and warm in microwave or on the stove.

Applesauce Cookies

1 cup brown sugar
½ cup shortening
1 egg
1 tsp. cinnamon
¼ tsp. cloves
½ tsp. salt
1 tsp. baking powder
½ tsp. baking soda
2 cups whole wheat flour
1 cup applesauce
1 cup chocolate chips
1 cup raisins
1 cup walnuts, chopped

Directions

1. Cream sugar and shortening, then add egg and mix well.
2. Add spices, salt, baking powder, baking soda, and flour.
3. Stir in applesauce, chocolate chips, raisins, and nuts.
4. Drop dough by teaspoons onto greased cookie sheet, and bake for 10–12 minutes at 350 degrees. If you like square cookies, (like Erica) press dough into a greased 9x13 pan and bake for 20 minutes at 350 degrees.

Tropical Fruit Salad

- ¼ cup mayonnaise or salad dressing
- 1 Tbsp. sugar
- ½ tsp. lemon juice
- Dash salt
- ½ cup whipping cream
- 1 large red apple, chopped
- 1 large Yellow Delicious apple, chopped
- 1 large banana, sliced
- 2 kiwi, peeled and sliced thickly. Cut slices into quarters.
- 1 cup pineapple tidbits, drained
- 1 can mandarin oranges, drained
- ½ cup walnuts, chopped
- ½ cup toasted flaked coconut, divided. Use ¼ cup for salad and the rest on top as a garnish.
- Lettuce, enough to line salad bowl.
- Apple slices, to garnish

Directions

1. Blend together mayonnaise or salad dressing, sugar, lemon juice, and salt.
2. Whip the cream till soft peaks form; fold into the mayonnaise mixture.
3. Gently fold in red and yellow apples, banana, kiwi, celery, walnuts, and ¼ cup toasted flaked coconut. Chill salad.
4. Line salad bowl with lettuce; spoon in the chilled fruit mixture.
5. Top with apple slices in a circle, and garnish with toasted coconut.

Creamy Chicken Noodle Soup

2 Tbsp. butter
1 cup chopped onion
1 cup chopped celery
¼ cup fresh chopped parsley or 1 Tbsp. dried parsley flakes
2–3 cups cooked chicken, diced or shredded
5 cups chicken broth
1 can (10 ¾ oz.) cream of chicken soup, undiluted
1 can (10 ¾ oz.) cream of mushroom soup, undiluted
1 scant tsp. poultry seasoning
¼ tsp. dried leaf thyme
1 tsp. salt
½ tsp. garlic powder
2 tsp. chicken bouillon
¼ tsp. pepper
2 cups frozen peas and carrots
3 cups dry egg noodles
1½ cups heavy cream or half-and-half

Directions

1. In a large pot or Dutch oven, melt butter over medium heat.
2. Add onion and celery, and sauté until onion is tender.
3. Add parsley, chicken, chicken broth, soups, poultry seasoning, thyme, salt, garlic powder, chicken bouillon, and pepper. Bring to a boil.
4. Add the frozen peas and carrots and the noodles, cover, reduce heat, and simmer for 10 minutes.
5. Stir in the cream or half-and-half.
6. If a thicker soup is desired, mix 3 Tbsp. cornstarch with ⅓ cup half-and-half, and stir in some of the broth. Add to soup. Cook 2–3 minutes or until thick.

Oven-Baked Potato Wedges

4 medium-to-large russet potatoes
3 Tbsp. olive oil
½ tsp. paprika
Salt and pepper to taste

Directions

1. Preheat oven to 400 degrees.
2. Scrub potatoes. Cut in half crossway, then cut each half twice lengthwise. Rinse, and pat dry.
3. Mix oil and seasonings.
4. Add potatoes, and toss.
5. Place potato wedges in a single layer on baking sheet, and bake for 30 minutes or until tender.

Bacon-Cheddar Deviled Eggs

12 eggs
4 slices bacon
½ cup mayonnaise
2 Tbsp. sour cream
1 Tbsp. mustard
¼ tsp. salt
2 Tbsp. finely shredded Cheddar cheese
Paprika for garnish

Directions

1. Place eggs in a saucepan, and cover with water. Bring water to a boil, turn off heat, and let sit for 10–12 minutes. Remove from hot water, and cool by rinsing under cold, running water.
2. Cook bacon in a large skillet until evenly browned. Cool, crumble into small pieces, and set aside.
3. Peel the hard-boiled eggs, and cut in half lengthwise. Put yolks in a small bowl. Mash egg yolks, slowly adding mayonnaise and sour cream. Stir in mustard and salt, then add crumbled bacon and cheese. Fill egg white halves with the yolk mixture, sprinkle with paprika, and refrigerate until serving.

Beef Casserole

1 lb. ground beef (can substitute shredded beef)
2 Tbsp. brown sugar
1 Tbsp. fresh or dehydrated minced onion
½ tsp. salt
1 can (16 oz.) pork and beans, drained and pork removed.
¾ cup barbecue sauce
1 can refrigerated biscuits
1 cup cheese, grated

Directions

1. Brown beef, and blot grease.
2. Stir in sugar, onion, salt, beans, and barbecue sauce. Pour in a 9 x 13 casserole dish.
3. Flatten biscuits slightly, and place on top of casserole. Bake for 15 minutes at 350 degrees. Turn biscuits, bake another 10 minutes. Sprinkle cheese on casserole, and return to oven for 5 minutes or until cheese is melted.

Coconut-Walnut Carrot Ring

1½ cups all purpose flour
1½ tsp. baking powder
½ tsp. salt
1 tsp. cinnamon
½ tsp. nutmeg
½ cup packed light brown sugar
½ cup granulated sugar
1 cup oil
2 eggs
1 cup grated carrot
½ cup walnuts, chopped
½ cup raisins
⅔ cup coconut
2 cups coconut, to garnish

Directions

1. Mix flour, baking powder, salt, cinnamon, and nutmeg.
2. In a separate bowl, beat sugars, oil, and eggs.
3. Add flour mixture to egg mixture. Blend until smooth.
4. Stir in carrots, nuts, raisins, and ⅔ cup coconut.
5. Pour into greased and floured 9-inch Bundt pan or a 6-cup ring mold. Bake at 350 degrees for 35 minutes, or until toothpick comes out clean.
6. Remove from pan after 15 minutes, and cool completely.
7. Frost with cream cheese frosting, and cover with remaining coconut.

Frosting

1 (8 oz.) package cream cheese, softened
½ cup butter, softened
1 tsp. vanilla extract
3 cups powdered sugar
1–2 tsp. milk

Directions

1. Cream together cream cheese and butter.
2. Mix in vanilla, then gradually stir in powdered sugar.
3. Add enough milk so frosting is of the right consistency.

Author Biography

MARLENE BATEMAN WAS BORN IN Salt Lake City, Utah, and grew up in Sandy, Utah. She graduated from the University of Utah with a bachelor's degree in English. Marlene is married to Kelly R. Sullivan and lives in North Salt Lake, Utah. Her hobbies include gardening, dog-walking, card-making, and reading. Marlene has written a number of nonfiction books, including *Gaze into Heaven: Near-Death Experiences in Early Church History* and *Heroes of Faith.* She has also written three novels. Her first was the best-selling *Light on Fire Island.* Her next two novels are Erica Coleman mysteries—*Motive for Murder* and *A Death in the Family.*